79

the

judas

figures

the
judas
figures

by Audrey Erskine Lindop

appleton-century-crofts, inc.

new york

To

Dorothy Clark

the
judas
figures

Chapter 1 ~~~~~~~~~~~~~~~~

A CAR SPED ROUND A BEND IN A MOUNTAIN ROAD. IT HIT AND
killed a goat. It skidded and threw up a fountain of dust
that made a white fog in the headlights. It started noisily
forward again to bump twice over the dead body of the
goat.

Behind the wheel an American cursed out loud. He
picked up a bottle and took a long pull from it. Then he
prayed aloud. "Okay, put it this way," he said to his God.
"Call it a deal if you like. I never said a prayer before—I
don't go for that kind of crap—but if this one gets answered
here's what I'll do. If you let him live I'll give up this stuff."
And with his left hand he corked up the brandy and threw
it into the back seat.

The car made the fourteen-hour journey in just under
twelve. At times the road fell away so steeply that it seemed
as if the rear light would tip over the hood. It passed no
one else on the road which was pitted and rutted, rattling
the bottles in the back and shaking the soft unhealthy flesh

1

beneath the American's chin. There were tears on his cheeks newly shed. He repeated, "Let him live and I give up the alk." The moon picked out jagged mountaintops and made playful monsters out of the ungainly maguey plants. The car racing round the corners all but turned over twice.

It had been light several hours when the town showed up in the distance like a dirty scar across the countryside. It would still take an hour to reach. The American swore wearily, "For chrissake! For chrissake!" Dark stains like bruises showed under his eyes. He pressed the accelerator down again and twisted his neck to ease the stiffening muscles. His legs buckled under him when he drew up outside the Palacio Municipal and stepped out. His tongue and his lips felt swollen and dry. He held on to the car door for support, and called out to a passing mestizo: "Hey! You! Lopez—the priest! Father Lopez, where do I find the priest?"

The half-caste was sociable. He smiled widely to show off gold teeth. Nothing could speed the directions. "This is Huapan," he explained. "It's a town where you find good things. Many hundreds live here—it's not just some little place you might find by the road. No indeed, there is a telegraph office and from there one may send small pieces of paper all over the world, for a little something paid, of course. I am saving to send one myself. I have an uncle in Texcoco who would be proud to receive such a thing."

The American wetted his lips and choked out, "I don't want a telegraph office—I want the goddam priest."

"Ah! That will be Father Lopez. He is much liked around here, that priest." The mestizo raised a delicate finger and pointed it down the street. "You will see where the man with the burro is turning—now, that is a pity, he's

2

not going to turn after all. A burro is an obstinate beast. Never mind, it was only a small thing to show you a way that it's not wise to go." The American closed his swollen eyes. When he opened them he saw an Indian bringing his goods to market piled high on the back of his wife. He called out asking the way to the house of the priest. The Indian made three concise movements of the hand, one forward, one left, and one right. The American said, "Thanks." Then he willed the last remnants of his strength into his feet. Somehow they moved forward. He managed to run down the street. He was fat and short and red hair clogged in the sweat of his forehead. He had gone only a few yards when the priest came out of a grocer's shop. He was carrying a jug of goat's milk, his tongue caught between his teeth with the effort of trying not to slop it. He looked frail and his Roman collar stood out from a withered brown neck.

The American lurched towards him. "You Father Lopez? Sam Frankenson here from Quantana. You have to come back there with me now."

"Come back with you, Señor Frankenson?"

"It's Father Keogh—he got himself shot. He's dying and he wants a priest."

The jug shook, covering the feet of Father Lopez in a sticky bluish fluid. His lips fell open. "Shot!"

"Well for chrissake get a move on. Don't you care that a priest wants a priest?"

"Señor Frankenson, I must fetch the Sacraments."

"For the love of mike, he'll have them, won't he?"

"Yes—yes. I suppose—how bad is it?"

"So bad I'm going to wring that chicken neck of yours if you don't quit this gibbering around."

3

"I must make a few arrangements first. I'll be as quick as I possibly can."

"Quick is just not fast enough. You're coming with me now." The American snatched the jug of milk and put it on the ground. Then he took the priest by the arm and propelled him up the street. Father Lopez shouted instructions to the small crowd that trotted beside him: ". . . do not forget, Silvanito, the baptism will now be tomorrow, and, Tavio, tell the sacristan . . ."

Sam Frankenson bundled him into the car. "You'll have to drive. I'm all in."

The little priest got into gear. "This is terrible, terrible, Señor Frankenson. You must tell me exactly what happened."

Sam Frankenson sat in the back with the bottles. There were three and two were empty. He opened up the third. "If Mac lives—I call him Mac—I'm giving this up for good. Yeah, I'll tell you what happened but first I have to get some sleep." He lay back, his mouth loose, crushing the crown of his panama hat. It was some hours before he woke up. He touched the little priest on the shoulder. "Look, pal, this isn't the snail stakes. We have to get there sometime." He climbed out and changed seats with Father Lopez.

The car raced forward so that the goat tracks that invaded the mountainsides shot past the windows in a flickering series of spiky brown twigs, and the vibrant green of the pepper trees seemed to merge into one long winding ribbon. When the road climbed and the car curled round the edge of a stark drop Father Lopez closed his eyes. When he opened them he asked, "Might I hear about it now, please?"

"Sure," said Sam. His forehead creased, trying to recall the details. "Mac walked right into an ambush last night. The hell of it is I don't remember it all that well. I must have killed a bottle or two since then and I guess I had my own brains knocked around in that fight. I kinda have blanks in my head."

"Where did it happen?"

"Tephuango. It was Malo and his lousy bunch, of course."

"Of course."

"You'll be glad to hear the dirty bum's dead." The little priest said nothing. In his head he was praying for Father Keogh. Sam suddenly asked, "Suppose we're too late for you to hear Mac's confession? Does that mean he goes to hell? If it does, hell takes in a pretty nice type."

"I can give Father Keogh Absolution after he is dead."

"That's fine. It could be that would comfort him. Did you know Mac finally had Malo on the run? It looked as if he'd put the skids under the whole darn lot of them."

"Yes, I heard. It was a very considerable achievement."

"Yeah! But we should have known Malo. Whatever you like to say for the bum he wasn't the kind to quit."

"No, he was not a coward," Father Lopez said.

"When you said that you said it all for him." Sam shivered. "That guy made my flesh crawl the way he'd creep around so it seemed like he never had any soles to his feet. I used to call him Pussyfoot. It's going to feel kind of strange without Pussyfoot around."

"Let's hope it'll bring peace to the town."

"Yeah! Let's hope. Well, here's the way I think it happened. I reckon it would've been around eight last night—it's like I told you, I'm kinda hazy about it—Mac gets a message from Tephuango. Some Indio's wife is sick.

5

Well, straight away I think it's a trap but Mac won't listen. Says he has to do his duty, and he can't risk not to go in case someone really is sick. So I go along with him just in case. It was a trap all right. They get us inside this Indio hut and all hell breaks loose. I must have gotten slugged pretty early. I get the blanks right after that and the darn thing keeps fading away from me."

"Was it only Malo there?"

"Nope, I seem to recall he had his pals with him— Vito, Porfirio, and that little creeper the Jeep. The next thing I know is these three hyenas have gone and only Mac, Malo, and me are left. Malo looks like he's dying and Mac is trying to get him to confess or something. Mac fussed like an old hen over that roughneck. Who the hell would want that soul saved?"

"Our Blessed Lord," replied Father Lopez and asked, "Who was it who killed Malo?"

"Search me. It was an accident, of course. It was pretty dark in that lousy hut; they must've meant to plug Mac and got Malo instead. Then one of them comes back and gets Mac just as he's sweating his guts out trying to save Malo. When they see Pussyfoot is punctured as well, they beat it and leave the two of them to bleed it out. Tell me, does the Lord want that bunch saved?"

Father Lopez answered, "Yes. What do you think of Father Keogh's chances?"

"Damn little."

Father Lopez spoke gently. "This must be very painful for you, Señor Frankenson. I know how attached you were to Father Keogh."

Sam shrugged his shoulders. "Mac's okay." Then he said, "X marks the spot."

They had reached the village of Tephuango. The

6

light was fading fast so that the shadows of the organ cactus plants were faint across the narrow mud street.

Beyond Tephuango the countryside stretched cruel and impenetrable towards the foothills of Arenales. The great mountain ranges fell back in tiers, line upon blue line of them until they were lost in the sky. The country which spread towards the feet of the Arenales hills was tangled and dark. It was said that no white man could find his way out of it if he ventured too far in and even the Indian trod it with care. It was said that a madness took hold of the head of someone who tried to fight his way out of the denseness, so that he floundered and retraced his steps even when freedom had come within sight. It was called the Great Green Walk of the Wandering Dead, for legend held the mazelike valley to be a testing ground for unquiet souls. Only the spirit which could discover a path to the foot of the hills would be able to free itself from earthly ties. At night the more sensitive ear was able to detect the cries of the lost ones seeking their way, calling to the living to rescue them from their plight.

Malo alone had been credited with the power to find his way about in the Great Green Walk of Death.

Father Lopez forbore to ask which of the straw-roofed huts had housed the crime of the night before. But when they left the parched poverty of Tephuango behind them he asked, "Did none of the Indians try to help?"

"Did anyone ever turn out against Malo? He had 'em all too scared, excepting for Mac of course."

"And yourself."

"Oh me," said Sam. "The devil looks after drunks."

They were silent when the car turned down the steep hill to Quantana. The lights were switched off on the plaza and the town lay in an inky-black well. Sam shot a sleeve

7

up to check with his watch. "Must be nine if the dump's in darkness. Yeah," he said, "just nine. That mean's it's been twenty-four hours. Well, now we see whether I have to give up the booze or not. Say, do you believe in prayers?"

"Naturally," said Father Lopez.

"Then give 'em all you've got," Sam told him. "I left Mac pretty sick."

Chapter 2 ~~~~~~~~~~~~~~~~~~~~~~

THE BISHOP HAD BEEN EXPECTING THE TRAGEDY. ONLY A few days before the cable from Father Lopez he had received a report from Father Keogh himself warning him that just such a situation might arise.

While the young priest he was interviewing read the report the Bishop sat back to study him. Father Marcelino Dominguez Lasques y Alonso was young and stern-faced. He brought with him into the room a dignity which sat at odds with his years. His superiors had written nothing but praise of him, and they had not seen fit to add a warning that the expression habitual to Father Lasques was a deep and perpetual scowl. His frown seemed permanently stamped on his face and his manner was coldly self-sufficient. He was exceptionally tall and the head held high and the straight shoulders gave a confidence bordering on arrogance. He appeared to be troubled by no sense of humor whatsoever.

8

He smiled dutifully at the Bishop's attempt at a quip to put him at his ease but he left the Bishop with the somewhat uncomfortable feeling that Father Marcelino Dominguez Lasques y Alonso was giving him time to pull himself together. He made a mental note to study the recipient of these little quips more carefully in future. He had hoped that the interview might have been relaxed and informal. He asked the priest to join him in a glass of mezcal.

"Thank you, my lord, I would rather not."

The Bishop held out his cigarette case. Father Lasques declined. "I'm afraid I'm not as strong-minded as you, Father," the Bishop smiled. "I wish I had so few vices."

"Your lordship has studied the opinions upon lung cancer?"

The Bishop had studied them with considerable apprehension—and pushed them into the farthest receptacle of his mind. "I'm not a chain smoker," he said defensively. "I smoke quite a few"—he studied the tip of his ash and thought it wiser not to include cigars—"er—cigarettes a day—perhaps ten to fifteen. You don't feel that excessive, do you? I mean if one hasn't a cough?" The Bishop became defiant. "Well, if I reach the heavenly gates and find *No Smoking* on them, I shall know that I'm bound for the other place."

He felt the young priest's eyes upon him. He looked up and met their sober depths. Father Lasques had thin and finely chiseled features. There were pictures of his Spanish ancestors in his mother's home: armor-clad soldiers with dark curls and stiff black beards; young high-ruffled vizcondes in braided doublets. Father Lasques had the same long-boned face, the same melancholy low-lidded eyes, and, the Bishop could not prevent himself from thinking, the same remote look of disdain. The Bishop's

9

family were frankly plebeian. He recalled that in one of the revolutions the Lasques had been impoverished and he reminded himself sharply that had the Lasques still retained their fortune Father Marcelino would have already relinquished his inheritance of his own free will.

He was well aware that there was a danger in sending a man of so little experience to Quantana. Father Lasques had not been long ordained. But a supply priest was urgently needed and the young man was anxious to go. The Bishop's foremost apprehensions were reserved for the priest himself.

He asked, "You have studied Father Keogh's report?"

"Yes, my lord."

"It was only a short time after I received that report that the shooting took place. So you'll see that Father Keogh's premonitions of disaster were not misplaced."

"Have you had any news of him?"

The Bishop shook his head. "The last I had was that there was no improvement. They were giving another blood transfusion and they managed to get a surgeon up from Milpahuaca. He would never have survived the journey if they had moved him. Quantana is greatly isolated. The operation was carried out under appalling conditions. He had not regained consciousness when I last heard."

"Do you think, my lord, it would have helped if Father Keogh had not been a foreigner?"

"They showed no more good will towards a countryman," the Bishop said. "Father Gomez fared worse before Father Keogh took over from him."

"I could have understood it if it had been in the time of the persecution."

"We could have all understood it then," said the Bishop. "The Church is no longer persecuted as such, but it was persecuted through Father Keogh by a single man. Malo was no ordinary bandit. Those who worked with him were ordinary enough—thugs and thieves and cut-throats—but he was not as simple as that. His real name was Anacleto Gonzales Flores Comachi Alvarez, but in Quantana they called him Malo, the Bad-One-of-the-Cats. I believe he had a passion for the creatures. He showed respect and even kindness towards them, something he seemed incapable of showing to a fellow human being. Father Keogh had a great admiration for him in a way. He felt it infinitely saddening that a character capable of such indomitable dedication could not be used in the service of God. I think myself that Anacleto had a fear of the Church. It would account for his inborn hatred of it. He knew that faith was his greatest enemy. If the people had faith he would lose his power over them. When Father Keogh revived the faith Anacleto was fighting for his life."

"One cannot help thinking," the young priest said, "that the police must have been very slack."

"The police were most vigilant," the Bishop said. "The Jefe is a man of the greatest integrity. He fought as untiringly as Father Keogh to try to reduce the menace, but Anacleto had half the town in his pay and the other half threatened into submission by fear. Not a soul could be found to give evidence against him. On the contrary, everyone was only too willing to provide a false alibi for him and distort the facts in his favor in order to keep in his good books. The Jefe's hands were bound. I am not certain that Don Pedro, whose official capacity is that of magistrate, has the same integrity as the Chief of Police. I fear that you may come up against many examples of this both in the higher and the lower stratas of life in Quantana. It is something I should like you to remember if you

11

take over Father Keogh's duties, either temporarily or permanently. It is safe to say that this Anacleto made of Quantana a challenge to Christianity."

Father Lasques looked through the report again. It was written in excellent Spanish and dated a fortnight back. He lingered over one section:

...your Lordship is already aware of the unfortunate scandalmongering which has been rife in the town concerning myself and the young Señorita de Cortinez, but not perhaps of the excellent use to which Anacleto has put it to discredit me. He managed to give a sinister implication to something which was merely foolish and young. I take considerable blame insomuch as I was blind to the feelings that were developing in the girl and must admit that even had I noticed them at the onset her extreme youth would not have predisposed me to take the matter seriously. Nevertheless, her misplaced affection for me could have been ignored and would doubtless have died a natural death if Anacleto had not made it his business to acquaint the entire town with her feelings. In a manner of speaking I deserved to be made the victim of this pathetic passion for I made her my especial protégée. She was a child when I came here first and badly in need of care. The mother, Doña Marian, an American woman unhappy in her own life, was fond of the child but quite incapable of understanding her. Don Pedro, the father, was an icy recluse whose books meant more to him than his own flesh and blood. It was only natural that Locha should turn to me for attention and guidance. I became her only friend, so perhaps it is also only natural that I should later come to represent something more to her. Matters are now in control, however, and by the time your Lordship receives

12

this letter she will, I trust, be happily married and have left for the United States. Unfortunately I doubt if the scandal will have departed with her and if I include it amongst matters of so much more vital importance and gravity, it is only to warn my successor of the gossip he is likely to encounter. I refer to my successor, my Lord, for I feel it my duty to warn you that if I am successful in my final attempts to outwit Anacleto it is more than likely that he will not allow me to survive.

When Father Lasques looked up, he asked, "Will there be any of Malo's men left?"

"Let me see," said the Bishop, and counted up on his fingers. "There used to be six, I think. One was killed in a fight, Lorenzo murdered a policeman and was sentenced for life, Pablo left them and went back to his home state, so if there are any left it will be Vito, Porfirio, and the little cripple they nicknamed the Jeep. But they would be of no account without Anacleto. His leadership was masterly."

"It would certainly call," said Father Lasques, "for a masterly leadership in return."

The Bishop detected in Father Lasques' voice a suggestion that he felt that there might have been better methods employed than the ones Father Keogh had chosen to counteract the evil. It was a poignant moment; for he recalled a not unsimilar attitude in Father Keogh himself when he read of the failure of Father Gomez. Sympathetic, respectful, but puzzled that such a thing could have come about; confident perhaps that a younger, more resilient man might achieve better results. The Bishop did not blame Father Lasques. He could not be expected to understand the crippling enmity that had been Malo's. He could have had no conception of the arduous battle Father Keogh had been forced to fight over the last seven years. He could not be expected to imagine the paralyzing influence that one man entirely dedicated to evil could have had over an isolated mountain community. That man in his lean, intimidating flesh was dead and only the tales of him lived. Father Lasques had never encountered the narrowed eyes of Anacleto. He had never in his short life met anyone who snuffed up the aroma of cruelty as if it had been a perfumed bouquet. The Bishop had met Anacleto only once and had remembered him ever since. He warned Father Lasques gently:

"You will not have to face what Father Keogh faced. The worst evil has been removed and the people are freed from fear, but although Anacleto is no longer a power, and the town can no longer be intimidated by him, he has only been dead a short while, and you may find he has left in Quantana traces of an evil hard to combat. It may have left an indelible mark."

Chapter 3 ~~~~~~~~~~~~~~~~

It seemed to Father Lasques that he had traveled half across the world before he reached the arid town of Huapan. Father Lopez was waiting to greet him. It was some time before they met. The train backed in to allow first-class passengers to leave the station untrammeled by the rabble, then shunted to let off the second class. Father Lasques was traveling second.

A three-man guitar band accosted him. "A little something for lightening your journey, Father?"

"But you didn't play in my carriage."

"No, but we played extra loud in the next."

Father Lasques relinquished a peso. It was easier than arguing. The band went off cheerfully to decide upon the most likely compartment in which to begin the return journey. They would move up the train as it stopped.

Father Lopez ran forward to meet Father Lasques.

"Oh, my word, you're late! Now we shan't have time to talk."

Father Lasques consulted his watch. "But the bus doesn't leave for an hour or so?"

"There are no times for the bus. It goes when it's ready and it's ready now."

Father Lopez shared the handle of Father Lasques' suitcase. Because the older man ran, the younger one was forced to jog in step with him.

"What news of Father Keogh?" he asked.

"He was alive, Father, just alive, when I saw him last. He's conscious now but he doesn't know anybody."

A tempestuous hooting was heard from outside.

"Oh come along, come along," Father Lopez urged. "I expect Doña Florencia has gone back for something. She usually does. So we might be in time to catch it. That is Roberto-of-the-Bus calling for her."

The bus had a name: "No Me Olvides"—"Don't leave me behind." Twelve people were waiting to board it. Most of them were attended by livestock. An Indian carried a wickerwork basket of tightly packed chickens and a boy

15

led a white goat on a string. A fat woman carrying a baby was running across the plaza.

"Doña Florencia!" Father Lopez puffed. "You'd better run for it. Although she is fat she is fast." He was clasping a brown-paper parcel and a bottle of lemonade. He pushed them into the young priest's hands. "Tortas," he said, "to eat on the journey, and something to quench your thirst."

Father Lasques thanked him, shook hands and arrived at the bus stop shoulder to shoulder with the panting Doña Florencia. She seemed in danger of dropping the baby at the sight of him. Several other persons turned round to gape. It was not a reception to which Father Lasques was used. His former parishioners would have expressed cordiality and respect towards a new priest. But in the hearts of his fellow passengers to Quantana he appeared to have excited nothing but distress. The driver did his best to dissuade him from making the journey at all.

"Well, it's not a nice place. It isn't a nice place like this, is it?" he inquired of his passengers.

A strong chorus answered him, "No."

An elderly man was more voluble. "It's a good thing to take what Roberto says, Father. Roberto knows both places well."

The bus itself, square and snorting, was not an inviting vehicle in which to travel over a hundred miles.

Nevertheless Father Lasques said firmly, "I should like a *single* to Quantana, please."

A voice from behind him said complacently, "Now I call that *most* unwise."

There was a girl at Father Lasques' side. She was bold-eyed and dimpled; an upturned nose added impertinence to her face. A blouse was drawn tight to emphasize her breasts and she wore a great waxen red flower in her hair.

16

It took Father Lasques only two glances to sum up her character. He guessed at her age, fourteen. She made him a coquettish bow, missed her step and knocked against him. When she recovered her balance she smiled.

"Do you come from Quantana?" he asked.

"Yes, if you please, I am Candalaria Fernandez, typist to the Señor Dentista, and very good he says I am."

"But not at the typewriting," somebody said.

A thin, bothered man took her arm. "My daughter," he admitted. "Yes, my daughter." And he sighed.

The journey took fourteen hours and the stench in the bus was severe. It was evident that no one had wished to sit next to Father Lasques. There was a scuffle that struggled to retain a semblance of politeness in which the small boy with the goat and three Indians were finally forced to his end of the bus. All efforts at conversation failed and while they pressed on each other repeated refreshment no one made the same gesture towards the priest. He was grateful for Father Lopez's thoughtful provisions. He offered a slice of the thick bread with the chorizo sausage filling to the boy with the goat at his side. The boy refused, button-eyed shyness puckering his face, but the goat accepted before Father Lasques was able to withdraw the sandwich.

The goat lost its foothold so frequently at the swing of the bus that it spent a considerable portion of the journey between Father Lasques' knees. He found the atmosphere conducive neither to prayer, contemplation, nor the study of his breviary, and when the whispering started he could not help but overhear it. It made strange conversation for a people who were reputed to be newly released from fear.

"Santa Madre de Dios! This will mean trouble."

17

"And we are the ones who will catch it most if we are seen with a priest on the bus."

"It would have been better for Roberto to refuse to take him, better for him as well."

"Yes, but not very polite."

"It might be possible to get off at the Huapan Ledge and walk down the rest of the way by oneself."

"It is not safe to be out in the night."

"For myself I would rather be out the whole night than be seen with the priest by the Bad One."

"If we are lucky," an old woman said, "we might get in before the Bad One's about."

"There's no chance of that, Bernandina, unless Roberto flies."

The small boy beside Father Lasques suddenly released the goat, threw himself down on the floor and howled. The goat, making the most of its freedom, trotted the length of the bus and butted the driving seat playfully. Roberto lost control at the wheel. The bus plunged sideways towards the side of the road and came to an abrupt halt at the edge of the ravine. Women screamed, men shouted and the child continued to howl. The more Father Lasques attempted to pacify him the more hysterical he became. He lay on the floor in a hunched-up ball of protest against the hands that were trying to lift him up.

"No, no, not by the window. The Bad One will see me if I sit by the priest."

Someone said sensibly, "The Bad One will *hear* you if you do not shut up."

The child was silenced instantly but would not resume his seat.

Roberto strode down the bus. "A fine thing, Manuel," he told the child sternly, "to let the goat take a run at my back. You could have had us all down the side of the mountain."

Doña Florencia stroked the boy's head. "Poor little Meme, he is frightened of the Bad-One-of-the-Cats."

Father Lasques broke out, "The Bad One? But I understood that Malo was dead."

Roberto made no answer. He went quickly back to the driving seat. But the three Indians sitting in front of Father Lasques, still apathetically smoking cigars, turned round in unison to stare at him with fathomless blue-black eyes. The boy passed the rest of the journey beneath the seat. It was old Saturnino the grocer who kept hold of the goat. Father Lasques overheard Doña Florencia say, "If you ask me, this very near accident is a sign that the Bad One is already displeased."

Hostile glances were turned upon Father Lasques. A deep and uneasy silence reigned and when the bus drove through Tephuango everyone ducked out of sight. Even Roberto lowered his head. The Indian settlement lay in darkness but through the hut doorways the fires were glowing like flickering earth-bound stars.

Then the bus took a steep nose downwards. Far below him Father Lasques saw descending steps of light where the town dipped towards the river in terrace fashion. The road descended so fiercely that he was forced to brace his knees. By the time the bus drew up the lights of the plaza had been switched off. It was shortly after nine. Father Lasques had never seen a group of people leave a vehicle with such speed. The passengers were out with their baggage and animals before he had stretched his limbs. When he himself stepped down on the plaza there was not a living soul in sight, but he could still hear the sound of footsteps running to the narrow back streets.

19

He turned to ask his way of Roberto, but Roberto was already in gear. He shouted above the engine, "You'd better hurry, Father, it's not wise to stay out in the dark."

And he drove the bus away. The night wrapped itself about Father Lasques as if a black hood had encased his eyes. The houses were shuttered and barred but he saw across the plaza a thin slice of wedge-shaped light. It was shining from under a door. He stumbled his way towards it. A guitar was playing behind the door and he heard the throw of dice. Men's voices were raised and a girl laughed. "Maria is growing too old for love, but those are the ones who hold on to it."

A woman's voice answered her, "Slut!"

Father Lasques collided with something soft. A squeak of anger proclaimed it alive. He bent down and discovered a small white cat mewing to get in at the door. He picked it up and turned the handle. The lamplight danced in his eyes at first and the noise stopped. He could hear human breath in the silence.

He said, "I am Father Lasques. Is this your little cat?"

No one answered. He appeared to have walked into a drinking bar. Smoke lay under the ceiling, greenish grey; stark murals covered the walls. They struck Father Lasques forcibly as expressing Communistic ideals but he was impressed by them artistically. There were only two women and four men in the bar. At first Father Lasques believed the men to be charros; they all wore cowboy dress, braided jackets, and tight-fitting trousers. Down the seams there were silver horseheads. Four black sombreros hanging on pegs had silver and gold threaded into the crowns. A fat man was polishing glasses behind the bar. A woman leaned plump elbows on it, and the guitar player, a man of great size, had emptied a bottle of pulque. At the same table a

20

smaller man chewed at his nails, nervously rolling two dice. The fourth, not much more than a boy, had a keen and narrow face. On his hand a big amethyst winked. Candalaria Fernandez slid off his lap. She avoided Father Lasques' eye as she asked him, "Why have you come here, Father? Do you want a drink?"

All four men stood up. It was when Father Lasques saw that the smallest was crippled that he realized where he was. He recognized the Jeep. He was in Porfirio's bar amongst Malo's men. The narrow-faced boy must be Vito, the one behind the bar Porfirio, and the big guitar player Pablo, returned from his home state.

It was the boy Vito who seemed to have taken over the leadership. He ordered, "Maria! Get rid of that cat."

The woman came out from behind the bar. She walked with a sensual grace. She took the cat and went off with it into the back of the house. But as she passed Candalaria she struck the girl's cheek.

Fat Porfirio blew out his lips and laughed. "I warned you, Chata, that Maria's hand is hard."

His use of the nickname "Snubnose" left Father Lasques aware that the girl must be on the friendliest terms with the men in the bar. Vito, big Pablo, and the Jeep called her "Chata" as well, and by the brightness in her eyes and the sway in her walk he suspected that she had shared Pablo's pulque.

The little Jeep giggled nervously. "Well, Father, come for the funeral? I don't think you'll find he'll last long."

Vito asked, "Who, the Padre Keogh? Surely he's already dead."

"That's right," said the Jeep. "This morning, wasn't it?"

21

Porfirio shook a solemn head. "A terrible loss," he said.

Pablo's guitar was inlaid with shells. A bird design covered the back. He struck up a tune and sang to it:

> *"Once upon a time,*
> *There was such a good priest,*
> *Such a very good priest,*
> *Such a very good priest,*
> *But a little señorita had such green eyes,*
> *Such very green eyes,*
> *Such very green eyes."*

Father Lasques ignored the song. He asked, "Will you tell me the way to his house?"

"They say he suffered greatly towards the end." The Jeep bit into a thumbnail. His face was heart-shaped and white. "It's a pity you couldn't have got here in time, Father. He kept calling out for a priest."

"He wanted to make his confession," said Pablo. "It would have eased his end."

"Confess!" said the Jeep. "Now what would a nice man like that have to confess?"

"Eh, Jeeponito!" Vito laughed. "You would find he's had his times. I would not mind hearing those sins." Then he said sharply, "Get this man out. We like to choose our company here."

Pablo and Porfirio seized Father Lasques. They bundled him towards the door. When it closed he was alone in the night again. Then Candalaria joined him.

"Come," she said, "I will show you the house."

Father Lasques thanked her. He was obliged to take her arm. His steps were uncertain following her but she found it easy to pick out the way.

22

He said, "You must have gone straight to that bar when the bus got in. You're much too young to drink."

"I do what I like," she said. There was no insolence in her voice. It was simply a statement of fact. Then she sighed. "It's a pity about the other padre. His eyes used to smile when he talked to you. This is the house."

Father Lasques knocked. There was silence until soft footsteps crept towards the door.

"The old one is listening," Candalaria whispered. "It's not wise here to let people in from the street. Give her some sign who you are."

Father Lasques called out clearly, "I am Father Marcelino Dominguez Lasques y Alonso. Kindly let me in."

A woman's voice asked a question back. "If that is who you are then who am I?"

"It is Chela, the housekeeper," Candalaria whispered.

"You are Chela," Father Lasques called. "I've already told you who I am. Please open the door at once."

Chela's voice was wary still. "It is possible to give such names and not be the one who was baptized with them. A friend of my sister's husband once gave names to a woman that were not his own, so that she should not find out that he was married."

"Old fool," Candalaria shouted, "this one is really the priest. He has come to take the dead one's place. I know for I came on the bus with him."

The door was opened suddenly. He had not time to thank Candalaria before a thin hand had pulled him inside. As he stepped over the threshold ears of garlic crushed under his feet. He carried the odor of them into the house on the soles of his shoes. Chela bolted and barred the door behind him.

"What a thing—to be seen in the dark with a girl of that kind. There is quite enough said about priests without that." She stood with a faded serape about her, a kerosene lamp in her hand. Her feet were bare and a plait hung down her back. "Mother in Heaven, it's a mercy you've still got your clothes on. That girl would steal the gold from your teeth if you smiled at her."

Father Lasques said, "Chela, I know what has happened. I've just heard the news."

She preceded him into a small whitewashed room. Worn primrose matting covered the floor and her feet made a singsong crackle across it. A Victorian medicine cupboard, gloomily curtained, took up half a wall. There was a desk against a window that was shuttered and barred on the street, and there was a straw mattress in the corner.

"I'm afraid this is all that we have for you, Father, but there aren't any fleas. I have personally seen to that matter myself. I took some of the doctor's cleaning poison. They say that the fleas do not like it. He sprays it all over the house." And she pulled back the blanket to show a wet patch of disinfectant in the center of the bed. Then she sighed. "Yes, it is terrible news. Nothing was ever so bad as this and it's not hard to find bad things here."

"I was told that it happened this morning," Father Lasques said.

Chela turned deep brown eyes on him. "Then it must have been el Choco who told you, Father. You shouldn't expect sensible talk from a half-wit. That one forgets his own name."

Father Lasques told her, "I heard the news in Porfirio's bar." He had to put out a quick hand to save the lamp.

"Porfirio's bar!" she squealed at him. "Mother in

24

Heaven, you might have been killed! You'd think they would all be inside the jail, well that's what I said to the Jefe. I said, 'Those ones should all be in jail.' And I'll tell you what he said. He said, 'Chela, I'm only the Chief of Police. I'm not the Lord God Almighty. It's His business to fix right and wrong. I have to have something called evidence.' You see it was this way, Father, there was only the padre himself at the shooting, and the Señor Frankenson who is someone who drinks too much. Well those two could say how the true thing took place but the padre was dying and the Señor Frankenson drank so much tequila and brandy to cheer himself up that afterwards he couldn't remember what happened at all. So that was no good to the Jefe. This Señor Frankenson is Americano, Father, he is barman to Señor Martinez of the Hotel de la Costa, a nice little place. The padre always liked him. Some people called them cuates, but I wouldn't call that one a padre's twin."

Exasperated, Father Lasques demanded, "Will you answer me at once—"

"Yes, well, give me a few little moments, Father, I am going as fast as I can. This means that the only ones left to tell the Jefe what really happened were the Bad One's men themselves, and they say that only the Bad One was there at the shooting and he must have shot the padre and then himself, so you see how they cannot be blamed! Some of the Indios have said this is true because they're afraid, and in this town there were people to swear that the Bad One's men were not with him that night. Can you think they could sleep in their beds with such lies? The poor Señor Frankenson is trying to remember again but something besides the tequila went wrong with his head. They say that somebody must have hit it at the time of the shooting. The

25

little Father Lopez has sworn to the Jefe that the Señor Frankenson told him that Vito, Porfirio, and the Jeep were most certainly there at the time, and one of these shot the Bad One as well as the padre, by mistake. The Jefe did put them in jail at first, but with the Indios, and so many people to say that they were all in Quantana that night, the word of the little Father Lopez wasn't enough against so many. So now these men are out again—kings of the town! Vito Castillo has Malo's place."

"Chela!" Father Lasques shouted at her. "I insist that you tell me about Father Keogh."

"He is a little better thank you, due to myself I think."

Father Lasques sat down in a leather-backed chair. "Are you telling me that he's still alive?"

"Yes, well, you could call it alive."

"Where is he?"

"He is up in his bed of course, Father. Did you think I have put him to sleep in the street?"

Father Lasques took two steps to the door. Then he stopped, suddenly nervous of disappointment, afraid that he might have misconstrued the woman's involved account. "If he's alive why did they tell me in Porfirio's bar that he was dead?"

"They would tell you that the President was killed by a goat if they thought it would hurt your heart. You should not have gone into that bar, Father, it is not a nice place for a priest."

Father Lasques ran up the stairs. There were only two rooms from which to choose. One was shut off by a wooden door, from which long-faded paint had flaked, the other by a beaded curtain. Father Lasques opened the door. The room smelled of disinfectant. It was lit up by a single candle, lopsided in the draft. Beetles and ants buzzed

26

around the flame, occasionally dropping, a wing singed, to kick agonized legs in the wax. Over the bed a big crucifix hung. A lizard scuttled round it and, startled by Father Lasques, sped down the wall. A table stood under the window cluttered with bottles, but a space had been found for a vase of tuberoses. Chela appeared behind Father Lasques. She took a card from the flowers and showed it to him. It bore only two words, *From Locha*.

Chela tore the card across. "It is not a nice thing for a bride to come running back home to send flowers to a priest. What sort of a honeymoon for the bridegroom is that? And what will you have for your supper, Father? There is nothing to have except beans."

A broom was propped up against the end of the bed and from underneath the pillow the top of a pair of scissors showed. With the garlic scattered about the doorway they made three attempts to keep evil spirits at bay. It was Chela who put such faith in superstitious remedies.

She was still frowning disapproval upon the flowers.

"There is no higher family in the whole of these parts than the de Cortinez. You would think that the Señora Cortinez de Dyke Brown would know how to behave. But most certainly not. Only a few weeks married, Father, and to come running home like that! The whole of the town is talking about it. It was just because the padre was sick. I said to Josefa who used to nurse her, I said, 'The next thing the Señora will do is to shout to the world that she has given her heart to a priest.' You ought to keep those things quiet. Of course her mother, Doña Marian, is just some ordinary gringo lady without very nice blood in her veins but a daughter should have her father in her as well." She closed the door quietly behind her, grumbling loudly beneath her breath, "A fine thing to come running

27

home for a priest. What is the husband going to say?"

There was nothing else in the room except the bed. It took courage to reach the side of it. Father Lasques became aware that he was unconsciously holding his breath.

No movement came from the bed. Father Lasques' own shadow fell over the face. It came as a shock to him to discover that Father Keogh's eyes were open, patiently appearing to study him. They were black and fine untroubled eyes but they were sightless. Father Keogh was unaware that anyone stood in the room. Father Lasques bent closer to look at him. It was a face which physical weakness had not deprived of strength. Clearly marked eyebrows lay dark on the forehead and the mouth showed a powerful calm. It was not surprising that a young girl could love him. Father Keogh in health must have had very considerable charm. The hair and the eyes that could make no response to the light had a Celtic darkness which could have passed for Mexican.

The Bishop would not have thought of an arrogant aristocrat if he had seen Father Lasques then. He would have thought of his own younger brother. There was no remote look of disdain, solemnity had fled, and tenderness mingled with the curiosity as Father Lasques bent over the bed. A lock of fine hair had slipped out of place, reducing his twenty-four years. His lips were apart and his eyes were bright. Father Lasques looked eighteen. He had practiced expressions in front of the mirror before the Bishop's interview. A frown brought a line between the eyes and would serve to belie the age, reserve would suggest wisdom, self-assurance would inspire confidence. The fear that the Bishop might consider him too young and too inexperienced had been a constant and nightmare companion to

28

Father Lasques; gravity would serve to divert the attention from lack of experience. He had longed to accept the glass of mezcal. It would have helped to soothe overwrought nerves and dissolve apprehension, but on the other hand it might have loosened his tongue to his own detriment and it would not have been wise to give the Bishop the impression that he was someone to leap at the first chance of alcohol. It would also be better not to smoke. Lack of restraint might prove prejudicial. Father Lasques had been determined that the Bishop should not perceive that Father Keogh's report upon Quantana had caused him considerable alarm. To do that would have been to give the Bishop the chance to decide that he was unprepared for the duties he so longed to undertake. He had not meant to belittle Father Keogh. He had meant only to show the Bishop that he considered himself competent.

Father Keogh stirred. The young priest jumped back guiltily as if he had infringed upon the other man's privacy. The black eyes were searching the ceiling and sometimes the forehead creased. The head turned slowly from side to side as if there were some form of tracery on the white square above that an unblinded eye could not see.

Chela came in with a tray of beans. "Here you are, Father, frijoles. It's a long time since we saw any meat in this house." There was a brown-paper parcel beside the plate.

Father Lasques said, "Chela, the padre moved his head, but he doesn't appear to be able to see."

Chela unwrapped the parcel. From it she took an unfragrant morsel. It was green-skinned and dark-fleshed and not far from decay. Father Lasques leaned forward to examine it. "What have you got there, Chela?"

"It is a piece of iguana, Father, that was cut up by the

29

witch. She is a white witch, a good curandera. If you place one of these pieces somewhere near to the sick it will keep the black magic from going to the eyes."

Father Lasques said sternly, "A good Catholic should not believe in these superstitions. Surely you ought to know that."

Chela stopped to put the section of iguana beneath Father Keogh's bed. "The Señor Doctor is a good Catholic, Father, as good as we get round here. But what has he done for the padre? Like a log he was as if there was nothing alive in his head. There were little moments when I thought his poor chest was too weak to make the breaths. So I said to myself, 'This Señor Doctor is not a good man.' Time and time again he has been here to stick a big needle into the padre's arm. Now I ask you, is that a nice way to make a sick man well? So I went to Mother Montezera, the witch." Chela made her usual return in her own good time to the question he had asked. "Yes, he can turn his head. This was not so before I went to the curandera. But the eyes are full of darkness still." Chela waved a finger in front of Father Keogh's face. "You see, it makes no difference. He does not see the shadows pass but he knows me if I touch him." Gently she ran her hand, brown and dry-skinned, over the sick man's face. Something near to a smile moved Father Keogh's lips. "If you touch him he will soon learn your fingers. He can tell between the doctor's and Señor Frankenson's. I do not say he knows who we are, but he knows we are someone to trust."

"Does he speak at all, Chela?"

"Sometimes. But it isn't how you and I would talk. It is all muddled up in his head, and always the Bad One—the Bad One! Have they said Mass for him? Did he get the Sacraments? Did they do this and that for him? As if

30

it wasn't the devil's job. And he prays for Malo too. The Bad One must sit on his brain."

Father Lasques told her, "Chela, when I came up on the bus today people were talking very strangely about the Bad-One-of-the-Cats. You'd have thought he was still alive." He noticed that she avoided his eye. "For instance, one woman said, 'If we're lucky we might get in before the Bad One's about.' What could she mean by that?"

"Well, Father, how am I to tell? I was not on this bus."

"But you know that Malo's dead."

"I know that they *say* he is, Father."

"Surely there's no possibility of his still being alive?"

"I am not here to decide such things, Father, I am only here to look after the padre." She picked up the tray and went downstairs.

Suddenly there was something else in the room, something he recognized, short though his experience of it had been. It was apparent to the innermost senses yet intangible to the touch and unseen by the eye. It was certain yet not determined. It was still to come and yet it was there as if it had always been. It was death. So forceful was its presence that Father Lasques went swiftly to the side of the man in the bed. There was no obvious change in the physical condition but in the face there was something which had not been there before. To the man in the bed death was not only welcome, it was long-cherished. It came as a prize. Its presence brought nothing but hope. There was no slackening of features, no tightening of breath. In the face of Father Keogh there was only a gentle and reverent acceptance of something held infinitely dear.

The boy by the bed was afraid. As he had never thought it possible he felt the black edges of fear and he

31

knew with embittering certainty that it was on his own behalf. The life that was slipping away from him would leave him behind the barricades he had thought to be impenetrable about himself. Useless and insecure, they would provide no defense. At the first onslaught they would fall and expose not only his own person but those whom he had thought them fit to protect. He had been so anxious to take on the task. He had considered his unworthiness but he had not considered his worthiness. The two had seemed inseparable but they were not. They were aeons apart. The one was not after all a logical outcome of the other. Doubts he had had in plenty as to his ability to succeed but not of his right to attempt success. ". . . It is safe to say that this Anacleto made of Quantana a challenge to Christianity." Words, words that had sounded so different many hundreds of miles away. "You may find left in Quantana traces of an evil hard to suppress. It will have left an indelible mark." Who was he to have challenged that mark? Who was he to have dared to try to trick the Bishop into entrusting him with the care and the guidance of souls so pertinently in need of more experienced protection? How dared he presume to be so anxious to undertake a task that could be better done by almost anybody else? All too plainly he realized how unthinkingly he had taken upon himself the responsibility not only of the salvation of those who could be harmed by his failure but of allowing the Bishop to share it. Both materially and spiritually the Bishop would receive half the blame. He needed, because of the need of others which he suddenly felt himself unfit to answer, the help of the man in the bed. If Father Keogh left him naked in front of himself and alone with the urgency of his own youth, he knew that he would be too keen a coward to give up the fight. He would lack the courage to face defeat. He could tell his God but not his Bishop that he could not stand alone. He would struggle on, bolstered by hopefulness posing as faith, determination masquerading as prayer, he would deceive both himself and his church and he would fail. He put out a hand in his agony to touch Father Keogh's face. And he prayed.

It was dark in the room when he touched the face. The candle had guttered and blown. The moonlight forced its way through the shutters in a series of thinly sliced steps. Father Lasques was still on his knees when the day broke but a change had taken place in the room. Death no longer filled every crevice, it had withdrawn as it entered, softly. Father Lasques felt a buoyant selflessness as if there were no weight in his bones and no blood in his veins, yet he himself was whole as he had never been before. He felt as if his complete being had been called a witness to things beyond the ordinary comprehension, retaining no valid recollection yet conscious of sublime privilege.

In the bed Father Keogh stared at the ceiling. Its height was exaggerated, seeming many miles off. At first he thought he must be in Ireland again and that the hazy white patches above were the great rain-filled clouds he had not ceased to miss. Then he thought that he must still be lying in the closely dark Indian hut; that the life so reluctant to leave the body was hampering the departure of his soul. He felt impatient with it for delaying his spiritual release, and he strained to remember whether he had or had not confessed to the tall young priest at his side. Then he fell a prey to a sudden fear that he might not after all be dying, that time had passed without his knowing, that the voices he heard, the hands he felt tending him might have succeeded in saving him. He realized that the fear was a sin against a God whose will it must be that he should continue to live. If he had done well he would have been granted rest in the eternal arms for which his soul so craved. He was too weak to resist the temptation of wishing that he might have achieved his goal. But his work was not done in Quantana yet. There was need for him somewhere still. It was as if Quantana had stretched out its very fingers and touched him on the cheek. He felt the despair in that touch. Somehow from somewhere he must gather the will to live. It might be that God in His all-seeing goodness was granting a second chance, mercifully protecting him from being taken to rest in his sins.

At first he knew neither the names nor the identities of the persons beside his bed. Then suddenly all names were clear to him. One in particular was written across the dingy white envelope that was the ceiling above his head as if it were on a letter addressed to him: *Anacleto Gonzales Flores Comachi Alvarez.*

He lay drowsily, listening to the questions of the anxious young priest. He caught only snatches of the doctor's low-voiced replies:

"... and the bullets removed ... operation remarkably successful in the circumstances ... bruising of tissues and damage to nerve ... right arm may be affected ... too early to tell."

Then Chela's voice broke into his consciousness. "Señor Doctor! Señor Doctor! Look! The padre's eyes are well again. See how they follow my finger about."

Father Keogh painfully followed from side to side what looked like a brown cigar in his twilight world.

"Do you see, Señor Doctor? How the eyes go with it? It was the same with my sister's youngest child. Just two

34

days old, the one that was not its father's—they always say those ones are brightest."

In the bar of the Hotel de la Costa, Sam Frankenson said to a customer, "I said a prayer for him, didn't I? When a nonpraying man prays it's like a nondrinker taking his first shot. It has one hell of a kick to it." Then he tipped a glassful of brandy back into a bottle and patted the cork. "Honey, you and me have to part."

To Father Lasques it was a further proof of the infallibility of prayer.

In the kitchen Chela congratulated herself: "It's a good thing *someone* had the sense to fetch the curandera."

The doctor, administering an anesthetic, confessed to the dentist, "I never expected to pull him through. There was no co-operation at all at first, then suddenly, he put up a fight. I've forbidden them on pain of death to tell him what he's come back to."

Chapter 4 〰〰〰〰〰〰〰〰〰〰〰〰

FATHER KEOGH WAS SLOW IN REGAINING STRENGTH. HIS own impatience impeded his progress. There were relapses due to overexertion. The wounds in his body showed lively scars but he suffered most with his weakened right arm. The doctor expressed himself delighted. "It's excellent that you feel pain. If you did not we should have to worry. No pain would show serious damage done to the nerve. It will trouble you certainly, but in time if you're careful you should regain the full use." He was severe in his warnings of what might occur if the priest took insufficient rest. "Not only in body, it's essential in mind. We must have you relaxed and at peace. Mental as well as physical strain will make you aware of those wounds and that arm."

"Well, how long will the wretched thing be out of action?"

Doctor Juarez was cheerful and bustling. "It may take months, it may be sooner—but for the time being it stays in that splint and that sling. Get it?"

"I get it," Father Keogh sighed.

"And remember what I said about worry. There's nothing to worry about. Everything's fine around here. You're not to trouble your head about church affairs. I don't care what the Pope says, you're under doctor's orders now. Let the curate take care of everything. That's what he's here for, isn't it? Another thing, don't go listening to anyone's tales—you know what this town is like for tales."

Father Keogh told him, "I heard Mother Montezera takes credit for my recovery."

The doctor laughed. "Oh, sure. I get no kudos at all. It's she alone who's cured you. You know what they're like for superstition round here. There's nothing they won't believe. Her reputation's gone up in leaps and bounds. The whole of the town is flocking to her. They're queueing up for spells."

"I'm glad somebody gets something out of it," Father Keogh laughed.

"Don't forget what I told you—no worrying and not too much praying!"

In Ireland Father Keogh's favorite sister knew nothing

of what had happened to him. In his wallet he kept a picture of her, of wide Irish eyes and springing black hair and a smile that he frequently smiled at, himself.

There were many irate notes from Ellen-Dora, accusing him of neglect. Her big hand slipped sideways over the paper. *What the* hell *are you up to, Mickey?* There was little or no punctuation and considerable confusion of subject matter. *Cora has foaled. It's a beauty. More sire than dam unfortunately. Darling, I'm worried to death about you. Are you ill? Have those awful people wrung your neck? Or have you eloped with that murky little bundle of chilly passion from the Casa Grande?* Ellen-Dora had never liked Locha. She had sensed the girl's feelings towards him long before he became aware of them himself. Her only visit to Quantana had been tarnished a little by his constant defense of Locha. It was one of the few disagreements he had ever had with Ellen-Dora. *The very last time I heard from you she was about to marry that cousin of hers, poor lad. He'll catch his death of cold!*

He dictated his reply to Father Lasques: "I have had a slight accident but I'm well over it now. My arm was injured, so I couldn't write. Delighted to hear about the foal—but I agree it's hard that we never seem to be able to reproduce Cora herself. I always did say there could never be two of her. You're still a little unkind about Locha! Yes, she did marry her cousin Dyke Brown. She's left Quantana and is living in Washington now."

Father Keogh inquired when the younger priest's hands hesitated on the keyboard, "Anything wrong?"

Father Lasques shook his head. But he seemed reluctant to type the words.

Living in such close proximity with Father Lasques, bringing with it as it did opportunities of self-abnegation, the lack of which Father Keogh had often felt a privation, nevertheless brought its difficulties. They had little in common outside their priesthood. There were few discussions upon matters unconnected with their common cause which did not show a wide divergence of taste and opinion.

Father Keogh's interests in painting were confined to the old mastery of canvas which expressed the artist's viewpoint in a manner visible to the untrained eye. Father Lasques was hotly defensive of the merits of modernity.

Father Keogh smiled at him. "I know what you're thinking—you think I fall into the Little Bopeep class. Well, I'm not particularly fond of sickly shepherdesses. I'm no fonder of Watteau and Fragonard than I am of those oddities with holes in their middles and eyes in their foreheads but I am, if it excuses me at all, able to appreciate Cézanne, Lautrec, and Degas."

Father Lasques leaned forward in agitation and his fingers appeared to be wrestling. "Only now are you able to appreciate them. But at the time you would have despised them as contemporary art. You would have been the first to criticize, the first to look down upon them. You would have been brought up on your English 'The Light of the World' and 'Bubbles.' "

"Heaven forbid," Father Keogh said.

"You would have looked on Lautrec as holes in the middle and eyes in the forehead."

"But he got in hands and feet as well!"

"Father! Father!" The young Spaniard's eyes seemed alight in his face and two flushed patches appeared on his cheekbones. "Is it impossible to make you understand? At the time we are speaking of you would have failed to recognize them as hands and feet."

"What should I have thought they were?"

"You would have been blinded then as you are now by convention. Degas and Cézanne certainly played their part in releasing the world of art from sentimentality but we have progressed in its freedom since then."

"The only reason I should like to live for another hundred years," Father Keogh said, "is to be old enough to make head or tail of modern monstrosities."

It was the same with literature and music. They could find no common ground. Yet there were times when Father Lasques could not control a fit of despondency. He felt himself sadly inadequate as an assistant to Father Keogh. It seemed in his darker moments of hard-fought depression to which his nature seemed irrevocably in bondage, that Father Keogh was naturally equipped in personality with everything he himself lacked. There was an ease in Father Keogh's manner which had the power to lessen the shyness of others, and the simplicity with which Father Keogh could take the word of God into the home of the humblest or the proudest was something which Father Lasques never failed to admire. He himself had always suffered from the difficulties of personal contact. His was a shyness that incommoded him. He still mistook sternness for dignity. In prayer only he felt himself a true lover of souls. Confronted with the flesh that surrounded them, he was stiff and at a loss.

Father Keogh was aware of the young Spaniard's social shortcomings, aware that the inherent shyness must obviously bring disquiet. But in its very struggle Father Keogh could sense an intuitive spirituality, to achieve which he himself must strive to the end of his days. Father Lasques had to fight unrest, Father Keogh had to fight content. He found it difficult not to become the victim of a sense of well-being even in adversity; not to enjoy the

39

sacred privilege of combating evil. He was fully aware that he should have been saddened by the need for it. He thought at times that of the two of them Father Lasques would be of greater use than himself to Quantana.

Oddly enough it occurred only to the Bishop that Quantana might have a need for both of them.

There were visitors at first—Sam, the Jefe, sad-faced and heavy-shouldered, and Roberto-of-the-Bus. It was Chela who guarded their tongues.

"Nothing is to be said to the Father about how things go on in the town. He will have to know soon enough."

They were stiffly uncommunicative. Even the Presidente Municipal, sly-eyed and perspiring in his tight alpaca suit, was not to be drawn out. It was upon the Presidente that Father Keogh had most relied for gossip. Don Agapito's young wife Arcelia had harbored a strong partiality to Malo-of-the-Cats. Her eye had even strayed towards Father Keogh himself more than once. She brought the Presidente little peace of mind, so that it must surely have come as a relief to him that Malo was no longer a rival. But the Presidente made no mention of Malo-of-the-Cats. The sweat formed across his balding head and at the sides of a loose-lipped mouth.

He had brought the priest a present which touched his heart at first. Father Keogh recognized in the leery old parrot one of the Presidente's most valuable possessions. He had always taken considerable pride in the way in which it repeated his name and swore, "Don Agapito! Santa Madre de Dios! Don Agapito!" It was not until he had gone and the cloth was removed from the cage that Father Keogh suspected the reason for the sacrifice. The bird's vocabulary had increased. In a high woman's voice it shrieked, "Agapito! Agapito! Silly, bald old fool!"

The old mestizo who had been Locha's nurse came down from the Casa Grande bearing presents of flowers and books. She carried the books in a grey robozo wound round the back of her head. Someone had carefully chosen them with an eye to Father Keogh's tastes. The books had been newly bought.

Chela took pains that Josefa was not left alone with Father Keogh and it was Chela who answered the questions put to her. Josefa made many attempts to open her mouth but was nearly always forestalled by Chela.

"This is a wonderful present, Josefa," Father Keogh said. "To whom do I send my thanks?"

"Doña Marian," Chela snapped.

"Doña Marian!" Father Keogh was puzzled. Doña Marian read nothing but beauty articles and gossip columns. Had they come from Don Pedro he could have understood. "Well, it's really extremely kind of her. What news have they had from Locha?"

"The Señorita Locha is—"

"Fine," Chela supplied for Josefa. "Now then, Father, it is not a good thing to be tired out with talk."

"Are they back from their honeymoon?" Father Keogh inquired.

Josefa had come to rely upon Chela. She turned a squat and wrinkled face and waited for Chela's "Yes."

"Have they found somewhere to live in Washington? It was Washington they were settling in, wasn't it?"

Chela answered, "Yes." Then she bustled the mestizo out of the room. She returned to plump up a cushion which Father Keogh had just satisfactorily arranged in his back. "That Josefa could talk someone's head off. It's not good for you, chat, chat, chat!"

41

The Jefe was no more informative. Father Keogh put anxious questions to him:

"How do they seem now they're free of Malo?"

"*Free* of him! Oh!—Yes, well, everything is going fine."

It was the same whenever he asked any questions. "Everything's fine, Father, everything's fine." From Chela, the Jefe, the doctor, and Sam.

The young priest echoed them hollowly but it was he who worried Father Keogh most. His efforts to turn all conversation connected with Quantana into other channels were far from subtle. Father Keogh would have liked to discuss with him in detail the findings of his day. He would have enjoyed passing on his knowledge of the persons the young priest would encounter, not unlike the proud displayer of a family album pointing out snapshots of close relatives.

But Father Lasques fell back on the doctor's orders. "He says we're not to talk more than ten minutes. It's important that you shouldn't be tired."

And he was frequently saved by Chela. Always a competent eavesdropper, she must have spent her whole day with an ear to the door. Whenever the young priest floundered Chela came bustling in.

"Now, now, Padre, the poor Father has more to do than stand making chatter to you all day long."

Father Keogh suspected a liaison between them and he felt a slight touch of resentment that he had never managed to train Chela so well.

He watched Father Lasques closely and was surprised to find such frayed nerves in a man of so few years. His skin had the dry and dull look that comes from lack of sleep.

"Chela, you are sharing the food equally, aren't you?

You're not feeding me up and leaving yourself and Father Lasques out?"

"No indeed, Father, we have the same as you and any little thing that you leave on your plate I make up for the Long Father at night."

"Chela, please use the padre's name. It's discourteous to refer to his height. I'm worried about him," Father Keogh said. "He seems to be losing weight."

"He is young, Father, and the holiness is new. It was the same with my second sister's husband, only with him it was not the holiness of course, it was the truss. A great hard thing it was, Father, to keep in a small little lump. It is just the getting used to something which makes them take off the weight."

Father Lasques was never back until late in the evening and he made the long journey into Huapan in order to confess to Father Lopez in preference to Father Keogh. Rather than sit with Father Keogh he went upstairs to meditate. Father Keogh had hoped that they might have recited their Office together. He found his own breviary difficult to manage singlehanded and he had always been of the opinion that the Office was something which might be doubly beneficial shared. Communal enjoyment of it was confined to the regular clergy. It was rare that the overworked parish priest had a chance to share the rigors and the privileges of the rewarding but demanding Office. He found Father Lasques unreceptive to the idea and forbore to press it. When unable to escape, the young priest gave the impression of edging towards the door and kept a perpetual eye on the watch he had borrowed from Father Keogh. He could not find his own. The house had been turned upside down for it. He recalled having used it at Huapan station.

"Didn't Chela tell me that you came up on the bus with young Candalaria Fernandez?" Father Keogh inquired.

"Yes, Father."

"Did she happen to get close to you at all?"

"She did bump into me—by accident of course."

"Of course," Father Keogh said. "She practically got my wallet off me as a baby in arms when I baptized her. You'd better pay a visit to the market. Have a look at the 'courtesy stall.' Quaintly enough, it's next door to Mother Montezera. Goods are displayed on that stall for about a week to give owners a chance to retrieve stolen property."

Father Lasques was shocked when he discovered the watch and looked even more so when Father Keogh laughed.

"Well, it's better than no form of restitution at all."

Father Keogh privately nicknamed the younger priest "Marcelino the Merry." Father Lasques had not smiled once and noises seemed to irritate him abnormally. Outside the window a barrel organ played all day. There were only four tunes: "Alexander's Ragtime Band," "Lily of Laguna," "Annie Laurie," and "Little Gray Home in the West." The organito, a Spanish dwarf, toothless and grinning, was called many names in the town—el Jorobado the Hunchback, el Choco the Half-wit, and sometimes el Pesado the Nuisance.

When Father Lasques put his hands to his ears Father Keogh sympathized.

"He bought it off some wretched sailor in Veracruz. It's his idea of cheering me up. It's good of him really. He doesn't make anything out of it this end. Later we might put it tactfully to him that we can't have him sacrificing his career."

44

He became even more perturbed about the younger priest. There was a bruise on the side of his face for which he seemed at a loss to account.

"You weren't ambushed by any chance, were you?" Father Keogh asked. "There used to be a rather disquieting little habit in this town of waiting in dark corners and dotting unsuspecting priests over the head. It was a fashion I hoped might have died out."

"It's quite all right, thank you."

Father Lasques seemed incapable of answering a straightforward question.

"What is the attendance at church?" Father Keogh asked. "You should be packed now they're free of Anacleto."

"I am not as popular as you, Father."

"It depends on what you mean by popularity," Father Keogh smiled. "As things turned out for me I rather hope you'll be gravely disliked. What was the collection on Sunday?"

"It—it hasn't been counted yet, Father."

"Not been counted yet? Well, that's something an old crock like me might manage to take off your shoulders if you're pressed. By the way, has the Rodriguez baby arrived?"

"Yes, Father."

"I was worried about that. The doctor expected trouble. Is Señora Rodriguez all right?"

"I think so, Father."

"But surely you called on her, didn't you?"

"Yes, Father, I went to the house."

"What was it?"

Father Lasques seemed lost in thought. "What was what, Father?"

45

"The baby of course."

"Oh! It was a boy—I mean a girl—well, I don't really know, Father, but it was either a boy or a girl."

"I'm glad," Father Keogh said.

Neither Chela nor Father Lasques could keep from him the poverty-stricken straits of the household finances. Their share of the benefices would have been little enough in normal times but it was obvious to Father Keogh that their impecunity could be attributable to only one thing: to lethargy or total abstinence from church on the part of the faithful. There could be no Sunday offertories, no stole fees, no Mass Intentions. They must be dependent for their existence entirely on the small allowance made by the Bishop in view of their peculiar circumstances. It was not a new position to Father Keogh. He had been forced on occasions to make door-to-door appeals to enable him to pay Saturnino the grocer. He had written articles upon Mexican life for the Irish market and taught English to the children of the Señoras Solano and Ferreira to augment his income.

When he questioned Chela about their finances she said, "Well, Father, this week is not such a good week because of the buying back of the Long Father's watch. You know how they charge on the Stall of Politeness—but next week we are sure to pick up."

Father Keogh confided to Sam, "I can't make head nor tail of my new curate. He leaves the house first thing in the morning and according to himself he does nothing, sees no one and goes nowhere. But he comes back completely exhausted by it all. Sometimes I think he's deliberately keeping something from me."

"Now why would he do a thing like that? Say, Mac, did you know you could have a hang-over on the wagon?"

46

"Is it very hard going, Sam?"

"And how," Sam replied. He gave Father Keogh's uninjured shoulder a playful punch. "Oh, I don't have any regrets about it but I guess I kinda got used to liquor and my blood keeps singing out for it. It seems when you give up alk you get yourself a whole set of new problems as well. I don't fit in with my pals any more. The kind I used to booze around with bore the pants off me now."

"It'll sort itself out. But it's improving you physically, Sam. You're in fine shape now."

"Oh, sure, it has compensations." There was a new care of his appearance in Sam. The beer stains had gone from the old fawn suit. His hat, still battered, sat straight on his head and his tie fitted close to his throat. The face was still gross and its color high but the eyes were clearer. "There's some things I like about it," Sam admitted. "But it scares the hell out of me at times. Suppose I do booze it up, suppose I go on the bat—how does that work out for you?"

"I shan't get the hang-over," Father Keogh pointed out.

"Did you forget that I made a deal with that God of yours? He takes the skids from under you and I give up hooch—that was the deal. Well, suppose I let my side slip someday?"

"Forgiveness is part of God's love."

"Yeah! It better had be."

"You would find that another prayer would ease things up."

"Talking of easing things up, you've been pretty sick, Mac. It seems like a good idea to quit the joint for a while, just until things—well, just until you're okay again."

47

"I'm coming along nicely, thank you, Sam. All I want is to be up and about again. I feel such a useless lump, stuck in this chair watching that boy taking the brunt of everything. It's not doing my nerves any good."

"Why not try praying to 'ease things up'?"

"Good advice, Sam," Father Keogh smiled.

The visitors ceased to call. Only Sam, the Jefe and the doctor came to the house. The little street which was so narrow that the shadows of houses made a black winding line down it was deserted. Nobody passed the window. Even the barrel organ moved away.

"What's happened to the organito, Chela?" Father Keogh asked.

"Well, Father, it would not be safe for him to—" Chela caught herself and her tongue wet her lips. "It would not be safe for him to play in one place all the time. It would make all the other places jealous."

"Was that what you were really going to say, Chela?"

"Yes, Father, certainly it was, but a little hiccup came up to stop me. My stomach has been upset."

She accompanied him when he was allowed to take gentle walks. He made an effort to increase their length each day but although there was not yet much heat in the sun his feet dragged and he found himself short of breath. He could not walk as far as the town itself. They followed the winding road that trailed into a goat track and crossed down by the maguey fields. Sometimes they wandered towards the River of Small Receptions where so many children were drowned. The air was sweet with the smell of the heavy-scented nardos that grew white and wild on the banks. The gay mirasoles embroidered the hillside, lifting their small colored faces towards the sun.

Sometimes they followed the high white wall on which

48

the vultures sat. His aim was to reach the church. Each day he shortened the distance to it. He could see the tamarindos that filled the churchyard. But the hill was too steep to the church itself. In the distance he saw its wash-pink tower and the tall tapered cypress that blocked out the front. To sit and hear the bell toll seemed a double renewal of strength.

It was strange how few people they met. Those they did rarely greeted him and none of them stopped to talk. Only the beggar who slept at night rolled in a filthy serape in the doorway of the Banco de Comercio asked a blessing or passed the time of day.

Once when they returned from an attempt to reach the church they found a Cadillac parked outside the house.

"Santa María Purísima! It is the big Americano car from the Casa Grande—now I wonder who we shall find in that—" Chela shaded her eyes and then smiled her relief. "It is only Don Pedro's driver, Victorino."

Victorino had brought a letter. It was written in a big hysterical hand and it read: *Do you have the energy to come up here? I'd be glad if you could make it. There's something I want to say to you that I wouldn't want to leak around the town.* It was signed *Marian de Cortinez* and there was a postscript. *Don't send the tall priest, it has to be you or no one.*

Father Keogh said to Chela, "I'm going up to the Casa Grande."

Chela's reply surprised him. "No, Father, you are certainly not. You are not strong enough for visitings yet and with Doña Marian it will not be possible to say no to the whiskey drink and still keep polite. She's a lady that drinks these things all day and not to take one would only offend her."

49

Father Keogh laughed. "My dear Chela, I'm perfectly capable of refusing an old-fashioned with the acme of old-world courtesy but I've not the slightest intention of doing so. I feel like a pick-me-up."

"Yes, and what else are you going to pick up? Silly tales that will start you off worrying—and besides it will not look quite nice to the town."

Father Keogh adjusted his sling. "What won't look nice to the town? I shan't be asked to imbibe in public, shall I?"

Chela blew on the top of the medicine cupboard and gave it a vigorous rub with her sleeve. "They will think you have gone to see—well, they will *think*."

"I should be only too delighted," Father Keogh said, "to be the means of bringing that unlikelihood to pass. Who will they think I am going to see?"

"Doña Marian," Chela said sulkily.

"Well, then, their intuitive powers will be justified. Really, Chela, I'm not sure that either of us quite knows what you're talking about."

Victorino's behavior was strange. As the car threaded its way through the town he wound down a window and called out to friends, "Good morning, Edmundo, good morning, Señor Ferreira. It is on the orders of my mistress that I'm driving the priest. You must not think that I take him about myself."

Father Keogh leaned forward and inquired of the man, "Why do you have to explain, Victorino?"

In the mirror the chauffeur's eyes were expressionless. His voice was polite. "It would not do for people to think that I use the car for my own pleasure, Padre."

The Casa Grande stood high on a rock. Terraced gardens tumbled poinsettia and bougainvillaea down to an artificial lake that shone like a splinter of glass in the sun. In the formal Italian gardens classical figures raised green-stained arms, or bent bow and arrow to take shot at a deer. The grounds were not well kept. Neither Don Pedro nor Doña Marian took a personal interest in them. Neglected summerhouses and tiny ornate pavilions were covered with creepers blocking the doorways; dark-mouthed, they stood yawning, to show cavelike interiors, a harbor for nothing but insects and rats. The jacaranda trees, flowering as blue as the sky, were strangled by climbing honeysuckle and the Casa Grande itself in spite of its colonnaded front and giant impressive doorways did not look a wholesome place. For all its architectural magnificence, the great house looked shabby in the pitiless inspection of the sun. The strong light played on it, giving it the look of a tired-faced woman from which age and neglect had chased all the traces of beauty and charm.

Father Keogh never failed to experience a sense of dolefulness as he approached the high iron gates. Even when Locha had played the self-contained games of a lonely child her laughter had failed to enliven it. It was as if she had fought a losing battle against the habitual silence of gloom and the atmosphere still carried her scars. There could be a gloom more destructive, Father Keogh thought, in the pressure of eternal sunshine than in the mournful greyness of a fog. Perhaps because the glare of it clarified the inner deficiencies within an already weary self, showing up the soiled patches on a soul like dust upon a polished table top. There was about the Casa Grande something else. There was a callousness in the neglect. Lethargy and poverty could not be blamed. The air of decay was not casual. It was deserted while still inhabited as if the house took its being from the man who lived his silent life within it, oblivious to any other world but the world of books.

Don Pedro emerged on occasions, thin-lipped and cold-eyed, to put into action his magisterial duties. If forced to disturb his hermit studies he was capable of returning to the living world of words with a chilling concentration. Father Keogh had never been easy about his administration of justice. Individual circumstances which might have put a different complexion on a case failed to influence his judgment. He was too grudging of time to be swayed by a nuance. Sometimes, Father Keogh thought that in his capacity of Juez de Primera Instancia Don Pedro turned a deliberate blind eye to things which he should have investigated with more thoroughness. But it was not for the innocent whom Father Keogh feared the most. It was for the souls of the guilty. Don Pedro took the surface view and delved no deeper. He had no wish to create a volcanic disturbance which might have shattered his own precious solitude. There was no doubt in the mind of the priest that Don Pedro would lean towards the side of evil if to expose it would disrupt his well-ordered existence. He would have turned a blind eye towards murder itself to preserve his peace and quiet.

Father Keogh never walked into Doña Marian's smoke-filled room without being sorry for her. The inevitable phonograph was playing tunes from another age. A jazz band of the twenties, still commendably clear, conjured up visions of bright young things while a singer wailed, *"Sometimes I'm happ-ee, sometimes I'm bloo-oo!"* Doña Marian wrote all over the world in her search for old recordings. They arrived months later, crated and straw-packed, at Huapan, to be collected by Roberto-of-the-Bus.

It must, Father Keogh thought, be due to a desire to return nostalgically to a time when her charms had been able to claim Don Pedro's attention. She was middle-aged, and well-preserved. Blond hair, naturalistically tinted in Mexico City once every three months, sat sleekly round her head. Her appearance earned her Father Keogh's admiration. She could receive few enough awards for her pains. It was unlikely that she saw her husband more than twice during the day and it was well known that he continued reading into the far reaches of the night. Hard lines round the eyes and mouth proclaimed her a woman at odds with the world.

She switched off the phonograph and came forward to greet him. "Why, Father, you're looking fine."

"Oh, I'm well on the mend now, Doña Marian, and thanks very much for the books."

Her blue eyes were dulled by the yellowed whites. She opened them wide at Father Keogh and one scarlet nail tapped her teeth. "I never sent any books."

Father Keogh sat down in the chair she pushed forward. "Then it must have been Don Pedro."

"It would never be Pey. He's so greedy with books I never knew him to loan one, let alone give."

"But Josefa told me they came from here."

She put an old-fashioned into his left hand and sighed. "Then I guess it's that daughter of mine you have to thank."

"But Locha's in Washington, isn't she?"

Doña Marian sat down opposite him. "Father, you have to help me. Locha is here. Repeat, right here," she said, answering his startled eyes. "Maybe I'm working against the mother-in-law gag but I don't think you'd find a nicer boy than that husband of hers. He's crazy about the kid."

"Isn't he with her?" Father Keogh asked.

"Oh, dear me no, it's only Mrs. Dyke-Brown that came home. She left him flat, Father, just walked out and left him flat. Incompatibility!" Doña Marian said the word bitterly.

"*Incompatibility!* But they haven't been married long enough to look up the word in the dictionary."

"I wouldn't say that was the reason anyway."

"What would you say it was?"

Doña Marian rose to pour herself another drink. "I'd say the reason was you."

Father Keogh said, "You don't mean that all that nonsense—"

Doña Marian interrupted him. "I wouldn't pretend I have the low-down on my daughter. I never got to know her that well but there's one thing I do know. She has a lot of her father in her. Their hearts aren't very big. One love is all they can take. Unfortunately with Pey it's been books."

Father Keogh stood up. Doña Marian lit him a cigarette.

"Milady moved out on Dyke the minute she heard you were sick. She drove all the way down herself. The way she acted I thought she was crazy. She said she had to be near you and she was never going far away from you again."

"What had Don Pedro to say?"

"Oh, he just told her to get the hell back to Dyke but he didn't notice she never went. You have to talk to her, Father. Somebody has to make her see sense."

Father Keogh was struggling against a desire to avoid

54

an embarrassing scene. He was ashamed of shirking his responsibilities. He said, "Would you like me to see her now?"

"Sure," Doña Marian said. She rang the bell and warned Josefa, who answered it, "Have the Señorita come down and don't tell her the padre is here."

Locha came into the room. She looked from Father Keogh to her mother and tightened her lips. "You just can't help interfering, can you, darling?"

She had a snowdrop frailty. Her hair, palely gold, was swept back from her face and fell limp from a black velvet knot. Except for her height which her slimness accentuated Father Keogh could still see the child in her. Sophistry sat ill upon Locha. He was immeasurably sorry for her. She had not often been happy. Her own close nature, an inheritance from Don Pedro, made it hard for her to have any friends. Pride also had come from Don Pedro. It was evident in the face with the broad forehead and the high cheekbones and the reserve in the clear grey eyes. From Doña Marian had come the fair, translucent skin. But there was a gentleness and a need for protection that came from within Locha herself. There's nothing so lonely as the loneliness inside one's own head, Father Keogh thought. He said to her, "You've lost weight. Did you find Dyke couldn't cook?"

"I wasn't with him long enough to find out." It was like her to challenge him first. She mixed herself an old-fashioned. "I'm sorry about the arm."

He was grateful for her casual sympathy. He never found himself in the company of Locha without feeling a quick understanding of her. It was possible that no one had fathomed her as easily as he.

Doña Marian refilled Father Keogh's glass. "Locha,

55

honey, I want you to listen very carefully to what the padre has to say. After all, he's your religion, your father's religion and your—"

Locha interrupted. "You're not going to lecture me, Father, are you? It will fall on stony ground."

"Why should I?" Father Keogh asked.

"Don't clerical gentlemen usually feel it their duty to give a few words of advice to runaway brides?"

"Clerical gentlemen *have* been known to mind their own business," Father Keogh said, "providing they're given a big enough hint."

Locha gave the long, slow smile that softened the whole of her face. "How awful for you, Father. Has Mama been disturbingly frank? If it's the slightest comfort to you, I don't intend to write you little tear-drenched notes and hang around your house."

"I'm sorry for that," Father Keogh said. "There's rather a dearth of visitors."

Locha filled her glass.

Doña Marian said, "Honey! That's your second."

Locha took off her mother's accent. "Darling! That's probably your sixth."

Doña Marian ignored the jibe.

Father Keogh controlled his own annoyance. It was apparent to him in every gesture she made that the girl felt a desolate insecurity. He shook his head when she offered to refill his glass.

"No thanks, I'm doing fine."

"Father, you certainly are. And I admire you for it. Not a bat of an eyelid, not a flicker of shocked surprise. I never saw such a competent worldliness." Her voice betrayed irritation with him. "But if you're the smallest bit interested, I'm still very fond of Dyke."

"I doubt if that comforts him much at this distance."

" 'Fond' is not good enough, is it?"

"Did you give yourself time to find out?"

"Could we drop the subject please, Father?"

"Certainly," Father Keogh said.

"Nothing you could do would make any difference."

"Then that's that," Father Keogh agreed. He could feel Doña Marian's eyes on him, bewildered at the attitude he took.

Locha returned to the subject herself. "It's something so personal and private I have to work it out my own way, and forgive me for saying so, Father, but you're the last person in the world I should care to discuss it with."

"I can understand that."

She turned on him, grating the words out. "Wouldn't it make a delicious change, Father, if you weren't *quite* so understanding at times?" She left the room, slamming the door.

Doña Marian jumped to her feet. "Why, Father, I just don't know how to apologize. Oh, she's Pey's girl, all right. It's that way with him all the time. They take things so quiet you think they have ice in them and then all of a sudden they go up in flames. I did so hope that she'd let you talk to her."

"She will," Father Keogh smiled. "There's nothing so infuriating as meeting with tolerance when one's been looking forward to resenting an attack! The more I tell her it isn't my business the more determined she'll be to see that it is. In the meantime I'll write to Dyke."

Chapter 5 〜〜〜〜〜〜〜〜〜〜〜

In the car he said to Victorino, "Will you wait while I go into church?"

"I was given no orders to stop, Father."

"Then just drop me here and I'll get myself home."

Victorino put him down at the gates. He closed his eyes with a sense of excited relief at being able to enter the church again. It was tidy and scrupulously clean. Someone had darned the tabernacle curtain. The sacristan, old and half-blind, was nowhere in sight. There was a deep yet voiceful silence. He prayed that he might be endowed with success in his attempt to persuade Locha not to jeopardize her happiness. He held himself gravely at fault. In making of her a special protégée he could well have been guilty of pride in her development. He prayed that the intensity of her feelings for him might be due to nothing more serious than the outsize emotions of youth and that as they were the more painful because of it, so they might be healed by it.

When he left the church Quantana, shimmering in the sunlight below him, felt a hundred miles away. He doubted his ability to reach it. The steep hill told on the muscles of his legs and his breathing was hard. Halfway down he was forced to rest.

A grotto lay back from the road. A statue of the Virgin Mary stood in a niche, a misshapen wax lily between her clasped hands. The rains had streaked the deep blue of her gown and the winds had piled sand at her feet. Father Keogh picked a bunch of mirasoles which covered the bank and laid them beside the figure. Then he sat down to regain his breath.

Behind the grotto a jilguero sang, reminding him of the full-throated notes of an English thrush.

A girl came swinging along the road. It was Candalaria. She was as vital as Locha was dreamily aloof. She seemed a ripe and garish chili to Locha's flower petal. She stopped and called out to Father Keogh, "It's not safe to sit on those old stones. A scorpion will come out and bite you." He explained that he was gathering strength. "Poor Father, I will go and fetch a burro to save you the walk. There are plenty tied up in the market place, doing nothing but kicking at flies."

"Candalaria," Father Keogh asked nervously, "you will ask permission, won't you? I don't want to be seen jogging into this town on stolen goods."

"It would just be a small little loan."

She rode the donkey back herself and dismounted to help Father Keogh up. "It is Silvanito's burro. He is having his teeth pulled out. He will be a nice little time under the gas."

A woman climbed laboriously up the hill below them. Weariness sat on her shoulders and showed in her tread. Her arms were full of brightly yellow zempasuchitles, the flowers which the Indians believed had the power to cheer the dead. It was Maria from Porfirio's bar. She was a big woman, handsome and upright. She had none of the mischief of Candalaria. Her beauty was powerful but bovine. She looked away from them as she passed.

59

"She is taking the flowers to the grave of the Bad One," Candalaria explained.

"The poor woman must love him still," Father Keogh said.

"Oh yes, she still loves him. But Maria is someone who must have a live man. She's Vito's woman now—that is when she can get the chance," Candalaria added, and Father Keogh was disconcerted to find himself the recipient of an outright wink. "There are others to take up his time."

Father Keogh spoke sternly. "Candalaria, I hope you have nothing to do with Vito Castillo Rivera. Maria is old enough to look after herself but you are not."

"Maria is growing too old to amuse him. See how tired she is going up the hill. She will be twenty-four when it comes to the rains."

"Yes, that is rather crippling," Father Keogh agreed. "You are not a friend of Vito's?"

"No I am not his *friend*."

"If I see you about in his company I shall make it my business to tell your parents."

"You will not see me about with him, Father. I'm at work in the day." And again he received the alarming wink.

Father Keogh found the burro difficult to guide with one hand, and Candalaria offered to lead the beast. He asked her, "I thought that you worked for the Señor Dentist?"

"Yes, I am assistant to Señor Campos. I hand him the little things he needs."

"Why aren't you assisting him now?"

"Oh, I can take a day off when I please."

"Doesn't he mind you doing that?"

60

She slid him a bubbling sideways glance. "He likes me too much," she said. Then she smiled up at Father Keogh. "They say that the Señorita Locha has left her new husband for love of a priest. It cannot be the Long Father, he isn't one you would love."

"How on earth do these tales get about?"

"Well, Josefa said this to Alfredo, the mozo at the Casa Grande, and the mozo spread it round."

"I see," Father Keogh said.

She lead the burro right up to his door. He was conscious that she was one of the few persons who had shown him an open kindness. When he thanked her he called out after her, "Be sure to take that burro back." He watched her riding up the street. She sat the beast straight-backed.

He was greeted by the Presidente's parrot when he went into the house. "Don Agapito! Don Agapito! Silly bald old fool!"

The young priest was typing a letter. He did not rise when Father Keogh came into the room. "Why didn't you tell me that Locha was back?" Father Keogh inquired.

Father Lasques did not turn round. "I—I thought—"

"You thought it might embarrass me?"

"I thought it might worry you."

"Is that the reason the town is boycotting me?"

The young priest bent closer over the typewriter. "No, Father, it's not. It isn't that."

His voice was unnatural and strained. When Father Keogh went to his side he deliberately moved his head away. Father Keogh turned him round by the shoulder. Over Father Lasques' eye there was a deep and freshly inflicted cut. "Now then," Father Keogh said, "who was it that didn't throw something at you this time and what made them not do it?"

Father Lasques looked distressed. He had his handkerchief pressed to his eye. "It was Alejo, Father."

"The goatboy? What were you doing, pinching his flock?"

"No, Father, I was just passing by. I think I must have frightened him."

"Frightened him into slinging a boulder at you?"

"It was quite a little stone."

"Let me see." Father Keogh examined the wound. "Well, it's not quite a little cut." He went to the medicine cupboard and took out a chipped first-aid box. "Had Alejo anything to say after this charming gesture?"

"No, he just ran off."

Father Keogh called to Chela for some hot water and when she brought it cleaned the gash. "I think you'll mend all right." He stuck a piece of plaster over the dressing. "Would you like to lie down for a bit? Has it given you a headache?"

"No, I don't think that is the cause of it, Father. I am subject to headaches in any case."

"I dare say the stone hasn't helped."

"Just fancy, Alejo!" Chela said. "His mother should take a stick to him."

Father Keogh asked Father Lasques, "Would you mind telling me with no beating about the bush exactly what is going on in this town? If their attitude isn't connected with my supposed romantic adventures what is it connected with? Why are they avoiding me? Why are they up against you? Why, now that they're free of Anacleto, isn't the church attendance good? Why is there no collection? Why were you unable to see the Rodriguez baby? Why if 'everything is fine' have you been physically assaulted twice? Sit down," Father Keogh added, "and take your time."

It was not easy for Father Lasques. He had been forbidden both by the doctor and the Bishop to trouble Father Geogh in his convalescent state. Father Keogh leaned forward and smiled. "I know that you're trying to spare me but don't you think it would be more satisfactory to my peace of mind if you told me the truth?"

The young priest broke down before the kindness in Father Keogh's eyes. It had been an increasingly difficult task to present matters in a favorable light. Bewildered and harassed, he had longed to confide in the older priest. Father Keogh, listening, blamed himself for not being more perceptive to the boy's urgent need of help. He deeply regretted the unjust nickname "Marcelino the Merry." Father Lasques had had no cause to laugh.

"Nobody goes to church, Father, I'm there every day by myself. I've been round to try to find out the reason. I've knocked at the door of every house. I've tried to ask people in the street but they shoot away from me as if I were carrying the plague. That is why I had no news of Señora Rodriguez or even the sex of her child. When they would not let me talk to them I wrote to them—dozens and dozens of letters—and pushed them under doors."

"Was that," Father Keogh asked sadly, "what you've been doing when you've shut yourself upstairs to 'meditate'?"

"Yes, Father, and it's the same in Tephuango. The Indians scuttle into their huts, and you were right about that bruise of mine. I had been up to Tephuango. Coyotito's mother was gravely ill. I wanted to give her Extreme Unction, but they wouldn't let me see her. They drove me off. It was all the more tragic, Father, for the

63

woman herself was asking for me. I went back to make another attempt. I kept out of sight until I saw Coyotito leave the hut—he went for her brothers, I think—I managed to slip in. She was too weak to make a verbal confession but she understood and gave an assent by a nod. On the way home someone followed me. When I turned round I was struck in the face. It was too dark to see who had done it and he'd gone by the time I had picked myself up."

"Do you know what happened to Coyotito's mother?"

"She died. From the look of her I expected it. The doctor had been out twice but they did nothing he told them, of course. The curandera had concocted some kind of a spell. It was an obnoxious brew. It probably finished the poor woman off."

"I don't doubt it and I also don't doubt that Mother Montezera is blaming the failure of her spell upon your interference."

"Yes, Father, that is why Alejo stoned me this afternoon."

Father Keogh hit the flat of his hand against his forehead. "It's hard to conceive what the trouble's about now that they're free of Anacleto."

"They talk as if they're not."

"What?"

"If you could hear them you would think he had never died." And Father Lasques gave in detail a description of what had occurred on the bus. "It's the same everywhere else in the town. That's why they won't open their doors to me or acknowledge you in the street—because *he* might get to hear of it. That's why they ran away from the bus so fast on the night I arrived. They wanted to reach their houses before he was about. That's why they don't come to church. Some of them do ask for the Sacraments and some of them make their confession but I have to meet them secretly. Even so there are only a handful who are willing to see me." Father Lasques used his long fingers to count up the faithful. "Don Timoteo and his wife, Doña Florencia of the bakery, Josefa and Victorino, the chauffeur from the Casa Grande, Domingo-of-the-Hired-Car, and Salvadore of the cinema. They will not come to see me together for fear that a group might attract attention. I go to their houses after dark."

"You've not been hearing the women's confessions alone?"

"No, Father, there's always been someone else in the house. Even Chela won't come to the church."

Father Keogh sent for her. "Why do you receive the Sacraments here, Chela?"

"Well, Father, someone must stay and look after you."

"That's nonsense. I'm nearly fit now and you leave me on other occasions."

"It's so sad in church all by yourself, Father, your voice sounds too loud in your head."

He knew that she was lying and he knew why. She was afraid. He had seen enough fear in Quantana to recognize the symptoms at once. "Chela, you do believe that Anacleto's dead, don't you?"

"I believe what I am told, Father."

"And what are you told?"

"I do not listen to tales, Father. I am not Josefa to gossip on street corners."

"Where did they bury him?"

"I am not the gravedigger—I did not put him in— but they *say* it is out on the mountain up by the Huapan ledge. They did not want him too near the town."

When Chela had gone, Father Lasques said, "It's

Vito Castillo who seems to be leading them now. Apparently they make no open trouble so the Jefe has nothing to charge them with. They're careful to keep on the side of the law."

"Vito Castillo!" Father Keogh repeated. "He was never anything more than a loose-living, swaggering, young braggart. He drank too much pulque and chased women about in his teens. He's a nonentity compared to what Anacleto was. He was just a greedy weakling who hitched his wagon to Anacleto's star."

"The wagon's well loaded without the star. They seem to be prosperous enough. It can't all come from Porfirio's bar. Vito has a suite at the Hotel Martinez. Old Martinez himself gets nothing out of it and he has to live down at the Hotel de la Costa to keep out of Vito's way. Vito also has a brand-new Cadillac."

"But if it's Vito wielding the Big Stick, why don't they seem frightened of him? Why still be afraid of Anacleto? That part of it doesn't make sense to me."

"It does seem strange," Father Lasques agreed.

"It strikes me as being even more than that. I'm quite certain that neither Vito nor the others would have the power to terrorize the town as Anacleto used to do. I know it sounds ridiculous but I can't get it out of my head that Anacleto must still be responsible."

"You think that he might have survived?"

"It may be due to my state of health but I really don't know what else to think. If only I could remember what took place in that hut it might help. Sam and I have gone over it again and again but it's an absolute blank to both of us. I only have one recollection. I seem to remember that Anacleto confessed, but that might be due to wishful thinking."

Father Keogh sat suddenly forward. For a moment he believed that he had seen behind Chela the figure of Anacleto himself. The boy in the doorway was slim and tall with a narrow, impassive face. Then Father Keogh leaned back, relieved. It was only Vito who stood in the room: young Vito, el Lobo, the Wolf. It was only Vito who lounged in the doorway as Malo used to lounge, boneless and young and insolent; who affected the habit of narrowing his eyes as Malo used to do; who was using every trick remembered to copy Malo's ways. He carried the teachings of Malo. His back was held straight and his voice never rose. He was soft-mouthed and gentle with the impeccable courtesy of the Gran Señor who would say to the stranger, "Let your hat remain on your head in my house. Regard my home as your own." He had also the hypocrisy of the Gran Señor who would have been forever affronted if his invitation had been accepted. But, in all, Vito's was a crude imitation of Malo, whose devotion to evil had imparted an unquestionable dignity to one of the devil's scholars. Malo was coolly austere in his personal tastes. He would never have clothed himself as young Vito Castillo did in a costume to which he had no right. The boy gained from the extravagant splendor of the charro gala dress. His height and the smallness of his bones gave his body a whippet grace. A short braided jacket covered his shirt. A tie in striped cotton flowed in a bow and the leather belt was embroidered in heavy white thread. The soft kid boots, cut from a single piece, were tight-fitting and pointed over the toes. On his finger there winked the big amethyst ring. His initials were cut into the surface.

Father Keogh said, "Well, Vito, for a second I thought you were Anacleto." Father Lasques stepped forward in-

67

voluntarily in front of Father Keogh. Chela screamed and ran out of the room.

Vito removed his hat. He threw it by the crown so that it spun through the air to alight on the typewriter, scattering papers. He sat down without bidding and proffered a full cigarette case. Both priests shook their heads.

"I heard you were better, Father, and I thought I would come to tell you how happy we are."

"That's kind of you, Vito. May I ask on whose behalf you are making the call?"

Vito studied the tip of his cigarette. "Why, certainly, on behalf of the town of course."

"Since when did you come to represent it? The last time I saw him, Don Agapito didn't mention that he was no longer Presidente Municipal."

It was cool in the room with the blinds partly drawn but the sun crept under the lower half of the window and made snapping lights of the silver horseheads down Vito's trousers. He looked up, grinning, at Father Lasques. His mouth was thin, twisting to one side only, well up into his dark-skinned cheek. "What did you do to your eye, Father?"

"He was stoned," Father Keogh said.

Vito made a noise with his lips. "You should have the offender up before the Juez de Primera Instancia, Father, and see that he's scolded and fined. But if you shouldn't get satisfaction there—" Vito trod out the butt of his cigarette on the pale primrose mat on the floor.

"Where else should we be likely to obtain it," Father Keogh asked, "except from the magistrate?"

Vito leaned his arms on the back of the chair and on

68

them he placed his chin. He hummed a snatch of a tune and kept time with his foot. Then he sang:

"When the river is full up with big fish,
Where can the small fish swim?

Well, Father, you would prefer that your curate was not hurt again?"

"Naturally," Father Keogh said.

"I have a little influence." Vito made a flutter of fingers. "Not much, but I think it would help. I will see that you are not molested."

"I need no protection from you," Father Lasques snapped.

"On the contrary," Father Keogh said. "If Vito has any *good* influence in Quantana we shall be only too glad to see him use it."

"No one will touch him, if—" Vito broke off and when Father Keogh was silent continued, "If nobody makes any trouble. We are a peaceful and happy town now, Father."

"It depends on how the 'peace' is enforced."

"There are no disturbances, no fights, no killings."

"But there *are* illegal taxes, threats of reprisal, and fearful hearts."

"I will tell you one funny thing that I have noticed, nobody goes to church."

"So we've observed for ourselves."

"Such a nice old-fashioned custom should not be allowed to die out."

"Quite."

"There's just a chance that I could use my good influence."

Father Keogh leaned forward, his deep voice inquiring, "There must be something you would like us to do in return for these favors. Won't you explain what it is?"

Vito spread long fingers out. "Why, Father, there's really nothing except—just to keep the peace. It would be a pity to stir up trouble in a place where none exists. But then you always preach so nicely, Father, and if you did that, shall we say to a full church once more, I am sure you'd preach nothing unwise."

"And on those terms I should be allowed a congregation?"

" 'Allowed' is a funny word, Father, when people in Quantana are free. Let's say they could be *persuaded*."

"But only if I could be persuaded to get up every Sunday and tell them not to kick against you, to accept what is wrong in return for no violence and not to risk fighting for what is right."

"Well, you would know best what to say, Father. I am not used to sermons."

"Yes, I should know what to say. What would happen if it was not what you wanted to hear?"

Vito looked up, his eyes narrowed. "Vito," Father Keogh said, "I feel I ought to warn you that you will get nowhere by trying to copy Anacleto."

"I've no need to copy him, Father. Anacleto can speak for himself." And Vito went out smiling at them.

Father Keogh sat silent for several seconds, then he said to Father Lasques, "We're going to the Jefe. I'm becoming more and more convinced that Anacleto must be alive."

Chapter 6 ～～～～～～～～～～

IT WAS THE FIRST TIME HE HAD WALKED AS FAR AS THE market place. He refused to take Father Lasques' arm. A rehearsal was taking place in the bandstand. The band were not always in harmonious agreement but were none the less enthusiastic for that. The guitars played a tumbling drum-broken tune which raised Father Keogh's spirits. By the side of the Stall of Politeness squatted the witch. She might have been as old as the mountains that rose to their shimmering peaks behind her. A blanket sat round her shoulders, full of holes that cigar ash had made. Her snake eyes pivoted backwards and forwards in a crinkled, dried-up face. Father Keogh stopped in front of her. "Mother Montezera," he said, "it was good of you to apply your healing powers to my interests." She bowed her head in receipt of the compliment. But she was not looking at him. She was looking at Father Lasques. Her skin was as dry as the cigar that resembled it also in color. She made a mumbling movement with lips that seemed hooked into her mouth. She said the words slowly with thought, and she pointed towards the younger priest. "That one will die of this town."

"Well, he's got to die of something," Father Keogh said. "And he'll probably die of it at a ripe old age."

Candalaria glided swiftly from stall to stall. An Indian selling pottery called, "Policia!" as a form of pro-

71

tection as soon as the girl approached. An agente in blue
and a peak cap immediately went to his aid. Candalaria
laughed at the Indian. "Silly old fool to call the police, I
would not have your pots if someone paid me to steal
them." Then she saw the priests. She made them each a
bob and inquired of Father Keogh, "You're not sore from
the burro ride?"

"Not at all," he laughed. "I should have been much
sorer without it."

"I am glad that the Long Father discovered his
watch."

"Candalaria," Father Keogh told her, "it's not very
courteous to refer to someone by their height or their
breadth. How would you like me to call you 'fatty Candalaria'? The padre has a name; you must surely know it?"

"You may call me Chata," she smiled, "if you like.
But, yes, I do know the Long Father's name." She made
Father Lasques a second bob. "It is Marcelino Dominguez
Lasques y Alonso. It was all on the back of the watch. Such
a lot to put on it, I thought."

"Where did you see the watch, Candalaria?"

"When it lay on the Stall of Politeness, of course."

"Very well," Father Keogh sighed.

The noise in the market was not made by the vendors.
They were never heard to call out their wares. They sat
silently in their accustomed positions according to the
classifications of their goods. Fruiterers, vegetable sellers,
and makers of pottery were grouped together, and those
selling wickerwork baskets or cloth. They squatted, apparently indifferent as to whether or not they made a sale.

Chickens clucked and donkeys brayed, dogs in great
numbers nosed for scraps. Barefooted children smoked
cigars or chewed at sugar canes. Garish serapes intended

for tourists dazzled the eyes. The serape of the weaver was invariably somber. His own tastes were more sedate than those for which he believed he was catering. Greys and browns and dignified greens ran in and out of his own garment but he had woven for the visitor scarlets and yellows and hummingbird blues.

No one except Candalaria passed the time of day with the priests. If spoken to, people nodded quickly or furtively glanced away. A few of them crossed themselves openly or made a small sign with the fingers to keep at bay ill luck. Father Lasques felt none of Father Keogh's affection for them. "They're hard to like," Father Keogh admitted, "but exceedingly easy to love." He could sense in their attempts to avoid his eye their efforts to cause no offense to him. Although they wished to dissociate themselves with him it grieved them to be impolite. He stopped and addressed Coyotito, who squatted in front of his wares. "I am sorry to hear about your mother."

The young Indian was tall and impeccably clean. The hard white of his cotton trousers and shirt seemed to jig in the sun. He rose from his heels and continued to plait a straw hat. On his head he already wore four of the completed articles perched on the top of his own black felt. He directed a steady impassive stare at some far-off point between the priests. He made no reply and sank swiftly down on his heels again. There was no interruption to the work on the hat. Sometimes Father Keogh wondered if anyone would ever fathom the depths of the Indians' blue-black stare. Did they plan? Did they hope? Had they any regrets? Or had they in their inheritance of ancient magic discovered the profoundest secret of nothingness?

The Jefe's room was whitewashed and bare. He sat behind a plain wooden table and his shadow fell big and broad on the wall. In the window a hummingbird hung in a cage. It hovered, a speck of electric blue and vivid green, above the perch. The Jefe fed it with honey and sugar syrup. He had caught it himself in the woods. It was one of the few things which had been known to bring a smile to his face. He looked up from beneath heavy eyes and said, "If it's about Alejo it's no good. Five people have already written in to say that they witnessed the scene and that the boy threw the stone at a buzzard. It was only by 'accident' that he happened to hit the priest. Here are the statements." The Jefe opened a drawer and slammed five sheets of writing paper down on the table. "You'll observe that they've all come off the same pad. They must have held a meeting and written them out together. They all say exactly the same. 'I personally witnessed this thing.' " And the Jefe read out the names.

"They're telling outright lies," the young priest said.

"I don't doubt it, but I can do nothing unless you can prove it. It's only your word against five." The Jefe sat back, disgusted. "It was the same with your own 'accident,' " he told Father Keogh. "Vito and the other two had cast-iron alibis. Four respectable citizens of Quantana, and sixteen Indios! I sit here and grind my teeth at times. I know perfectly well what's going on. Vito is levying illegal taxes—they live like fighting cocks up at the Hotel Martinez—but the people are too scared to complain for fear of revenge. I've questioned people I know to be paying Vito heavily but nothing will make them admit it. They're so scared of him they'll band together to protect him against me."

"He offered us his protection this afternoon," Father Keogh said, "provided we turn a blind eye and promise not to try to tickle a few consciences up."

74

"You'd better accept it, Father; it'll do you more good than mine. You could be murdered in the middle of the plaza during the evening parade and unless I was present myself or one of my men had a firsthand view not a soul in the place would see it happen. I thought up a scheme sometime ago. I'm offering five pesos each for information, and double to anyone who can bring the offender in."

"Is it working?"

"Not yet. One or two have tried to get it by concocting a trumped-up tale but nothing of value's come in. In fact nothing has changed for the better since Anacleto Comachi's day. He might just as well be alive."

"I suppose, Jefe," Father Keogh said, "there's not a chance of that?"

"He was pretty far gone when we arrived on the scene. But I can't say we worried ourselves—we were too concerned with you. The doctor did give him a quick look-over, but it wasn't more than that. He had his work cut out saving you. We left Comachi where he was. His body remained in the hut that night while we brought you back here. He was reported dead the next morning all right. No one would bury him; my men had to do it in the end. Old Don Timoteo could tell you more about it. He made the coffin and took it out to Tephuango. The town was too scared to have the body brought here."

"Don Timoteo!" Father Keogh said. "He's upright and honest enough himself but he *is* Vito's father. If by any chance Anacleto had survived and the Indians hid him out of fear, it would be easy to put pressure on old Don Timoteo. Are you sure it was Anacleto they put in that coffin?"

"I didn't see him in it myself," the Jefe admitted and shouted towards the door, "Sarjento! Come in here a

75

minute." The sarjento wore a pistol on his hip and a cartridge belt over his chest. "You were in charge of Comachi's burial. Did you see the body yourself?"

"Not since the night he was killed, Jefe. Don Timoteo had him boxed up when we got out there next day. You know how they like to do that quickly to keep the spirit from getting away, especially when it's Malo's."

"Did the men make any remarks about the coffin? Did they think it the normal weight?"

"No, Jefe, they said it was unusually heavy and I remember Carranza saying that it must be the Bad One's sins."

"H'm," said the Jefe, "stones might weigh as heavy as sins." He turned to Father Keogh. "You think there's a possibility of his carrying on somehow through Vito?"

"I don't think Vito would be capable of operating on his own. But if Anacleto were working through him and the town knew it that could account for everything."

"Well, there's a quick way to check," the Jefe said. "We'll open up the grave."

Chapter 7 〜〜〜〜〜〜〜〜〜〜〜〜〜〜〜〜

AT BREAKFAST THE NEXT MORNING CHELA SCREAMED. "SOME-one has made black-magic signs. They must have come into the house in the night or maybe climbed over the wall."

Father Keogh was the first to reach the patio. At first

he was unable to see the cause of the disturbance. The outsize leaves of the elephant ears which Chela grew in old kerosene tins obscured the view. Then, to the left of the well, and laid in a line with the blue-washed wall, he saw that several dozen pebbles had been carefully arranged on the ground. He examined the wall. "They came over here. You can tell by the scrapes."

"Mother in Heaven," Chela squeaked, "we might all have been killed in our beds."

Father Keogh went down on his knees. "I think it's a message, but it's not easy to make the letters out at this level. Marcelino, could you go upstairs and look out? You might be able to read what it says from up there."

Father Lasques leaned out of the window. "Yes, it does make a message," he said, and carefully read the words out: " 'If you wake Anacleto someone will die.' "

"Good heavens," Father Keogh said, "what a painstaking way of doing it. They must have taken hours."

"It's quite possibly someone who doesn't want us to find out that the grave's empty," Father Lasques said. "But we'd better warn the Jefe."

The Jefe was not impressed. "It's a way of avoiding detection. Handwriting could give them away. There are all kinds of dodges in this place. I once had a note in peanuts stuck onto a board, and if it isn't that—six or seven people get together and send a message by forming one letter each. More often than not they can't even write, they just copy what's put before them. So it wouldn't help if you could ask everyone in the town to write his name; there'd be nothing to check it against. I've checked most of these stones for fingerprints but your correspondent wore gloves."

"Do you think it's serious?" Father Keogh asked.

The Jefe raised his shoulders. "It could be a threat or it could be well-meaning. But if it's proved correct I only hope to God someone dependable will be around to catch a glimpse of the crime."

"You're a hard-hearted brute," Father Keogh laughed. "I really believe you'd bait a trap with a baby if you thought it could prove anything."

"Certainly, Father," the Jefe said. "Do you think you'll feel strong enough to accompany me tonight?"

"I'll be ready when you are," Father Keogh said.

The Jefe called for both priests in his car. Two policemen and a corporal following them carried acetylene lamps and spades. The Jefe had left the oficial, his lieutenant and second in command, in charge of Quantana. The sarjento remained to support him and six agentes were patrolling the town. "I'm expecting trouble tonight," the Jefe said. "They're sure to make some kind of protest against opening Comachi's grave, especially if he isn't in it. I've posted a man at the church. It's quite likely they'll do damage up there."

The white dust on the upward-curving road made a ghostly path in the Jefe's headlights. A cloud of turtle doves rose from a maize field nearby and flew blinded towards the car. Some hit the windshield and some were sucked past. Father Keogh was worried about the injured birds. He tried to peer through the back window. "The poor things might be suffering," he said. "We ought to go back and wring their necks."

The Jefe turned solemn eyes on him. "The torcaza is the worst enemy the farmer has got. The damage it does is untold."

"Yes, I know, but where I come from it's considered

unsporting to wing a bird and not follow it up and put it out of its misery."

The Jefe slowed up. He sent Father Keogh a pitying glance.

"Let us at all costs be 'sports.'" When the police car drew level he called to the corporal, "Cabo, go back and destroy all the torcazas you find in the road. And, Cabo, bring them back with you. They are good for the table, these birds."

The corporal backed down the road. The Jefe turned round to the younger priest. "I have always heard that the Irish were mad. And now I have proof," the Jefe sighed.

"My mother was English," Father Keogh remarked.

"That makes it worse, Father. It's well known that the English are far up the pole." The corporal came back with four turtle doves. "May we go on now?" the Jefe inquired. "There is nothing you feel you should do for their souls?"

"I was concerned with their material welfare only," Father Keogh smiled.

It was cold on the side of the mountain. The wind chased black clouds across the bland face of the moon and far below them Quantana winked with lights. The grave was on the side of the road by the treacherous Huapan ledge. It was marked with a plain wooden cross. Father Lopez had sent it from Huapan.

Far down in the valley began the awesome Green Walk of the Dead. It stretched for a hundred miles or so, a dense blanket of tangled black foliage. Even under the moonlight the forest seemed solid. The searching white light seemed to find it impossible to pick out individual trees. The two agentes dug their spades in the earth while the cabo held up the acetylene lamps. Ants and beetles attacked the glass round the flames, their weird dances

79 .

making an eerie shadow show. The agentes put ropes under the coffin and hauled it out. The Jefe gave the order to open the lid. No one spoke as they prised up the nails. The sandalwood split under the pressure with a snarling crack. When the coffin was opened the moonlight fell straight into it. It shone on the surface of stones tightly packed.

"Good God in heaven!" the Jefe said.

Father Keogh went forward to look in the coffin. "Help me to clear out these things."

"Tip it over," the Jefe ordered.

"No," Father Keogh said, "don't."

Father Lasques helped the agentes. They tossed the stones behind them and the thuds on the earth kept in uncanny time with the beat of Father Keogh's heart. The wind wailed round the mountain and a fall of rock came lumbering in protest down the side. It was as if the mountain's savage spirit resented the disturbance of its close and secret grave. When the coffin was cleared the moon and the lamps showed a plain white linen shroud. It was Father Keogh with his left hand who gently removed the winding sheet. The corporal swung the lamps closer and Father Lasques bent curiously forward.

"It *is* Anacleto," Father Keogh whispered.

"Yes," said the Jefe, "it is."

"The stones will have been to weigh down the spirit so that it couldn't escape," the corporal explained.

Father Keogh recognized another superstitious belief. Someone had had a more kindly thought for Anacleto. No one had loved him except Maria—it must have been she who had taken the trouble to see that his corpse should lie on a cross of lime and thus shorten his soul's stay in purgatory.

Death had hardly touched the features. The body lay straight and soldierlike. No one had bothered to cross the hands. The moonlight as if it too were curious seemed to examine the face. Father Lasques was surprised at the beauty he saw in it. What to expect he had not known; corruption perhaps of both life and death, but not this austere asceticism. Indian blood had built the cheekbones high in the face. It was narrow and long and unlined. There was a patient but vital strength in it still. He looked like the carved-out figure of a sleeping Aztec god.

Father Lasques broke out in spite of himself, "He looks more like a saint."

"He was in his way," Father Keogh said. "He was one of the devil's saints."

Father Keogh had not realized how much he had been hoping that Malo would be alive. This man who had chosen to be his enemy he had so hoped to make his friend. He found himself suddenly sad to the point of exhaustion that he had failed to bring this about. It was impossible to look down upon the strangely living face of death as anything but a friend. A verse of a song which Malo loved came into and stayed in his head:

> *Out on the mountain he lay alone,*
> *Out in the wind on the mountain,*
> *There was no one to weep save me, save me,*
> *Out in the wind on the mountain.*

Father Keogh placed his rosary in one of Malo's hands. It had been a gift from his sister in Ireland and he had had it for twenty-five years.

When they arrived back in Quantana there was news for them. Victorino was dead.

81

Chapter 8 ~~~~~~~~~~~~~~~~~~~~~~~~~~~~~~~

No one had witnessed the crime, but Chela had an explanation for it. "They say the Bad One is angry that you opened his grave. You should have taken more notice of what the little pebbles said."

It was Domingo-of-the-Hired-Car who had come running in with the news. Outside in his car the corpse lay across the back seat. He had fetched Señora Solano from Huapan and just as he passed the Casa Grande he had seen a body at the side of the road. He repeated his tale to the Jefe. "Scared! Well, just imagine it. I thought, 'They will say it is I who has done this terrible thing.' But I was at school with this Victorino. We were together at one little desk until we were old enough to leave. For we never moved up in the class at all."

Father Keogh told him, "Domingo, I'm terribly sorry you've lost your friend."

"Thank you, Father. I said to Señora Solano, 'Well, never mind how it will feel, Victorino cannot be left on the side of the road as if he was someone that nobody cared for, he will have to ride beside you.' I told her that I would not charge for this part of the journey but even then the poor lady was sick."

The Jefe said, "You should have called the police to the body, Domingo, and not brought the body to the police. Now both you and Señora Solano will have to show us the exact spot where you found it."

82

"It was up where our lovely Lady stands and someone just lately put flowers. It's a nice holy place to die."

It was the little grotto where Father Keogh had sat and heard the jilguero sing.

Both priests were present when the doctor examined Victorino. Father Lasques went back for the Sacraments. Extreme Unction could still be administered. Victorino had not yet been dead two hours.

"Do you think someone ran him down in a car?" Father Keogh asked.

The Jefe shook his head. "This was done with a jagged instrument, probably one of the grotto rocks. Someone must have been waiting for him when he walked back from the cinema. That would be about half past ten. Can't you imagine," the Jefe sighed, "the alibis this town will think up? There won't be a soul without someone to prove that he was somewhere else between ten and eleven o'clock."

"The warning was right after all," Father Keogh said.

"This time," the Jefe agreed. "Yes, but there was an occasion when Señora Ferreira was warned that a death would take place in her house and all that happened was her cook gave birth to twins in the kitchen. You can't always rely on these things. I've checked with the agente who was patrolling the church end from ten to half past. The grotto was screened by the wall and the trees, but even if he could have seen nothing he would have heard something. But Victorino made no sound." The Jefe took out a pencil and pad. "You would know who his friends are better than I, Father. Can you think of the people he went around with?"

Father Keogh's dark eyebrows contracted. "It's Dom-

ingo I seem to remember seeing him about with chiefly—
but I think he was quite friendly with the manager of the
cinema?"

"Salvadore would not have left the cinema by then."

"Then I've seen him out drinking with Edmundo
Arrieta."

"The baker! Yes, he might prove interesting. He's
drunk most of his time and he'd do anything for an extra
glass of pulque."

"I've seen him occasionally at Alfonso Herrera's but I
don't think there was any particular friendship there.
Alfonso made his uniform. Then he was fairly friendly
with Alfredo, the mozo at the Casa Grande."

"That is a thought," the Jefe said. "Coming from the
same house, the mozo would have known what time he
was coming back from the cinema. I think a friend might
have been employed as a decoy while someone attacked
from behind. He must have struck before he had time to
cry out."

The houseboy Alfredo had been on duty and had
served dinner at a quarter past ten. There were three
people to swear that Salvadore had not left his cinema until
half past eleven. Alfonso Herrera had dined with friends
and Edmundo Arrieta's wife said he had not left the house.

"Asleep he was, Jefe, dead on his bed. I know that for
I had all the work to do. He was too stupid with pulque
to hit anyone's head but his own."

Eight agentes made door-to-door calls. "The only
person who hasn't an alibi," the oficial reported, "is the
beggar who sleeps in the doorway of the Banco de Comercio. He says he was in the Avenida de Cortinez at half past
ten but nobody's bothered to prove it for him."

"Someone must be lying," the Jefe said. "A man

doesn't usually hit himself on the back of the head with a rock."

The oficial went to Porfirio's bar. He declined Vito's offer of a glass of real pulque of Apan. The bar was full and had been full, Pablo said, from rising six o'clock. There were countless people to swear that the bandits had not been out of its doors. The Jefe was inclined to believe them. "That's probably true," he told the lieutenant. "They'd be careful to work it through someone else."

Father Keogh went up to see Victorino's widow. She lived above the garage at the Casa Grande. The Jefe had lent the priest his car. Victorino's widow had seven children. They slept in one room across four iron bedsteads with planks in between to make extra room. She had a thin viper face and her eyes snapped with hard lights. Her coarse black hair was disheveled in a bun. She pulled open the door and scowled.

"Only a few hours he's been dead and I've had no peace. First the police and now the priest. When does a body find time to sleep?"

"I came to offer my sympathy, Señora Elizondo, and to see if there's any way I can help."

"What kind of help would I get from you," she said.

"I have given Victorino Extreme Unçtion, Señora Elizondo. I am sure you will take comfort from that."

"Comfort!" she spat at him. "Comfort! He was no good alive and he's no good dead but at least when he lived he brought money in. It is you who have stopped that." And she shut the door hard in his face.

Locha was waiting for him at the foot of the stairs when Father Keogh climbed wearily down.

"I wanted to spare you that. She's already had a go at poor Mother."

85

"How could your mother be blamed?"

"Oh, well, it was she who sent Victorino to fetch you in the car and apparently it's risky to be seen about with you."

"Poor Victorino," Father Keogh said. "He was worried about it himself."

"That wretched woman accused Mother of causing his death and you know what Mother is. We've had her in floods of tears. Some of it's booze, of course—but if it's anyone's fault it would seem to be mine."

"I don't quite see how."

"Well, if I hadn't left Dyke Mother wouldn't have wanted a heart-to-heart with you and Victorino wouldn't have had to drive you up here. His death appears to be a direct result of my sins." She was twisting a chiffon handkerchief. It smelt of a French perfume. Her hair had the same subtle scent.

Father Keogh told her, "You can put that out of your head. To send for me wasn't your idea."

She walked with him towards the gates.

He was unable to rely upon being able to keep up his former speed. It was necessary to allow himself more time to walk from one place to the other. He looked at his wrist watch and hurried.

She said, "Father, do you think it is godly of you to try to outstrip me when you must know how badly I need your advice?"

Father Keogh chuckled. "I hadn't thought of godliness in terms of sprinting, but aren't I the 'last person' in the world with whom you cared to discuss the matter?"

"That wasn't true and you know it. I've thought everything out very carefully and I now know that I couldn't possibly live anywhere except somewhere near you."

Father Keogh answered, "Rubbish."

She stepped in front of him, making him halt. "What harm could that possibly do?"

He smiled at her when he told her, "It's notoriously unwise to go and sit in a tobacconist's when you're trying to give up smoking."

He was amused at the tone of her voice. He had heard it so often used by Don Pedro when he wished to make his presence unpleasantly felt. It was coldly and imperiously reasonable. It was not hard to see what might deprive her of sympathy amongst her friends. The autocratic lift of the chin, the coolly rebuffing glance of the pale green eyes were not easy to forgive. He wondered whether it was because she sensed that in himself she could find an understanding of it that her affections had been transferred to him. She said, "As I can guarantee that it won't inconvenience you, Padre, may I ask whose business you think it is but mine?"

"I think it's Dyke's."

"Dyke has gone out of my life."

"He's been pushed out of it. You'd better pull yourself together and learn to appreciate him before someone else makes a better job of it than you. You might be sorry when it's too late to get him back."

"How vulgar, Father!"

"You must accept my apologies." He side-stepped her and walked towards the gates.

She took short running steps to keep up with him. "You wrote to him, didn't you? He told me you had. You said my feelings hadn't got anything to do with you."

"I didn't put it quite as ungallantly as that."

"Well, perhaps it will surprise you to hear that Dyke thinks the whole thing is *your* fault."

"It would surprise me much more if he didn't."

She forced him to stop again. "Father, I'm terribly sorry. I know I'm being very rude."

"Couldn't you try again with Dyke, Locha?"

She was pale and blue circles showed under her eyes. "I'll make a bargain with you, Father. If you'll go away from Quantana, I'll go back to Dyke."

"My work is here, my place is here—I can't just turn round and desert."

"Why can't that gangling youth take over?"

"That's no way to refer to Father Lasques. He's only been sent here to assist me until I can get on my feet again. Quantana's my problem, not his."

"Well, if anyone's going to be shot at again I'd prefer it was him and not you." Her voice shook and on her lashes he saw the start of tears. "Father, I'm so scared for you. I am, I'm really scared. If they do this to Victorino just because they thought he was in with you what will they do to you yourself?" She kept her eyes lowered, hoping to hide the tears.

"Locha, don't think I don't appreciate your offer—it would be a sacrifice to go back to Dyke at this minute, I know. But I want you to *want* to go back to him, not in the spirit of sacrifice but lovingly, sure that you'll make him happy, and in doing that make yourself happy as well."

She stamped her foot when she answered him testily, "Oh, why aren't you toothless and bald?"

"It won't be long," Father Keogh smiled.

88

Chapter 9 ～～～～～～～～～～～

CHELA WAS ALSO CONCERNED FOR HIM WHEN HE RETURNED to the house. "A nice thing about Victorino! So those are the games they are going to start. Who is it going to be next? I am worried about Victorino's spirit. I've told Don Timoteo that the stones on the Bad One were not heavy enough, so I said to him, 'It must be something stronger to keep Victorino down.' I have suggested a little sharp stake."

Father Keogh was reading a letter that the young priest had left him to sign. He turned to her sharply. "What?"

"This Victorino, Father, may be very annoyed with you. 'Just through the shoulder,' I told Don Timoteo, 'to pin him inside the box.' We do not want his spirit following you around."

"Chela, that's a disgraceful suggestion and unworthy of one of the faith. I must see Don Timoteo at once."

On the way he met the doctor.

Father Keogh complained, "My own housekeeper, if you please! She's a very good Catholic in most ways and yet I can't get these ridiculous ideas out of her head."

"If anything happens to you," the doctor warned him, "neither Malo nor Vito will be to blame. It'll be your own fault. You're a sick man still and when I told you to rest I meant it."

Don Timoteo had nailed down the coffin when Father Keogh reached the house. He was a gentle, distinguished old man. He was the maker of artistic fireworks. There were half-finished structures all over the workroom, great cutout figures with fireworks wired into the limbs, and a five-foot bird of paradise which when it went off would fire up in a shower of magnificent glowing plumes. Father Keogh had seen many a colorful example of Don Timoteo's skill.

His wife brought a cup of coffee and a plateful of marzipan mixed with ground peanuts. She looked distressed at his lack of enthusiasm. "But, Father, you used to like turron de cacahuete."

"I still do, Doña Urquandina. It's extremely kind of you."

He had been slightly put out by the fact that she had laid the little feast on the top of Victorino's coffin. He realized that to mention it would cause her embarrassment and put the disrespect down to professionalism.

She tapped the side of the coffin and told him, "This boy was a cousin of mine. They say you would hardly have known him, the way he was battered about."

Don Timoteo laughed out loud when Father Keogh brought up the subject of the stake. "That Chela of yours is a foolish old woman. I don't play those kind of tricks. But I said to her, 'Yes, I will drive in the stake.' Why not if it makes her feel happy? It was not me either who weighed down Comachi. The Indios took that precaution."

Father Keogh sat back, relieved. Then he said, "Don Timoteo, that son of yours seems to have stepped into Anacleto's shoes."

"Bad fit to them," Don Timoteo commented. "Father, Vito is only the child of our bodies, he is by no means the

90

son of our hearts. It was so late in life that he came to us, I have wondered at times whether it isn't a sign from the heavens that at our age it would have been better to leave such things alone."

"It's not your fault that he's turned out as he has. Everyone knows what good parents you've been. But how do you account for his hold on the town?"

Old Don Timoteo replied, "That's not such a very hard thing; he is working through Anacleto."

"That's what I always thought. But how can he when Anacleto's dead?"

"They say Vito talks to the Bad One, that the Bad One gets out of his grave. They say that every night he goes into Porfirio's bar and gives orders to Vito, and they say that he walks about in the daytime in a number of shapes so that no one is safe from his eyes. But at night he takes the form of a cat. Well, sometimes I think that it is nonsense but really it wouldn't surprise me if the devil himself went to visit that boy of ours."

"Does anyone ever see this cat?"

"Not many because they're afraid to be out at night, but Roncho Herrera the tailor who lives across from the bar has seen it every night. He watches behind his windows. He says strange things occur. For instance, as soon as the bar is closed there comes a small white cat. Some people are badly afraid of it."

"So you think, Don Timoteo, that Vito is deliberately using Anacleto's 'spirit' to help him control the town?"

"You must see how well it would work for him, Father. It's not Vito who tells them what to do, it is Malo! It's not Vito who takes the taxes from them—they go to the Bad One's ghost. If they disobey Vito they displease Malo, and they're frightened of doing that." He patted the coffin beside him. "Victorino was displeasing *Malo* when he drove you that day to the church." Father Keogh put a hand to his head. "The spirit gave my boy orders: No one was safe who befriended the priests."

"I see," Father Keogh said. "So that's why my visitors suddenly stopped and even the organito moved away."

"Oh, yes, they're afraid to be seen with you now, and it will be worse after the example of poor Victorino."

"But not everyone believes in such rubbish—yourself for instance and people like you."

Don Timoteo sighed. "Myself for instance and people like me! What good can so few of us do? There is Don Miguel of the Banco—he wouldn't believe in such things—the doctor, and Señor Campos—though I'm not one to like that dentist much—Don Pedro of the Casa Grande, and some others, but it's only a handful to the rest of the town. That will go on as it did under Malo. If it makes no trouble it gets none."

"But surely the people you mention wouldn't submit to illegal taxes?"

Again the old man's shoulders lifted. "Suppose I were to pay such taxes and I went to the Jefe or you about it? I might find my house would burn down or my wife would be hurt in the street, and what is more certain, I should do no more business."

"I see," Father Keogh said slowly. "He's employing all Anacleto's tactics."

"Anacleto will live while Vito lives. He was never a fool, that boy."

"But if only someone had the courage to give evidence against him the Jefe could do something about it."

"When so many people are willing to come forward and prove that the guilty one is innocent?"

The old man looked up at Father Keogh. "You will have to be careful. If Vito makes more threats in Malo's name he will have to see that they are carried out—it would be the end for Vito if the people no longer believed in the Bad One's spirit."

"Yes," said Father Keogh, "I quite see that. Don Timoteo, you don't feel it's safe to go to church yourself?"

The old man shook his head. "I have no way to live except by my business."

"People have to have coffins. They can't very well do without those."

"But they can buy fireworks anywhere, Father, and it's these I rely upon most."

"Would it distress you if I told the Jefe what you've just told me?"

"No, Father, if you think it would help him, but he cannot arrest the Bad One's spirit."

"It might give him a chance to break the superstition down."

The old man's voice was soft. "It's a funny thing—I pray for the Jefe as well as for Vito. I want him to catch that boy. I would rather he spent his life in prison than go on the way he does. The more he is free, the more sins he'll commit and the more he will have to answer for."

Father Keogh told him gently, "You must pray for a change of heart in him."

"Vito has no heart."

It was hot in the streets at midday. He walked slowly, aware of a heavy sensation about the heart and an ache in his right arm. Don Timoteo's explanation had saddened him. He who had so longed to change the flesh for the spirit and to leave the living world behind, had been re-turned to it only to find that in Quantana Malo had re-

93

tained his leadership even in death. He was a weaker influence than Malo still. The people's fear of the power of Malo's spirit was greater than their faith in the power of God. There was something else to trouble him. It was still impossible to recall the precise happenings of the night he was shot in the Indian hut but he was growing increasingly certain that Malo had confessed. The memory was tantalizingly close to him, somewhere above his head. In the church and on his knees in his own bare room he prayed that it might become clear to him. It was more important for him than to recall evidence which might help to incriminate Vito. It was more important than anything else. If Malo had died repentant, if at the last moment he had regretted the harm he had caused, then it was even more vital that Vito should not be allowed to further his own kingship in the realm of evil by using the dead man's name.

When he reached the Jefe's office, Father Keogh found Sam Frankenson inside.

He sang out, "Hi, Mac!"

The Jefe told Father Keogh, "Señor Frankenson just came in to report a conversation he heard in his bar last night."

Sam said, "That's right, the hyenas were in. It's not often they honor the de la Costa but they dump their lousy carcasses once in a while just to show no place is free of them."

"Did they all come?"

"No, big shot Vito doesn't travel around any more. He has to preserve his dignity. It was Pablo and the Jeep."

"It's not the only bar they visited," the Jefe said. "It's been the same line of talk all the way round. Trying to undermine police authority."

"Yeah! Such as what good does it do anybody to rely

on the police when a guy gets murdered right under their nose and they don't have a clue who did it! The Jeep says you might just as well holler for help to an alligator as call the police. Scared to go out nights, little Jack Nasty is."

Father Keogh said, "Has anything useful come in, Jefe?"

The Jefe shook his head. "No, we checked all personal motives but nobody had a grudge against Victorino except his wife. I have the cleaners on the lookout for bloodstained clothes but Victorino's friends would more likely go in for the river wash. Oh, what a dump!" The Jefe sighed. "The guilty can't talk and the innocent won't."

"I've found out what keeps the innocent mouths shut," Father Keogh said, and he reported in detail what Don Timoteo had told him.

The Jefe pressed a bell. When the corporal answered it he said, "Cabo, fetch me a bottle of mezcal." He turned round to Sam and apologized, "I'm sorry if it's putting temptation before you but this piece of news is the worst I could have. Comachi was less of a menace alive. That way you could catch him, this way you can't."

"Our only chance," Father Keogh said, "is to break down the belief in Anacleto's spirit and make them realize that the whole thing is a put-up job on Vito's part."

"A poor chance," the Jefe said. "With these people, superstition is as much a part of them as the blood in their veins. Vito can scare them with a dead Comachi better than Comachi could scare them himself if he came back to life."

"It's a gravy train," Sam agreed. "These dopes thought Pussyfoot could turn into a goddam white cat when he was alive. There's going to be nothing he can't turn into now that he's cold meat. Every time a door blows open it's gonna be Pussyfoot busting in, every time someone comes

95

home with a load on him and falls flat on his fanny it's gonna be Pussyfoot tripped him up. Vito sure knew what he was doing when he thought this one up. It's worthy of Pussyfoot himself. Those hyenas have a racket for life."

Chapter 10 ~~~~~~~~~~~~~~~~~~

FATHER KEOGH PAID NO MORE THAN COURTESY ATTENTION to the doctor's advice.

He convinced himself that activity was beneficial to him. He told Father Lasques, "I wasn't made for an invalid."

He and Father Lasques attended the evening parade. Music tumbled out from the bandstand and the barrel organ played. No one resented the challenge of the organito to the band. El Choco was something to laugh at and Quantana loved to laugh. The youth of the town circled the plaza, the girls on the inside and the boys on the outside. Only one couple flouted convention. Candalaria walked with her arm in Vito's.

Father Keogh found her swaggering bravado pathetic. It disgusted Father Lasques. Candalaria's head, like a dusky flower, was carried high. She was barefoot and she pointed her toes. She stepped out like a horse in a show ring. A man's hands would have met round her waist. A bottle-green skirt touched her ankles. Her hips swayed so provocatively that Father Keogh feared a parting of blouse and skirt. Her lips were a sticky vermilion that matched the great waxen flowers in her hair. She snubbed some of the strollers with a lift of her small brown nose and upon others she bestowed a gracious smile. The priests received the latter attention.

"That girl revels in sin," Father Lasques complained.

"She's drunk," Father Keogh replied.

He called her. She slipped her arm instantly out of Vito's, picked up her skirts and bobbed before them. She had the Indian's balanced grace. "Padre Michael Keogh! Padre Dominguez Lasques y Alonso! What a fine night it is, look at the stars! Vito has said he will marry me if I am good. I shall be first lady over all Quantana." Her youthful plumpness shook when she laughed. "Oye! Father, the old cats will not spit at me then. It is I who will do all the spitting. Maria says Vito is not Anacleto but what do I care for that? Vito is first man and Malo is dead." She gave a little shrill cry of gladness, twisted round throwing her skirts out and danced.

The evening parade came to a halt. The band reached the end of a pattering rumba and crowded together to see what had occurred. Only el Choco continued to play "Little Gray Home in the West."

Vito strolled up to Father Keogh. "There was something you wanted to say to my girl?"

"I wanted to tell her that she ought not to allow you to compromise her in the evening parade and I wanted to remind her that I've already threatened to warn her parents if I see her about with you."

"You think they'd object to me, Padre? Who else can give her what I can? What other girl rides in a fine new car?" He pushed out the side of his cheek with his tongue.

"Is it only the ladies, Father, who have such a need of God?"

"No one has a greater need of Him than you," Father Lasques supplied.

"But it's always the ladies with this priest. First it's the Señora Dyke Brown and now it's the little Chata who takes up his time. You have quite a reputation with the ladies," he told Father Keogh.

"Yes, I know," Father Keogh said acidly. "Isn't it exciting? But my time is at everyone's disposal, yours in particular. I shall be only too glad if you'll claim it."

Vito said, "Thank you, Father, but I'd rather claim my girl just now." He went to put a hand on Candalaria's arm but she flicked open her fan in his face. Every gesture she made had a drunken bravado but every one had grace. I wonder why it is, Father Keogh thought, that only the Indian knows how to move. He had noticed it often in Coyotito. It was a supple and fluid dignity which could not be made grotesque and clownlike even by too much pulque.

Candalaria forced Vito to retreat at the tip of her fan. Father Keogh asked her, "Do you know what Vito stands for?"

"Yes, Father, he is first man in this town."

"Do you know that he hurts other people?" She stretched her brown toes, making hills in the dust. "There are people who have been grievously harmed, and who are going to be even more harmed by Vito. Do you want to feel that you are helping him? Do you like to see children and old people frightened? Good people forced into sin? Do you want to be that kind of first lady?" She picked at a loose strand of lace in her fan. "Do you love him?" Father Keogh asked.

"Yes, Father."

"How can someone of your age be certain of love?" the younger priest demanded.

"Well, I have tried it with the Señor Dentist and some others and I like it with Vito best."

Father Keogh told her gently, "The padre was referring to the spiritual side of it, Candalaria. Are you fond of him? Do you like what he can give you or Vito himself?"

She considered it, dark brows contracted. Her drunkenness left her at once expressive and confused. "Father, this Vito is something. You don't find him anywhere else. He's not Vito because he is first man—he is first man because he is Vito." It had cost her something to work it out. Her gaiety was gone. "Liking has nothing to do with loving."

Vito joined the three of them. The band had struck up a halfhearted tune. The evening paseo continued. Vito stood with the lights of the plaza behind him. He beckoned Candalaria. She moved to his side as if she had moved in her sleep. She became defiant at once when she realized it. "You cannot tell me what to do." And she took three quick steps back to the priests.

Father Keogh looked carefully at Vito. It was a smooth yet irregular face. It was powerful, not in the austere way of Malo but in the commanding appeal of its youth. It was softer than Malo's but no less determined. It had in the great, black, begging eyes a plea, as if it detested its guilt and asked pardon for it. Its smile had a contradictory innocence. It could sway Maria from the love she still felt for Malo. It could command Candalaria however much she might set herself out to defy it. Father Keogh recalled dismissing him as a "loose-living, swaggering braggart." In comparing the boy adversely to Malo he had lessened

99

his own ability to protect Quantana against him. It was not
for him to judge the force of evil in Vito as less worthy of
his attentions. He felt himself presumptuous in claiming
a preference amongst the enemies of God. The boy was not
merely a killer of bodily life, he was a lasting destroyer of
souls. His influence would stretch beyond the graves of his
victims. A soul's stay in purgatory might be determined by
him. His corruption would spread like a tropical disease.
It would seep through the cracks from house to house. It
would spread from tongue to tongue. It would slowly but
surely annihilate faith. Vito was no cheap imitation of
Malo. He was able to stand alone.

Father Keogh censored himself for belittling Vito. He
had always felt his deficiencies keenly. In good health he
had used material as well as spiritual methods to rectify
them. Punctuality assisted him most. In the crowded life
of the secular clergy time could become an active hindrance
or a carefully accumulated blessing. He became a skillful
thief of stolen minutes. Books were left open, their places
marked so that in standing over them or in passing them
by, a passage or two might be read. Problems were written
out under eye-catching headings and left on the desk so
that a quick glance could refresh the memory. He had
always waged a personal war against time. He had a reverence for it. He was conscious of its shortness in the service
of a divine Master who gave sparingly of it in order that it
should be well used. An hour misspent in the service of that
Master was lost. It could be made up but never repaid. He
was bitterly aware that only in the offering of the Holy
Mass every morning, in the half an hour of preparation and
in the half an hour of thanksgiving, was his own time un-
hinderingly dedicated. He might spend the rest of the day
in the hopes of continuing his Mass Intention, and he

might be in prayerful or active communion with God, but he never reached the close of a day without feeling that he had wasted it. It was difficult not to confuse personal mis-appliances of time with the claims that duty made on it. It was difficult not to grudge the pastoral visits which had no more vital effect than that of doing less harm than good. A positive attack upon evil seemed imperative in Quantana, a negative hard not to minimize. It had even been difficult not to grudge the sometimes excessive demands of the confessional. But in his period of enforced inactivity he had lost sight of his reverence for time. Without peace of mind he had squandered it, resenting his idleness. He felt that he had made poor use of the chances which he would once have recognized as a gift from God, to devote himself to his own personal sanctification. A harassed mind had wasted the opportunities of contemplation and meditation. Even if the channels which should have stretched clear and receptive between himself and his God were so blocked that he failed to receive the divine directive, he could have heard it repeated in the voices of his doctor and his friends. But he had not chosen to listen. It was as if his God in an effort to make him aware of the necessity of rest had made use of the human tongue itself:

"Let the curate take care of everything. That's what he's here for, isn't he?"

He had not placed his complete faith in Father Lasques. He had fretted to take over the reins himself. He had given no full confidence to the well-laid plans of God. Arrangements had been made for him to be relieved of strain but he had refused to accept relief. He had been a prey to perpetual anxiety, robbing himself of the precious moments in which, undisturbed, he might have been forever fortified. So that now he emerged to face the new task ahead of him unrested, unworthy and weakened in spirit and flesh. He realized it, looking at Vito.

It was significant that he should have done so in the moment of challenging Vito for a single endangered soul. It was the moment for which he should have used his unaccustomed leisure to prepare himself. He had underestimated the task. Candalaria danced undecided between them as the whole of Quantana might come to dance.

Chapter 11

HE CALLED ON CANDALARIA'S PARENTS. THEIR EYES HELD continual consultations. They were both ill at ease with the priest. "She's a bad girl, Father. She was always bad."

"Then she needs all the help we can give her. Do you know that she's Vito Castillo's mistress? Do you know that she reels round the plaza at night drunk on tequila or pulque or beer or all three?"

The Fernandez had ten other children. They could afford to disown Candalaria. "You should forbid her to have anything to do with Castillo." He looked round the room. It was furnished with many small luxuries although the Fernandez were notoriously poor. It was not hard to discover the reason for their lack of parental control. When he left the old couple he felt dispirited. He had seen the corruption of Vito creeping from house to house. It was evident not only in the eyes but in the very possessions of the Fernandez.

His visit bore immediate fruit. He walked home with Sam, after hearing Don Timoteo's confession, to find Chela's voice sour when she greeted him.

"The Long Father is out and you have a visitor who is not very nice."

"Chela, will you kindly call Father Lasques by name."

The visitor was Candalaria.

She was waiting in the small whitewashed room. She sat demurely beneath a faded picture of Saint Antony de Padua and when she stood up she kept her eyes on the ground and made each man a prim little bob. "Padre, good afternoon! Señor Frankenson, good afternoon!" Then she asked, "Will you hear my confession please, Father?"

"Certainly," Father Keogh said.

"That should make a first-class movie." Sam whistled and when Father Keogh showed him out he said, "You want to watch out for that lapful, Mac, she's a bitch."

"I *beg* your pardon, Sam?"

"Skip it. Just watch out."

Candalaria had many sins with which to accuse herself. Father Keogh was troubled by the long list of crimes committed, it would seem, by the fourteen-year-old with alarming frequency and a certain amount of pride. "And I accuse myself of letting Vito make love to me not only because I like it but because it annoys Maria so much. Oh! And I accuse myself of selling the Long Father's watch to the witch and of buying scent for my hair out of my share of the money he paid when he bought it back Amen."

She did not strike Father Keogh as genuinely penitent and he was obliged to refuse her absolution. The refusal

103

made no impression on her. Even when the confession was over she chattered about her sins. She appeared to see no reason for changing her ways and had no intention of making restitution. "Give back what you steal, but that's silly! What would be the good of stealing?"

Father Keogh tried to reach her conscience through her heart. "There's never any good in stealing; sooner or later you'll be caught and sent to prison. But quite apart from that, do you ever think of the people you steal from? How would you like to have something stolen from you? Father Lasques for instance was very attached to that watch you took; his mother had given it to him. It cost him so much to buy it back he had to go short of food."

"Oh, but then he was foolish. He should have told me. I would have stolen it back from the witch." She sat upright and kept her eyes on him, her hands clipped together between her knees.

Father Keogh's voice was patient. "That would have made it very much worse. Father Lasques would have preferred to have lost the watch, however precious it was to him, than have you commit another sin." It was quite obvious from her expression that he had cemented an already poor opinion of Father Lasques.

"It's the wish of my parents that I come every day to take lessons in how to be good."

The information startled him. He had not considered his visit successful and neither Señor nor Señora Fernandez had struck him as being impressed by it. They had been among those who had shut their door in the face of Father Lasques and it was hard to imagine them willing to incur the displeasure of Vito Castillo.

"May I take the lessons from you, if you please? The Long Father looks down his nose."

Father Keogh was losing heart in his battle to hear Father Lasques correctly named. There were times when he was in danger of slipping into the use of the nickname himself, although he was aware that it referred to facial expression as well as to height.

"It will depend entirely upon which of us is free to see you."

"He will not want to be free." She grinned. "He's afraid I will take something from him again—and I could, I'm so clever at that sort of thing. Oh, look, your picture has come off its nail. It will fall to the ground and break."

In the few seconds Father Keogh turned his head in the direction of Saint Antony de Padua her fingers fluttered. He felt not even the lightest brush of them. When he looked round again she was laughing and holding out his fountain pen. He took it from her and restored it to his inside pocket. "Plenty of people in the world have a talent for picking pockets but no one admires them for it, Candalaria." He felt the observation somewhat hypocritical for he had been considerably impressed by her skill himself. He said sternly, "I realize that Mexican girls mature earlier than the ones that live in my part of the world, but even so you are too young to know what you do about life. You'll be spoiling your chances of making a happy marriage if you ruin your good name now."

Chela came in with a cup of coffee. When he asked her for a second cup she shook her head. "I am not going to wait on that one, Father. I've more respect for my hands and my feet."

Candalaria put out a small red tongue. "I wouldn't drink your coffee, withered old bean. I'd spit it right out on the floor."

"Burra!" Chela screamed at her. "You've no place in this house. The padres are not after your sort."

"Chela," said Father Keogh, "I think it would be more in keeping with our calling if you allowed Candalaria to think we aren't after anybody's sort. Now please apologize to one another and let's have that coffee." When neither of them spoke he stood up. "Very well, I will fetch it myself." When he came back Candalaria had gone. Chela remained with her arms folded. Father Keogh asked gravely, "Did you drive that girl out?"

"No, Father, the devil called her."

"I'm ashamed of you, Chela."

"And I am ashamed of you, Father, letting someone like that take a seat in your house."

"Well, she's going to take a seat in it for an hour a day for a good long stretch, so I think you had better get used to her."

Chela went grumbling out of the room. "Such a name you will get in the town."

Victorino's death gravely affected Quantana. Of the few who had received the Sacraments and made their confessions in the privacy of their own houses after dark, only Don Timoteo and his wife remained. The others found numerous excuses to close their doors in the faces of the priests again.

Victorino was deprived of a conventional funeral. His wife made it clear that she wished him to be buried with no religious rites. Don Timoteo's plain coffin was lowered into the grave without ceremony. There were no prayers said for Victorino except those which were said by Father Keogh and Father Lasques into the emptiness of the silent church.

The greater portion of the poorer classes were convinced that the spirit of Anacleto was something to appease and that the only true safety lay in co-operation with it. The professional classes and the more educated smiled at the absurdity of it but nevertheless recognized its power. The town was divided in opinion. The Presidente Municipal, the dentist, the doctor, the manager of the Banco de Comercio, his first cashier, Salvadore of the cinema, Pancho of the gaseosa stall, and Señor Martinez of the Hotel de la Costa were aware that it was Vito behind the supposed activities of Malo's spirit. But only the doctor was willing to say so in public. The others preferred not to cause Vito offense and to remain safely untroubled themselves.

The Presidente was courteous when he refused Father Keogh's request to impress upon the town that only living persons could have been responsible for Victorino's death. He sat in his flower-packed patio between the hammocks that hung from the upper story and kept his rocking chair gently in motion from the pressure of one slippered foot. Sweat sent a spreading patch under the armpits of his black silk suit and shone on his olive-skinned head. His wife sat beside him, pouring out chocolate. She kept a perpetual watch upon Father Keogh under thickly short lashes and smiled a slow, inviting smile whenever she encountered his glance. Her blouse of thin organdie showed lace underneath. She was flat-faced with overwide nostrils, but full lips gave her a heavily sensual expression. When she passed Father Keogh his cup of chocolate she took care that her fingers touched his. Father Keogh was doubly embarrassed by the fact that he was also under constant scrutiny from the Presidente. Behind the cigar smoke the Presidente blew out he could feel the suspicion of button-bright eyes. He guarded his treasure with every glance.

Father Keogh found it doubly pathetic that the plump Doña Arcelia, whose beauty for the Presidente eclipsed all others, should be, to the eye unbesotted by love, a not overattractive young woman. There were many who could surpass her in Quantana. Candalaria's swinging grace made a pudding of Arcelia's sly-eyed charms.

The Presidente's chair rocked faster, his irritation expressed in the nervous force of his foot. "My dear Father, if I were to appear on the steps of the Presidencia and tell the people not to believe in ghosts they would not listen to me. They have always believed in ghosts. It would only encourage them if they thought I was taking this nonsense seriously."

"This nonsense *is* serious," Father Keogh said. "A man has been killed to lend it conviction. Have you forgotten that?"

"It's possible that you and the Jefe attach too much importance to these superstitions."

"Señor Presidente Municipal, I should like to make it clear that neither the Jefe nor myself have any tendencies towards believing in witchcraft or evil spirits. But we both feel that too great an importance can never be attached to something which has provided unscrupulous persons with a weapon powerful enough to bring disaster to the whole town." Father Keogh had spoken with a certain amount of heat and sat back to run his handkerchief round the edge of his collar.

The Presidente knocked the ash from his cigar. "And you think it would assist if I in my mayorial capacity stood up and told them not to believe in fairies?"

"I do. They're preying on these people's ignorant beliefs and using them to their own advantage."

"I think I must set a good example and preserve my dignity." The Presidente smiled.

Father Keogh put down his cup of chocolate. "If you really wished to set a good example, Don Agapito, you could do it best by making an appearance in church."

"I am a lapsed Catholic," the Presidente replied. "It may be reprehensible, but it is comfortable."

"And safer?" Father Keogh inquired.

"Safer?" the Presidente repeated. "My dear Father, am I to understand that you consider that one might sustain some form of harm in practicing the faith?"

"I thought it possible that you had reasons for supposing so, Señor Presidente Municipal." Father Keogh turned round to the girl at his side. "And you, Doña Arcelia, are you a lapsed Catholic as well?"

The Presidente replied for her. "Arcelia is like all dutiful wives, Padre. She follows in her husband's footsteps. Isn't that so, my heart's pet?" He held out a fat, moist hand to her which she either chose to ignore or failed to see. He was left with it outstretched, pink-palmed and wet. He withdrew it and busied himself with a match. Father Keogh observed that the flame was shaking.

Arcelia kept her eyes on the ground. She whispered, "It would give me great joy, Agapito, if the Father would come to the house to hear my confession. It is such a long time since I received the Sacrament of Penance."

"Father Lasques would be delighted to come round tonight," Father Keogh told her, and was rewarded with a look of relief from the Presidente and one which bordered on spite from his wife. To the Presidente he said, "Don Agapito, I think you might find that by practicing your faith you would derive a far greater comfort than you do from lapsing in it. It is surprising how the most personal

problems can be eased by seeking the guidance of God."
He let his eyes rest for several seconds upon the bowed
head of Doña Arcelia.

Father Keogh and Father Lasques redoubled their
efforts to induce Quantana to give open support to its
church. When Father Keogh celebrated Mass in the morning Father Lasques went from house to house, into shops,
and made personal appeals in an attempt to persuade the
people to attend the service. When Father Lasques celebrated Mass it was Father Keogh who tried to induce the
town to place more trust in its faith than its fears. But
only one person responded.

Candalaria came to the church.

She dressed for the occasion as if she were attending
a fiesta. Her gayest rebozo was wound round her shoulders
and her heavy black hair fell unbraided from beneath one
of the largest horsehair hats Father Keogh had ever seen.
It was her practice to stick the flowers that she had gathered on the way into the band. It reminded him irresistibly
of a donkey at Margate. Gaudily cheap jewelry round her
throat, her ankles, and her wrist made a clinking distrac-
tion whenever she rose from or went down on her knees.
No piety showed in her bearing but friendly co-operation
shone out from her eyes. Her small voice, crystal-clear in
the empty church, was disturbing and it was impossible
to believe at times that she could make such a variety of
noises. She shuffled her feet, she coughed, she sneezed. She
dropped her rosary and her prayer book with unfailing
regularity and she could induce a remarkable collection
of creaks in the back of her pew. What she did with the
kneeler Father Keogh was unable to conceive. She could,
he thought, only be playing a form of football.

Father Lasques complained of the same distractions. They discussed between them whether their consciousness of these sounds might not be magnified by the fact that they had become accustomed to an empty church and whether this might not be the cause of Candalaria drawing their attention towards her unquiet ways of worship. At a moment so solemn and so exacting when the divine impact upon the human brought with it the attendant nervous tension so closely allied to the great privilege, it was difficult not to feel when celebrating the Mass that the strain was not lessened by the clamorous participation of the sole representative of the laity.

Father Lasques was doubtful about Candalaria's motives.

"I think," Father Keogh said, "that she's a very independent young woman. We might find that she has flicked her fingers in Vito's face. She may even have done it in defiance of him. Vito is very susceptible and that might be her charm for him. No one else has the courage to flout his authority. He might regard it as a novel experience."

"But why should she want to come to church? There's no point in our trying to ignore the fact that she has a notoriously bad character. She's a thief and her morals place her in much the same class as a prostitute. Does she come to Mass because her attendance is so conspicuous that it trains every eye on her piety? Is she mocking us? Is she enjoying the limelight it brings her?"

"Oh, I should think so," Father Keogh said. "It would account for that incredible hat. But you know there have been some bad people who have made good Catholics and some good people who have made bad Catholics."

Father Lasques hit his fist against the palm of his hand. The bones in his wrists stood out painfully.

111

"This girl is not coming to church for the love of God."

"No," Father Keogh agreed with him, "but she may be coming at the dictates of God. Candalaria does not like to see us deserted. That overwarm heart of hers is motherly. She cannot bear to see anyone fail if it's within her power to see that he succeeds."

"Does that apply to Vito?"

"Possibly," Father Keogh said.

"So that in her maternal instinct for us she is forging a passport to heaven."

"What makes you feel that a maternal instinct is forged?"

"Father, this girl is a bad girl. That has been proved time and time again. We're fools if we hope otherwise. It would be so easy for us because she has followed us to feel that we have triumphed. We have not—that girl receives the Sacrament of Penance and still reverts to her old ways. It's a waste of her own time and ours if she repeatedly commits the same sins over and over again."

"I know," Father Keogh said.

"And yet you are defending her? You're disguising her faults as virtues. You're investing her with holiness because she's appeared in the church. I would rather proclaim myself responsible for the followers of Our Lord amongst the people here who have not dared to make an appearance in church rather than claim for Him that this girl has appeared in His Name."

"This girl," said Father Keogh, "has not appeared in His Name. She has appeared as a quite unconscious disciple. She came because she felt that we needed support in a way that must surely imply that she is supporting Our Lord. And it's as well to remember that no one can enter the House of God however noisily without deriving some benefit from His Holy Presence."

Father Lasques agreed but he sighed a little. "I suppose it's better to have a nobody doing something than a somebody doing nothing."

Father Keogh smiled at him. He was interested in Father Lasques' last remark. The fact that he was hypercritical of Candalaria might stem from a snobbishness inherent in the well-born Latin. Strangely enough, it detracted neither from his holiness nor from his humility. It did not mean that his was not a true love of souls. It had, Father Keogh thought, nothing to do with religion, it had only to do with blood. The Latin aristocrat could be incapable of coming to understand the meaning of the word equality even in piety.

He was right in his conjecture about Candalaria. She took a delight in disobeying Vito. She could boast of her influence over him to the rest of the town.

In the suite at the Hotel Martinez for which he never paid Vito lay with his legs stretched out. He was playing with Candalaria's hair. He gave it a tug when he asked her, "Why did you go to Mass?"

She released her hair from him, scowling, and answered, "Someone should make them feel happy."

"I forbid you to go to church."

"I do as I please," she retorted.

"I shall be angry if you continue to go."

"That will turn your stomach sour, not mine."

The Jeep sat by a marble-topped table. He refilled his glass from a jug of beer. His face looked even smaller behind a jutting cigar. It wagged in his mouth as he spoke. "You'll displease the spirit of Anacleto, Chata, and it's not a wise girl who does that."

Maria sat curled in the opposite corner. Her big-breasted figure looked gross, reclined. "His spirit would not trouble with a creature of her kind."

The sun streaked through the window. It seemed to pay loving attention to Vito's smooth head of black hair. He took one of Candalaria's fingers and put it between his teeth.

"It was foolish to let her go down to the priest's house," Pablo growled from the corner. He was plucking the strings of the shell-covered guitar, sending a single-noted tune into the comfortable quiet of the room. Now and again a foot or a hand or a head kept time to it.

Vito bit Candalaria's finger and trapped it in his fist. "What a small brain for such a large head! That will be useful, big Pablo. In time even you should see that." He asked Candalaria, "You have made the priests think that your mother and father have sent you? They know what to say if they're asked?"

"They are to say that it is true that they sent me."

The Jeep made a sucking noise quenching his thirst. "But you have dropped it into the ear of the witch that Anacleto's spirit will have its revenge on anyone going to church."

Vito heaved over to put a hand on Candalaria's neck. His smile, lazy and bright, reached the Jeep. "Who's to say yet that somebody won't get hurt?"

Candalaria rose to her knees beside him. "What will you do to the priests?"

"Do?" sneered Maria. "What could he do? He's a puppy dog wagging a crocodile's tail."

Pablo struck a chord. "Maria is right. I wonder some-times if we shan't be the ones to get hurt ourselves. It was one thing to follow Anacleto and another to put our fate in the hands of a boy like this."

Vito sprang off the couch. By mistake he hit the side of Candalaria's head with his knee. She clutched his leg and put her teeth into it like a little savage cat. He kicked himself free and pulled her up by the hair. Then he gave her a sharp cuff on the chin which caused her own teeth to draw blood from her lips. He pushed her backwards onto the sofa. "Even you can play too many games with me. My temper is not always sweet." When he spoke to the others his voice was quiet but they could see the danger behind his eyes. "As for you, I should warn you to play no games at all. You have no ways to please me again like this child has. Your arms are not round and your breasts are not soft and I don't care for kissing your necks."

Porfirio's bellowing laugh broke out. "That is something we're sorry to hear, eh, Jeeponito?" Did you hear the bad news? We shall not have him kissing our necks!"

The Jeep doubled up, laughing, and hugged himself. "For myself I could cry with the disappointment. I was too shy to ask for such a favor but I must say I always hoped."

Vito's voice put a stop to their laughter as once Malo's had been able to do. The look of him made them uneasy. He bore an uncanny resemblance to Malo with his steady, narrowed eyes. The same thought was in most of their minds—that it might be as well to remember that this boy had been Malo-trained. It would be wiser to show respect for Vito. "Laugh," he said gently. "It makes a nice sound in the ears. There is no need for anyone to follow me who does not have the faith." He made his voice even more gentle and his eyes turned as soft as his words. "But I think even I should feel sorry for the fool who saw fit to turn against me."

The Jeep assured him quickly, "Vito, it's nothing like that. It was just that Anacleto was wise in such things."

"And I have told you that I, too, am wise. When the priest needs advice he asks his God. When I want it I ask Anacleto."

The Jeep's frown was worried. "But, Vito, *you* do not believe in his spirit yourself."

"That's a pity," Maria said. "What it could say might frighten him. Don't forget he was killed by that puppy dog."

"Vito meant to kill the priest," Porfirio said. "Anacleto would be sure to remember that."

Pablo threw his guitar to the sofa where it jangled beside Candalaria, who dabbed at her still-bleeding lip. "It would be a poor day if we came to believe in such rubbish. We should suffer from ojo ourselves."

"Anacleto would not put the evil eye on *us*." There was uncertainty in the Jeep's voice. Porfirio also spoke doubtfully. "Remember we left him to die."

Maria told them bitterly, "Not everyone forgets."

The Jeep swung his stunted body towards her. "Well, what was the use? He was dying in any case. If we had stayed we should all have been caught."

"The priest asked you to go for a doctor," Maria reminded him. "But instead you saved your skins."

"I heard what he said to that priest," Porfirio whispered. His eyes rolled in his great florid face. "He said, 'The rats are leaving. What did you expect of rats?'"

Maria's laugh was softly malicious. "You have cause to fear Anacleto's spirit."

Pablo banged a fist on the table. "His spirit does not exist except for superstitious fools. We are using it only to help get rid of these priests."

"His spirit does exist," Vito contradicted him. "You will find it alive in me." The eyes that stared back at him began to believe him.

He turned round and told Candalaria, "You will carry on with your going to church."

"But just now you ordered her not to," Porfirio blustered.

"And just now I'm changing my mind."

Candalaria stood up and stretched, catching her hands above her head. "I do as I please," she said. She wound her rebozo round her shoulders and slipped in a packet of cigarettes. The theft was too swift to attract attention.

When she had gone Vito smiled at them. "She will stay away from church now I have told her to go!" He rolled himself onto his back again. "I have watched Anacleto carefully. I have learned his ways. My eyes are all over the town as his were, and also my ears. There is always someone to tell me what they have seen or heard. I am not like the Jefe who gets no one to talk. I know before they have made up their own minds what those fool priests will do."

"They're not fools," the Jeep said. "That is the first mistake that Anacleto would never have made."

"When you think of the things they believe in, they are fools. They are more stupid than the half-wits who go to the bruja and ask her to make them love spells. What do they practice but magic, up at that altar of theirs?"

Pablo reminded him, "Padre Keogh has a way with him. He can make people listen to that idiot talk."

"He is sick," Vito answered. "His strength will give out. Chela told Domingo and Domingo told Mateo and Mateo told Alfonso Herrera who passed it on to Maria, that the doctor has warned him about his health. He will kill himself for us with too much work if we give him enough work to do."

"But he has the other one to help him," Porfirio pointed out.

Vito sent him a slow and lazy smile. "He will not have the other one long."

"Then they will send someone else. The world is full of these terrible priests."

"They are welcome to send whom they like," Vito said. "The town will be tired of them all by then. Already they are saying that a priest causes trouble. They will turn him out themselves. They will soon understand that it does not pay to side with the church against me. I make no trouble if the priest makes none. Already they're saying that."

"Supposing he gets them to talk. Someone could say something about the way Victorino died."

"That chicken could never come home here to roost."

"Why not?" asked Maria. "A bird can fly."

"Certainly, clever one, but that bird did not come from here in the first place."

"Those men that you paid could talk," said Maria.

"Those men that I paid did not know that I paid them. They have never even heard of me. They got a letter, that's all, with nobody's name on it, made out of newspaper print. It said that if this job was done the money would be found in an old tin box by Anacleto's grave. Half the money was put there before the job and half when it was done. It is true that I risked losing the first half, but I knew they would not miss the second. I told you how I watched Anacleto and how well I have studied his ways."

Father Keogh was unable to persuade Candalaria to

go to church again. When he asked her why she no longer attended she simply replied, "I got tired of it, that is all."

When she had gone Father Keogh enjoyed his first cigarette for many days. He said to Chela, "By the way, where did these come from? I found them on the desk."

"Someone must have put them through the window. I did not buy them," she said, "and the Long Father thought they were yours so he did not touch them."

"Oh dear," said Father Keogh. "And I thought they were his and pinched one immediately!"

Chapter 12 ━━━━━━━━━━

VITO HAD NOT BEEN MISTAKEN WHEN HE FORESAW HOW Quantana would feel. The town was alarmed by the belligerent attitude of the priests.

"It is not a nice thing to pay taxes but it is better than something worse."

"It is always the same when these priests begin working. Terrible things come about."

"It is not good for a place to be run by bandits, anyone knows that, but there is peace unless somebody fights them."

"If you went to the Jefe what would happen? You would never be heard of again."

"Well, perhaps if the Jefe could catch them red-handed—"

"Yes, but who wants to play the cheese in the mouse-trap? Myself, I should think it small comfort to know that my dead body would be the one to get them caught."

Few people thought it wise to go to church unless Father Keogh and Father Lasques agreed to carry out their duties without causing annoyance to Vito or Anacleto's spirit.

"One saw what happened to Victorino for just driving the priest about and you can say what you like, but it's a very strange thing that this happened when they opened the Bad One's grave."

When it was obvious that no one would come to church to hear a sermon, Father Keogh and Father Lasques came to the conclusion that Quantana must be attacked from the street corners and at the doors of its houses. While one preached in public the other made the visits. They chose different points from which to talk. Sometimes from street corners, where the roads crossed at the Avenida de Cortinez, and sometimes on the plaza from the rust-pitted bandstand. They delivered a daily address in Quantana and visited Tephuango. It was silent in the dust-thickened road that ran through the tiny settlement, an uncanny, listening silence that made their voices sound loud in their heads. There was nothing to be seen in the mud-track street except the grotesquely spiked shadows of the organ-cactus fences and the diving sweeps of the vultures that circled above. The Indians remained in their huts.

In Quantana it was necessary to shout at the top of the voice to be heard. Wherever the priests chose to speak they were joined by the organito. Attracted by the possibility of gathering crowds, he set up his barrel organ at their feet and turned the handle round incessantly. No entreaties would send him away. Grinning, he kept up his wrangling accompaniment, so that Father Keogh and Father Lasques were obliged to compete in volume with "La Banda de Ragtime de Alexander," "El Lirio de Laguna," "Annie Laurie," and "Una Casita Gris en el Oeste."

They spoke simply to reach the hearts of those whose faith was impaired by superstition. They spoke as they might speak to children who had an inordinate fear of the dark. They spoke as simply to those who were wiser but still believed more in the protection of Vito than in the protection of the church. Repeatedly they told Quantana and Tephuango that it was the spirit of Vito Castillo Rivera and not the spirit of Anacleto Gonzales Flores Comachi Alvarez which was causing the disquiet in the town. They said that no harm could be done by a man whose soul was in purgatory but that untold harm could be done by a living man organizing the evil to be perpetuated in his name. They accused Vito and those in his pay of inventing the orders which were purported to come from Malo and of seeing that they were carried out.

"Fear robs you of faith which is God's protection. Without that protection you place yourselves in the devil's hands. Prayer alone can renew that faith. If you are frightened to come to church pray in your homes and your hearts. Only God can hear the voice in your hearts. Claim His forgiveness, claim His guidance. You cannot be refused for God is Love. He hangs on the Cross again beside you when you shut him out of your lives. His will be the joy of the Father receiving the trust once again of a child who has deserted Him. Peter betrayed Him thrice and yet this was the man whom Our Blessed Lord sent forward to carry on His word. Prayer will give you faith and faith

will give you courage and by courage you can rid yourselves of this man who imperils your freedom."

"Was there ever such talk?" the Jeep giggled. "They
nearly had me on my knees."

"It will be interesting," Vito agreed with him, "when
you think that the opposite is going to happen to everything they say."

"Mac," said Sam to Father Keogh, "do you think it's
wise to go spreading all that angel food around?"

But Father Keogh and Father Lasques ignored the
warning.

"One man has no chance against a whole town full
of people if those people are determined to be rid of his
tyranny. Your best chance lies in collective attack. If one
man turns informer it's dangerous but if a hundred men
do so, it's safe."

They made their appeal individually as well.

"Mateo," Father Keogh said to the boy who worked
at the garage for Domingo-of-the-Hired-Car, "are you content to sit back like a weakling and let Vito Castillo tell
you what you may or may not do with your life?"

"You have three beautiful children," Father Lasques
told Maria-of-the-Post. "Will you let them be brought up
in the shadow of fear? If you and your friends joined together you could set them free once and for all."

"Salvadore, you work hard in your cinema. Your
family should receive all the profit you make. Are you
willing to share it with Vito Castillo by paying him illegal
taxes?"

"Coyotito, you could do much for your people by
helping them to recover the comforts of their faith. You
are an educated man, Coyotito. You can read and write
and you can spread these advantages to others of your tribe.

Are you going to tell me that a man of your understanding believes that a dead man's spirit can walk about inside the body of a cat?"

"Josefa, you used to come regularly to Mass. Since when did you last receive Holy Communion? Don't you feel a great loss in your life?"

"Roncho," they said to Alfonso Herrera, the tailor, "you have an excellent business. It's a waste of your time to make Vito's clothes free."

"Señora Ferreira, Señora Rodriguez, Señora Martinez, Señora Solano, you are women who receive much respect from this town. What sort of example are you setting it? By lapsing yourselves you are supporting Castillo and witchcraft."

They said the same things to Roberto-of-the-Bus, to Pancho of the gaseosa stall, to the chemist Anastacio, to every market vendor, to the two professional washerwomen who scrubbed clothes on the river stones, to the farmers who watered their mules at the fountain, and to Don Pedro of the Casa Grande.

"How can the Jefe protect you, if you deliberately try to hinder him when he acts in the name of the law?"

Locha sent a note down to Father Keogh. *Haven't you had enough trouble without asking for more? Why can't you leave Castillo alone? He is every bit as dangerous as Malo was.*

Father Lasques typed out the reply to her: *Because if we left him alone we should be leaving evil alone and the battle of Christianity against it is not yet won. Every fighter is needed, however humble. Every voice should be raised against it, however weak.*

The street campaign was wearing. Father Lasques was afflicted with severe headaches and Father Keogh felt pain

123

in his wounds and his arm. More often than not he was obliged to resort to a sling. The first sign that the town was listening came from a surprising source. The Señor Presidente Municipal was sitting on the old horsehair sofa in the little whitewashed room when Father Keogh returned with the dust of Tephuango thick in his trouser cuffs.

"Good afternoon, Don Agapito, what can I do for you?"

The Presidente raised brandyball eyes.

"You have been telling us to pray. If we did, do you believe that we should have any luck?"

"Certainly, if the faith is strong enough."

"I am willing to pray for a miracle," the Presidente said.

Father Keogh sat down uneasily. There was something in the expression of Don Agapito which warned him that the desired miracle was not to be in the general interests of the town. The parrot had recognized its one-time master's voice.

"Agapito! Agapito! Silly bald old fool!"

Father Keogh, embarrassed, covered the bird with Chela's discarded skirt.

The Presidente passed a hand over his sweat-gleaming head. "You will observe that I am a little thin on top."

"It's something we nearly all come to sooner or later," Father Keogh smiled. He felt acutely conscious of his own head of healthy hair.

"I do not mind for myself," the Presidente lied, "but it is something that worries my wife."

"Agapito! Agapito! Silly bald old fool!"

The Presidente glanced towards the cage. "An evil-natured bird. I cannot think where he picked such things up."

Father Keogh was silent, wishing that he had stayed preaching longer in Tephuango. With any luck it might then have been Father Lasques who walked into the problems concerning the decortication of Don Agapito. He was instantly ashamed of the thought. He realized that the few remnants of the Presidente's domestic happiness were probably at stake.

"It's that all her young friends make fun of her, Father, for being married to someone so old. If I had back my hair she would love me again, that is certain. For you will see that my face is still fine."

Father Keogh could see nothing of the sort but he pitied the small, perspiring man. "Have you tried all the usual remedies? Lotions, tonics, things like that. Have you had massage?"

"I have spent," said the Presidente, "a considerable fortune in trying to put things right. According to you there is only one course left open to me—prayer!"

Father Keogh suggested, "Surely, Señor Presidente Municipal, it would be possible to win back Doña Arcelia's regard in other ways? Physical attractions are bound to be lessened in time. Couldn't you draw her to you by more spiritual qualities? With—with your—your conversational powers, for instance, your knowledge, your consideration for her. Surely the fact that you are the father of her children creates an unbreakable bond?" He realized his tactlessness at once. There was open doubt about the parentage of the Presidente's seventh child. It was unmistakably possessed of the same smile, the same eyes, and the identical nose of the Señor Engineer who lived next door. He was also aware of the unlikelihood of Doña Arcelia's being attracted by spiritual means.

The Presidente eyed him steadily. "Miracles have occurred?"

"Most certainly."

"Do you think they could still occur?"

"Without doubt."

"Well then, Father, if I were to go down on my knees and pray that I might, in due course, receive a new head of hair, would I be wasting my time?"

Father Keogh replied emphatically, "No, Don Agapito, you could not be wasting your time."

It was Salvadore who brought about the "miracle." He offered Father Keogh and Father Lasques a free seat for the last house of *The Road to Morocco*. This was a second sign that they were regaining favor. Free seats had not been forthcoming for a long while. Salvadore was his own projectionist, and as he had also to assist in the inevitable dispute over tickets a performance rarely began other than half an hour late. There were many with so poor an idea of the technicalities attached to film making that they considered Salvadore responsible for the entertainment itself. He was held in great esteem.

The Señores Crosby and Hope were popular in Quantana, the Señor Don Bingo being an especial favorite. The cinema was full. Chickens wandered in from the street outside to peck at peanuts and popcorn dropped on the floor and hungry dogs scrounged round the feet. A large proportion of the audience, being uncertain what was taking place, felt compelled to clap at intervals to insure that the show did not stop.

Father Lasques leaned over to whisper, "You would

never think Crosby was wearing a toupee, would you? They are wonderful these days."

Father Keogh closed his eyes. "A wig!" he sighed. "A wig!"

It was the priests who took the measurements of the Presidente's head. He sat between them in the white-washed room, insisting that the door should be locked against intruders. "And what of the keyhole? That old woman of yours might peep in. It's not something I want to go all round the town."

Father Keogh told him, "I've already stuffed it up." He read out instructions to Father Lasques. "Well, you take the circumference first. That's it—now then, front to back! Shouldn't you start higher up on the forehead? He doesn't want a fringe. Next, it just says 'Nape.' Then temple to temple, ear to ear, and now across the head. I only hope that's right."

Two photographs were required of the Presidente, in his middle-aged baldness and in his youth with a full head of hair. A sample for color was also requested. There was none to be found on the shining head. Father Keogh suggested a piece of the eyebrow. "It'll set the tone if nothing else."

The Presidente's anxiety was detectable in his impatience until an interesting parcel was brought up from Huapan by Roberto-of-the-Bus. Then he appeared with so natural a head of hair that even the priests were startled by it.

It was impossible not to be aware that "the Miracle of the Presidente" had done as much towards bringing the town back to the church as all the words addressed to them. The greater proportion of Quantana had never seen a wig before. The Presidente was in no danger of facing awkward questions but he was under continual discussion.

"It is something I saw with my own two eyes. One minute he had the head of a pig's bare back and the next he was—well, you have seen him."

"Yes, and they say that he prayed for this thing."

"Well, it shows that the priests are right when they say that God hears your prayers."

The Presidente took a prideful part in the evening parade round the plaza. With Doña Arcelia on his arm he raised his hat to every slight acquaintance. Father Keogh had many a nervous moment when the "miracle" was exposed to a wind. Father Lasques tried to reassure him.

"It fits like a glove. He has to peel it off."

Father Keogh had forbidden the Presidente to claim that the hair was his own.

Don Agapito was quite unabashed. "I shall say that I have received a new head of hair in answer to my prayers. That would be true, wouldn't it?"

"Well, yes, I suppose so in a way," Father Keogh answered doubtfully. "As long as you don't say it grew."

Chapter 13 ～～～～～～～～～～～

HE WAS A LITTLE ASHAMED OF THE "MIRACLE" AND HE would have liked to forget it, but he received a sharp reminder the day after Don Agapito appeared in the wig.

Chela said to him, "An Indio has come to the house. Upon my word, such visitors! You would think we were not people who counted, to be disturbed when anybody likes."

It was Coyotito who had come to see Father Keogh. The Indian rose from his heels, lifted a battered bowler hat and sank down again in an effortless fluid movement. Father Keogh recognized the hat. It had once belonged to Don Pedro in his Oxford University days. Discarded, it had reached Tephuango many years before Coyotito was born. His father had handed it down to him and it now achieved place of honor on the household altar in Coyotito's hut. If anyone from Tephuango wished to visit the town in an official capacity, it was borrowed upon payment of a handful of grain. Father Keogh had seen it on many an Indian head. It was worn as a courteous gesture and as a personal badge of distinction.

"Is there some way I can help you, Coyotito?"

"You have seen the shadow picture, Father? The one where the Señor Crosby sings?"

"Yes," Father Keogh admitted uneasily.

"Splendid, wasn't it?"

"Splendid," Father Keogh agreed.

"I think this was amongst the most clever that Salvadore has ever put onto the great grey square that can show you living things."

"It was admirable," Father Keogh said.

"What a nice thing God has done for the Señor Presidente Municipal."

Father Keogh practiced flexing his right-hand fingers. He felt that it might be Coyotito's roundabout way of telling him that he had traced the source of the miracle to the Crosby toupee. He was apprehensive when Coyotito paused. But the Indian was smiling broadly.

"I, too, should like this miracle."

Father Keogh stared at the full head of wiry black hair and the pigtail that hung down the back.

"But, my good Coyotito, *you* are not bald."

The Indian patted the top of his bowler hat.

"It is not up there that I should like it, but down here." And he laid a long-fingered hand on his chest. Then he opened his cotton shirt. "Smooth, you see, Father, smooth, with no hairs. There is a girl I should much like to have for my wife. It is in the person of the daughter of my uncle's great friend Jesus Romero. Maria of the Seven Eyes they call her."

Father Keogh was frowning, bewildered. "But I don't see what that's got to do with the lack of hair on your chest."

Coyotito raised his bland, black eyes. "It has nothing to do with it, Father. She is only called this because she can see so many things. Never was one so young so wise."

Father Keogh asked him patiently, "Coyotito, *why* do you want hair on your chest?"

"Ah, well, Father, this Jesus Romero—six sons he has had, you would think he'd be pleased, but no, it is the girl he is glad about. There is nothing she cannot make him do if she chooses to smile in his face. And she did *not* smile when I asked for her hand. So this Jesus Romero said 'No' to me. I am to ask you, what a terrible thing! This girl should not be allowed to speak."

"And where does the Señor Crosby fit into this?"

"Well, Father, I should think it was easy to see. Don Bingo must have hairs on his chest."

"They were not apparent in the film."

"Gringos," said Coyotito severely, "are always proud of the hairs on their chest. I have looked at this shadow picture carefully. I am just as much of a fine fellow as the

Señor Crosby so where is the difference? It must be in the hairs on his chest that the little Maria could sense, for she has a love for him which she does not show for me."

Father Keogh told him gently, "Coyotito, if Maria has an admiration for the Señor Crosby I think you might find that one of the chief attractions is his voice. He sings," Father Keogh pointed out, "and there are many people who have a great admiration for his voice."

"I, too, am able to make these sounds." Coyotito emitted a strange howl at which Father Keogh found it impossible not to wince.

"How old is Maria?" he asked.

"Well, she is quite a young woman now. At the turn of the moon she'll be twelve."

"And you are about eighteen?"

"I will be coming to eighteen with the rains in this year."

"In June," Father Keogh said. "Can you support Maria of the Seven Eyes?"

Coyotito nodded.

Father Keogh thought for a minute or two. Then he said, "Coyotito, I think I know a way to make Maria proud of you, but it depends on the kindness of somebody else. You must be patient until I send for you."

Father Lasques typed a letter for Father Keogh. It was addressed to Doña Marian.

She sent back a postcard. It bore three words: *Okay. Any time.*

Father Keogh himself escorted the young couple to the Casa Grande. The fact that they risked placing themselves so conspicuously in his company gave yet another hint that the town was responding to the appeal. Coyotito wore the bowler hat and a quietly colored serape hung over his shoulder. Maria of the Seven Eyes came no farther in height than the young Indian's waistline. She wore a heavy collection of beads round her throat and her blouse was tucked into a long pleated skirt. A headband of twisted wool sat low on her forehead and earrings dragged down the small lobes of her ears. She was barefoot and as she walked she switched huge startled eyes from Father Keogh to Coyotito as if to lose sight of one or the other of them for an instant would leave her entirely alone in the world.

"Maria speaks no Spanish," Father Keogh observed.

"That is right, Father, she knows only her own tongue."

"Do you understand the Mixe language?"

"No, Father, she will have to learn mine, or some small bits of Spanish to help us along, but I am not much one for talking. I am a reading man."

"Will she be happy outside her own tribe?"

Coyotito shrugged his shoulders. "I do not get drunk and I shall not beat her. There are not many who could say such fine things for their man."

"That's true enough," Father Keogh sighed.

At the Casa Grande the mozo, Alfredo, looked surprised at the visitors. "We're all three expected," Father Keogh told him and he ushered the other two up the stairs. He had time to wonder whether he would encounter Locha and to hope that he did not before Doña Marian called out, "Hello there," in answer to his knock on her drawing-room door. She eased herself out of an armchair and came forward to greet him. "You look like you didn't sleep in weeks, Father, but Josefa tells me the arm is better."

"Oh, much, thank you. I can move the whole thing about now." And he raised it to show her.

"My," she said, "I am glad." Then she glanced at the Indians. "Do your pals speak Spanish?"

"Coyotito does," Father Keogh replied.

Doña Marian looked the Indian up and down. "You'd think the kid would go for him. He looks all right to me."

Coyotito returned her scrutiny. Father Keogh could not help comparing the nervously rapid gestures of Doña Marian with the solid patience of Coyotito who moved only his lips when he spoke.

Doña Marian addressed him, "Does your girl friend have any particular Crosby favorite? I have quite a selection here."

Father Keogh intervened. "I haven't told them anything about it, Doña Marian. I thought if you'd just be good enough to play a few, Maria would be so impressed with Coyotito's being able to arrange for Bing Crosby to put on a special show for her that it might endear him to her. Apparently she has a surprising influence over her father and one word from her could do the trick."

Doña Marian put six records on the phonograph. The ash from her cigarette fell in before she had closed the lid. "Darn it," she said and squinted as the smoke spiraled up to her eyes. "The kid'll probably think Bing's right inside, himself."

"That's quite likely," Father Keogh smiled. "I don't suppose she's ever seen anything like it before."

When the first record played and Crosby sang Maria's mouth opened and remained open until the second began. Then she crept slowly towards the phonograph. She touched it gingerly first with one finger. Then she squatted beside it, her ear close to the wood. Coyotito moved across to her side. He pointed to the phonograph and then to himself. She raised respectful eyes to him.

"I think it's working," Father Keogh smiled.

Doña Marian opened the phonograph, chose a record and made a sign for Maria to watch. The child raised herself slowly up on her toes and peeped apprehensively into the mechanism. Doña Marian showed her how the voice appeared only when a record was turning around. Then she took one off and gave it to her.

"Here you are, kid. You don't have anything to play it on but maybe you'd like a keepsake. Watch out!" she warned quickly. "It breaks."

She took the clutched treasure which the child was about to shatter in the tight pressure of her arms and showed by a sign that it was delicate.

Coyotito made them a speech of thanks. He inclined his head first towards Father Keogh and then towards Doña Marian. "It is a great thank-you I feel I must say to you, Padre. If there is any small little thing that I think I can do for you, you will not hear that Coyotito said 'No' to himself. And it is a great thank-you I say to the kind Señora. This gift will be something to show to our children. It will be fine to be able to tell them that it was on this particular little black ring that the Señor Crosby has sung just for our sakes."

When they had gone Father Keogh said, "It's a 'great thank-you' I have to say to the kind Señora, too. I am perfectly aware that no one else would have done me this favor."

"Oh, skip it," Doña Marian laughed. "It was worth it to see that kid's face. Her eyes shone like lamps. How come a Mixteca gets tied up with Coyotito? Don't they come from somewhere around Mitla?"

"I believe so. But she is the daughter of an uncle's great friend or something. He probably brought her over to Tephuango and there's some complicated bargaining in process. You know what that can mean."

"Oh, sure! It can go on for months." Doña Marian stubbed out a cigarette. "Talking of daughters and marriages, there's some complicated bargaining going on in this house."

Father Keogh's tone altered. His eyes were grave as he said to her, "Doña Marian, I sometimes wonder what we are going to do about that problem."

She put her face in her hands. A cigarette jutted from between her fingers and she blew out a column of smoke through them. "You know, it's kind of nice to hear you say 'we.' I don't get much co-operation around here."

"This is certainly *our* worry," Father Keogh assured her. "What's happened now?"

"Locha wrote Dyke that she wanted a divorce. She had a pretty rough letter back. He said she could whistle for it."

"Well, that's excellent. All we need is time. I'm absolutely certain she'll get over this ridiculous passion for me."

"But is it so ridiculous? I tell you, you don't know that kid. Nobody cares to mention it because it seems it is like some kind of disgrace, but Locha has a lot of me in her too. I fell for Pey at her age and it lasted all this time. Laugh that one off."

Father Keogh leaned forward. "There's surely a difference. You've remained with Don Pedro. The years have been able to cement your affection."

Doña Marian's smile struck Father Keogh as being the oldest portion of her face.

"Father, I remained with Pedro like a picture gets left on the wall that nobody looks at any more. Nobody bothers to take it down because they forget it's around.

135

Look, Father, I know Locha's young and you think she'll get over it, but I don't have all that faith."

"But surely she must know it's hopeless?"

"Maybe that's what keeps the thing going. You're the prince in the ivory tower to her, Father. I don't say she won't marry again maybe over and over. She may have a dozen affairs, but she's always going to go into it looking for someone like you and she's going to come out of it sour because she didn't find someone like you."

"Heaven forbid!" Father Keogh said. "If we can only get her to go back to her husband, she'll have the utmost difficulty in remembering what I look like in six months' time. She must have been sufficiently attracted to him in the first place to have thought there was a chance. She's used to being in love with me, that's all. I don't doubt her sincerity, but I think unbeknown to herself it might well have become a pose. Did you see the letter from Dyke?"

"Sure, but I had to snoop for it. Locha never tells me a thing. He was pretty mad at you, Father."

"He probably can't conceive that I'm not at fault somewhere."

"It has me worried. He said if it finally turned out that she decided to make the break because of you, he'd see you paid for it if he had to walk all the way from Washington to bust your face wide open."

"If it would solve anything, I'd be happy to stand up as an Aunt Sally for him."

"I'm kind of scared, Father. It looked like his blood was really up. He might do you some kind of harm."

"The most important thing, Doña Marian, is to try to keep harm from them."

136

Chapter 14 ~~~~~~~~~~~~~~~~~~~~~~

MARIA OF THE SEVEN EYES PERSUADED HER FATHER TO GIVE his consent.

Coyotito told the town, "It was so soon that my prayers were answered, for I tell you I went down on my knees for this thing."

No one admitted to being frightened of Vito and everyone denied believing in the spirit of Anacleto. But the town, encouraged by Coyotito, was impressed by the street campaign.

"It is quite a nice thing to hear the priests grumbling at you once more. It makes you feel that your sins are important again."

Maria-of-the-Post admitted, "My youngest has never been baptized. I worry about it at times. My Pepe wanted to take her to Huapan, but I was afraid of the evil eye."

"I am not of course so foolish as to believe in the spirit of Malo, but it would be much wiser not to annoy it."

"It would be a comfort to go to church again. There isn't a doubt about that."

"Vito Castillo has never said himself that he does not wish us to go. It is only the things that one hears."

Coyotito suggested, "It might be a good thing to ask him if he thinks that the Bad One would mind."

"Now there's a fine thought, Coyotito! We could say that it's not to offend the Bad One, but just to get married and buried and useful things. It would be fine to have a proper funeral again. It is not respectful to the dead to be put in the ground by the gravedigger and no one to do the right things."

"My Rosario is growing impatient for her wedding, but I said to her, 'Wait and see if there is some little sign that God will be helping the priests to let us go to church in Quantana again.' It's so expensive to hold a marriage in Huapan."

"Well, then, someone must go and ask Vito. Who should we send?"

Finally a small deputation consisting of Mateo, Alfonso Herrera, Coyotito, and young Alejo the goatherd called upon Vito at his suite in the Hotel Martinez.

Vito received them graciously. Mateo had been chosen as spokesman. The tailor, Herrera, had put on his best black suit, but he had cut it too close for economy's sake and he felt the strain across his chest. All four had hidden about their persons small talismen to keep off the evil eye. Neither had told the other. They had paid a secret visit to the adobe hovel which housed Mother Montezera and parted with five pesos apiece. Vito offered them each a glass of beer. They accepted and sat sipping in unison, as if to do anything alone in such company would single them out for unwelcome attention. Mateo had trouble in finding words. He bent the brim of a black felt in his fingers. He wore a highly colored American shirt. "Señor Castillo Rivera, we have come to say—that is, we have not come to say anything, we have come to ask—that is, there is something we would like to know about the church."

Vito pointed a thumb behind him. "Then you have come in the wrong direction. The padres live on the lower road."

The Jeep crossed the floor with his ungainly crippled gait to choose a cigar from a cabinet. "Did you think Señor Castillo had taken holy orders?"

Mateo made a second effort. "We were wondering," he said politely, "if the señor spirit of the late lamented Anacleto Gonzales Flores Comachi Alvarez would object if we went to church a little."

"Just to get married and baptized and buried, only for useful things," Alfonso Herrera put in quickly. "Not to go letting the priests make fools of us."

"Oh no, certainly not," agreed Mateo. "Roncho is right. Everyone knows what the church can be like with the money it tries to get out of you. It's no better than paying illegal taxes to—" He broke off, appalled, when he remembered to whom he was speaking.

"Worse, perhaps." Vito smiled at him. "You get left in peace if you pay your taxes, but the priests are always after you."

Young Alejo, the goatboy, edged his way forward. He held his hand up to show that he wanted to speak, a gesture he remembered from schooldays. "If you please, Señor Castillo Rivera, my mother would like me to go back to church because she is afraid that God will be angry with me if I stay away, but she is also afraid that the Bad One's spirit will be angry if I go."

Vito answered carefully, "How can I talk for Anacleto? All I know of this spirit I have heard from your priests. For holy men their teachings are strange. They are telling the town to fight a spirit. For myself, I am not quite sure such things exist, but even if I was as frightened of it as your priests seem to be, I could make no answer for it."

Mateo spoke out bravely. "In the town they believe that the spirit is always in touch with you and tells you its wishes from day to day."

"If they believe that," Vito smiled at him, "they can thank the priests for putting it into their heads. Does the town want to go back to church?"

"It would be a nice thing to do if it was something that would be sure not to upset this spirit. I am like you, Señor Castillo Rivera, I am not certain of this thing myself, but there are many who do believe in it. Some have laid eyes on it, some have heard it, others have had it speak to them. It takes so many forms, but most often it is in the form of a small white cat that goes to Porfirio's bar each night." Vito's eyes met the Jeep's and traveled past them to Porfirio's and Pablo's, then they turned back to Mateo. "And so, Señor, it is the feeling in the town, amongst the Indians chiefly of course," Mateo said, glancing at the expressionless face of Coyotito, "but amongst many others as well, that as this is the case it would be possible for you to discover the wishes of the spirit in this little matter."

Vito turned a cigar between long fingers. "There would seem to be only one sensible thing to do. Why don't you go to church and find out if the spirit minds?"

It struck the four petitioners as extremely good advice. Mateo was careful to put the second query with which Quantana had entrusted him. "And yourself, Señor Castillo Rivera, would you have any objections yourself?"

Vito stood up and smiled at them. "Now that is a question I *can* answer. As far as I am concerned, you could all take your beds to it. I would not care if you lived in the church."

A broad smile broke out on all four faces. They

bowed themselves backwards out of the room. Mateo rammed his hat on his head. "Now there's a satisfactory meeting! The priests will believe they have done it with their talk, which is always a polite thing to make people feel, and Vito has no objections. For myself, I cannot believe he is evil. That beer was exceptionally good."

"But he does see this spirit," Coyotito insisted. "When you mentioned it I saw him speak to his friends with his eyes."

They spread the good news around the town. "We are to try out the church on the Bad One's feelings and Vito does not mind!"

In the well-carpeted suite at the Hotel Martinez, the sun forced its way through the shutters and sent bright, dancing bars across the floor. Vito's young body was limp with laughing. "To think I was angry with poor Maria for putting down food for that cat!"

"Time and time again when she disobeyed you," Porfirio reminded him, "you said you would kill it. That goes to prove that you're not always so wise."

Vito refilled his glass with beer. "Yes, well, in that I'm not like Anacleto. I have no love for cats."

"Whose is it?" Pablo asked.

"Maria believes it was one that Anacleto used to give food to at times and that's why it keeps coming back."

The Jeep giggled. "Perhaps it is really his spirit."

"It will be from now on," Vito promised him. "Tell Maria to catch it the next time it comes. We must greatly encourage its visits. Find out what it likes to eat best and feed it that but see that it gets nothing else all the day. If it's hungry it will keep up its calls on us. Maria must take it down to the house of the witch and see that she keeps it locked up until nighttime."

Pablo sent out an arm for the shell-covered guitar. As he played he sang to himself:

> *"Out on the mountain he lay alone,*
> *Out in the wind on the mountain.*
> *There was no one to weep save me, save me,*
> *Out in the wind on the mountain."*

"Vito," Porfirio asked, "are you wise to give in to the church? These priests could make people believe in their lies if they are given a good enough chance."

"You heard what I said," Vito told him. "I said I could give my word, but not Anacleto's."

"How will you make Anacleto talk?"

"I shall not have to," Vito laughed. "Anacleto will speak for himself. A cat comes to my door and they say it is him—well, everything else that happens they will think is his doing. I need not exert myself at all, unless now and again I feel I should give the spirit a helping hand. But even that might not be necessary. Something is bound to go wrong for someone. Something always does." He was echoing Sam when he told his friends, "If a child falls over in the street, or is kicked by a burro, you will find Anacleto has done it. If somebody loses some money, or a business deal doesn't work out, or the seeds are slow in growing— Anacleto's been at work! If there's an illness, or a stillborn child, or even if the bus gets stuck on the hill, that 'señor spirit' is bound to be blamed. If the smallest thing goes wrong when the town goes back to church, it will be because the spirit of Anacleto disapproves." And Vito covered his face with a glossy magazine to keep off the sun and went to sleep.

On the following morning the church was so full that there were people left out on the steps. When Father

Keogh appeared vested in a black chasuble, there were whispers: "He will be offering up the Sacrifice for Victorino's soul." The conjectures were incorrect. Father Keogh was offering up the Sacrifice for Malo. It caused much comment afterwards. "Fancy saying a Mass for the Bad One like that. I should have thought it would have been wiser to try to keep that one out of heaven."

"Yes, and to put him before Victorino! That's not only surprising, it's rude."

"Perhaps," someone said wisely, "he thought the Bad One needed it more than Victorino."

"All I can think is the shooting affected him."

"Still, it was nice to hear the Mass again."

Father Lasques said the Requiem for Victorino. Mass was said daily in the church and Benediction was well attended too. Confessions were heard both in Quantana and Tephuango. The amount of work involved for Father Keogh and Father Lasques was formidable. Religious instruction in the school had been minimized over the last few months. It was necessary for either one or other of the priests to take a daily class. It was not easy to deal with the children of parents who had deliberately lapsed themselves. There was a certain amount of hostility and frank disbelief to be faced. The out-of-practice choir had to be rehearsed, the catechism classes had to be reinstated, there was the Sunday school, the Children of Mary, and there was such a procession of penitence that Father Keogh and Father Lasques were kept in the confessional for three and four hours apiece. There was a high demand for baptisms, churchings, and wedding presentations.

In addition to the mounting round of daily duties there was an hour's good advice to be given daily to Candalaria. They were making slow progress with her. What they defined as sinful she still regarded as skillful. They were aware that she lied to them and that she had made few efforts to improve herself. There were also numerous ceremonies which the town considered itself to have been done out of. The traditional Candlemas Day blessing of seeds in the church had been irrevocably missed. But it was still possible to give a ceremony in retrospect to the plantings. Crosses were set up in the fields, blessed with incense and holy water, prayers were offered, and in the church and in private houses offerings of incense were made to the saints. The sick calls were so numerous that it seemed that the whole of Quantana had suddenly found itself in need of the attention of the priests.

Then old Antonio Ibarra caught his trousers on fire. Ancient and senile, he sat nodding each day with his back against the sun-baked wall of his patio. A cigar rolled down between his drawn-up knees, smoldered and finally set him alight. His shrieks brought help from neighbors and the physical damage was slight. But his granddaughter-in-law was at Mass. No one said much about it at the time as he had been known to set himself on fire before, but it was the beginning.

Doña Marian slipped on the great broad staircase of the Casa Grande and fractured her forearm. It had been a matter of some surprise to Father Keogh that she had escaped an accident before. The stairs were highly polished and she was frequently unsteady in her use of them. It was the private duty of Josefa to support her on these occasions, but Josefa had gone to Benediction.

The second cashier of the Banco de Comercio was imprisoned for embezzlement. The manager had suspected him for some time, but it was unfortunate that his dishonesty was brought to account just after he had rejoined the choir.

A lizard ran round in a complete circle on the wall behind the bed of Roberto-of-the-Bus. Two days later he received a letter to say that an uncle, dying in Oaxaca, had changed his will and left Roberto out. It was only that morning that Roberto had offered up a special Intention for the uncle in Oaxaca. Maria-of-the-Post sent a parcel to Huapan which failed to arrive. Silvanito went to the dentist and found that his two gold teeth would not be ready in time for his wedding. Salvadore's ancient sound apparatus broke down in the cinema. It left the Señor Cooper mouthing words in the court scene of *Mr. Deeds Goes to Town* which no one could hear. Several persons thought it a trifle ominous that Salvadore's powers should have been impaired so shortly after attending a Missa cantata. A burro ran amock in the market and damaged one stall of refrescos and one selling radio parts. The fountain failed and lightning shot across the sky an uncommonly long time before the following thunderclap. Even so, there was only a murmurous apprehension until Doña Florencia had a heart attack.

Chapter 15

FATHER KEOGH HIMSELF WAS IN THE MIDST OF A DISCONCERT-
ing interview when he was called to her. He was hurrying
back from the churching of Señora Garcia. He rounded a
corner suddenly and came face to face with a young
American. He was big-boned, and his close-cropped head
was an inch and a half above Father Keogh. There was a
lazy look over his eyes and his smile as if he had only just
waked up and might stretch in the morning sunlight. He
was not smiling when he blocked Father Keogh's path.

"Do you have a minute or two you could spare me,
Padre?"

Father Keogh recognized him. "You're Locha's husband, Dr. Dyke Brown."

"Used to be," was the reply.

Father Keogh extended his hand to him. It was
ignored and he withdrew it.

"Doctor, I do hope you don't mean that you've started
divorce proceedings?"

The American shook his head. "We haven't come
unhitched legally yet."

"And I hope you never will. I realize you are not a
Catholic, Dr. Brown—"

The young doctor's eyes were unreadable when they
looked Father Keogh up and down. "I had enough of
Catholics," he said.

146

"Would you care to come back to my house for our talk?"

Dyke nodded. He seemed disinclined to walk abreast with Father Keogh. He followed at a short distance behind with his hands in his pockets. If Father Keogh waited for him, he signed the priest on with a jerk of his chin. Father Keogh was conscious of eyes and comments as they made their Indian file through the town.

"That is the Señor Gringo doctor whom the Señora Cortinez de Dyke Brown has left for the love of that priest."

In the small whitewashed room Father Keogh pushed forward a chair for the doctor, but the offer was declined. Dyke Brown flicked a cigarette from a packet and lit it for himself. The voice was not raised, but the words were forced out as if there was a power of breath behind them which the young doctor had stored in his lungs for the purpose.

"You lousy, hypocritical, goddamned Turk!"

Father Keogh said evenly, "Dr. Brown, when I wrote to you I thought I made it quite clear that I would do everything within my power to bring Locha to her senses."

"How come she ever came to lose them? Somebody must have encouraged her."

Father Keogh was silent.

"Look, I don't say you're actually sleeping with the kid—"

"Thank you. I appreciate such restraint."

"But can you look me right in the eye and tell me you were not responsible for that kid falling for you in the first place?"

Father Keogh found it hard not be be impatient with Locha for involving him so tenaciously in her own private life with no consent of his. As a child, her affections had

147

always been extraordinarily concentrated. One possession would absorb all her attention. If it was lost or destroyed she could never be persuaded to substitute anything else in her regard for it. If she could not retrieve it or mend it she would grieve for it, always secretly sad that she could never repossess it. It might perhaps be as Doña Marian feared, that her love for himself was a cherished belonging with which she could never be persuaded to part. He prayed daily that it might not be so. Yet under Dyke's angry scrutiny he felt an inexplicable pang. He was defenseless against its sudden thrust because he had not expected it. It reminded him that if these prayers were successful Locha would forget him. He would never himself forget Locha. She would be for him always the rebellious, lonely child who had placed her small friendship so trustingly in his hands. That she had grown up, that her figure was slender yet softly curved, that her eyes palely green had the still, dreamy wisdom of a cat, that there was about her skin and her hair an elusive scent as a night wind can carry the breath of flowers—these things were for others, not for him. He had his own picture, his secret bond with her past. The child in her still came dancing forward to meet him whenever he met her smile. Yet it was impossible not to wonder whether a more thorough search should be made in himself for the blame.

His voice was thoughtful when he asked Dyke Brown, "You think I've seduced this girl mentally, that I got hold of her affections and deliberately tantalized her with my inability to return them?"

"I couldn't put it better myself."

"Then would you mind helping me to discover if it's what I think too? Now, firstly, as Locha's whole feeling for me is based on our earliest relationship I must have started

148

my mental seduction about eight years ago, which would make her either nine or ten. Does that strike you as being something a grown man would do, always supposing, of course, that he wasn't a sexual maniac—and I take it you'll give me the benefit of the doubt for that? Secondly, it's possibly escaped your memory but I was largely instrumental in persuading Locha to marry you in the first place. Thirdly, I am still confident that if she will only give your marriage a second chance she could still make it happy for you both. Upon reflection I find myself innocent of your accusations. Had I known she was going to develop these feelings for me, you may be sure I should have managed to prevent it."

"Well, it's just too bad for you that you didn't, Father, because here's what I intend to do. I intend to sue you for alienation of affections and I am going to do it right here in Quantana. I guess the Church isn't keen on that kind of publicity? It wouldn't do you much good with your bosses, huh?"

"What I'm worrying about, Doctor Brown, is what good you think it could possibly do you. Even supposing you won this extraordinary suit, how could that help you with Locha?"

"It couldn't," Dyke Brown agreed. "But it could help me a hell of a lot with you."

"Personal revenge would recompense you?"

"I said it could help."

Father Keogh studied Dyke Brown's face. His normally pleasant expression seemed ill-suited to the words he was using. The kindly lines of the slow smile that were visible round the mouth and the drowsy eyes seemed at war with the tone of his voice. It caused Father Keogh a keen distress to feel himself responsible for the hatred which was struggling for supremacy over a naturally easy-going nature. Dyke Brown should not be threatening another man with ruin. If he were not at work he should be at play. His was a straightforward soul. It should have no shades of Vito or Malo. It would be bruised and bewildered in its efforts to emulate them.

Father Keogh stood up. "Am I never going to be able to make you believe that it is my dearest personal wish to see everything come right between you two? Do you honestly think that I've waited until I was in danger of blackmail before I tried to influence her?" He took out his last remaining cigarette, remembered that he owed it to Father Lasques and put it back in his case. "It would be to your greater advantage, young man, if instead of trying to get your revenge on me you made an effort to help me. You can do more for yourself than I can do for you. Instead of suing me for her affections, fight me for them! Fight me through her. Go up there. Stay at the Casa Grande. Your aunt'll be glad enough of your support. Talk to Locha, take her out, let her see what she'll miss if she forfeits your company for good. Use every trick you can think of. Good heavens, man, you shouldn't need me to tell you how to win back your own wife. Make her see what an obstinate fool she's been. And above all, be patient with her, be tolerant, be kind. Let her see what your love could mean to her in life."

Chela put her head round the door. "Father, quick, you're wanted up at the bakery. The doctor has asked you to come—something terrible has happened to poor Doña Florencia."

"What's the matter? Is it an illness or has she had an accident?"

"No, Father, it's something much worse."

Father Keogh was acquainted with Doña Florencia's matrimonial difficulties. The husband, a notorious drunk, left her to run the business and knocked her about in fits of sobbing, hysterical rage. Normally she was well able to hold her own with any weapon that came to her hand. But it was possible that on this occasion Edmundo Arrieta might have done her some serious injury.

"Has she been badly hurt, Chela?"

"No Father, it is something much worse."

To show exasperation was pointless. Father Keogh had been in Mexico long enough to know that only the one whose temper was lost was affected by it. It made no impression on anyone else.

"Very well, Chela, I'll go up at once." He turned round to Dyke Brown. "Would you care to continue our talk later or do you feel it pointless?"

"Anything further I have to say I'll make public. I'll give you a month. You see, I still think it's you who could influence my wife."

Father Keogh passed by him without further comment.

The bakery was close to Porfirio's bar. Edmundo Arrieta barred the priest's way. His face was puffed from too much pulque and smudged with flour. Edmundo had never received from Quantana the courtesy title of "Don." Respect was reserved for his hard-working wife. Father Keogh addressed him severely.

"Is what's happened to Doña Florencia your fault again?"

"*My* fault!" Edmundo shrieked at him. "No, burro! You are to blame. Why else should a nagual visit us?"

The heat of the primitive ovens invaded the whole of the house. Doctor Juarez was waiting inside.

"Oh, I'm glad you've come, Father. She's calling for you. She's had a heart attack. She'll be all right but it'll help her to talk to you."

"What's this about a nagual?"

"Oh!" The doctor made a noise with his lips. "That was the cause of the heart attack. Look!" He beckoned Father Keogh across the room. A great stone trestle stacked with loaves bore the white imprints of a cat.

Father Keogh bent to examine them. "Some cat has obviously walked in the flour and left marks on the table. Why should that give her a heart attack?"

"Well, you know what they are. Isn't a nagual supposed to bring bad health and trouble? I don't think it's confined to a cat. It can be any small creature, I believe, but isn't there a tale going about that Malo has put himself into the body of a cat? She thought he had paid her a visit and collapsed with fright."

"Oh, what *is* to be done with them?" Father Keogh sighed.

Arrieta came in. He put his face close to the priest's.

"You and your churchgoing, that is what's done it. Until she went up there praying with you again everything here was all right."

The doctor said, "Use what few wits you've got, Edmundo. As there is no such thing as a nagual, how could it possibly have brought harm to your wife?"

"These are the paw marks of a real cat," Father Keogh pointed out. "There's nothing supernatural in them."

"If there is no such thing as a nagual and it cannot bring bad health like they say, why was my wife struck down by it?"

"She wasn't," Father Keogh said. "She was made ill by her own superstitious fears."

Arrieta spat down at his feet. "This is not the only harm that the spirit has done. What of this poor old Tono Ibarra who nearly died when his trousers caught fire? Look what occurred in the Banco and up at the Casa Grande. The whole town is saying the Bad One is angry because you have pushed them all back to the church."

"Edmundo, misfortunes can occur in a perfectly natural manner. It's got nothing to do with evil spirits."

"My wife goes no more to your church after this and I forbid you to go to her now."

"Your wife has asked for me," Father Keogh said. "I shall have to respect her wishes."

Doña Florencia recovered quickly and seemed to suffer no lasting ill effects. But there was an uneasy feeling throughout the whole town. The congregation was noticeably thinner when Father Lasques celebrated Mass on the following morning and fewer people cared to be seen in the company of the priests.

Chapter 16 〜〜〜〜〜〜〜〜〜〜〜

FATHER KEOGH ASKED FATHER LASQUES, "DO YOU FEEL UP to a cat hunt? I think it has now become necessary for us to trap Anacleto's spirit."

"I wonder if that was the little white cat I picked up outside Porfirio's bar on the first night I came to Quantana."

"I hope so," Father Keogh said. "It might recognize you as an old acquaintance and walk trustingly into our sack."

"What shall you do with it, drown it?"

"*Drown it?*" Father Keogh said. "On the contrary, I shall bring it back here and cherish it. It shall sit on my knee, sleep on my bed and feed off my plate, and then provided coincidence doesn't choose to see that I drop dead with apoplexy, it should surely go to prove that the poor little creature can't hurt anybody."

"We shall need some sort of bait," Father Lasques said. "What we need is a really strong-smelling piece of fish."

"There's some for supper," Father Keogh said. "Ask Chela for it. She wouldn't give me so much as a fin but then I'm not in her good books. She thinks my morals went to pot when I told her to be polite to Candalaria."

Father Lasques came back from the kitchen with a fish head held between finger and thumb. "I think this ought to do it," he smiled.

"That ought to do anything," Father Keogh agreed. He held out his handkerchief and made a bundle of the fish head in his pocket.

It was dark when they reached the plaza. There was no one about and only the splinter of light through the iron grille on the opposite house front showed that Roncho Herrera was keeping his watch. The Indian laurels that fenced in the plaza semed to crouch like humped figures intending to spring. From the bakery next door Doña Florencia's voice made angry unmusical sounds in the night as she rated Edmundo for being drunk again.

"Nothing done! I must do everything—and so recently sick in my bed—while you sit round the house with your tongue lolling out. Are the geese fed? Has the pig been put in? Are the chickens in their house? Most certainly not. I am quite sure of that. I must do everything, I Florencia who could have married straight into the bank."

Porfirio's bar was closed. They could hear the Jeep's high metallic giggle and the clatter of glasses returned to the shelves. Pablo was playing the old guitar and singing a lewd little song. Vito was baiting Maria.

"Sometimes she is still Anacleto's woman. That is when I want something that *she* has to give. But it's a different tale, isn't it, Doña Maria, when it's something that you want from me? Then it is smiling and stroking and *my* woman. She forgets Anacleto then."

The door opened guardedly not more than a crack. The priests crouching on each side of it drew themselves back to the covering wall. Maria's hand placed a saucer of milk on the steps. The door was pushed to and the bar was silent.

Father Keogh leaned forward and whispered, "They obviously keep it shut up somewhere else and starve it to insure that it comes here each night." Father Lasques held the sack and Father Keogh the fish head. "Get the poor little beast into the bag as quickly as you can but be careful not to hurt it. Then get back to the house. Don't wait for me, I'll look out for myself."

"I will do what I can," Father Lasques said.

In the darkness Father Keogh smiled. "You sound on the nervous side. Are you?"

"I'm not at home in this sort of thing," the young priest admitted.

"Oh, I am," Father Keogh said. "My sister and I used to lure pheasants off a neighbor's estate when we were

155

children. We used to soak currants in brandy and get them tight."

They knelt a quarter of an hour in an uneasy silence. Their limbs grew stiff and their flesh was chilled by the fresh touch of the strong night wind. A faint mew from behind set their nerves on edge.

"Quick," Father Keogh breathed.

All that could be seen of the victim was an indistinct white blur. Father Lasques made a plunge with the sack. A loud squawk of terror turned the silent watchfulness of the night into a turmoil. Shutters flung open, women screamed. Doña Florencia's shouts were ahead of the rest of the noise.

"Drunken fool! What did I tell you. Someone is stealing the birds."

"Great heavens, we've got hold of a chicken," Father Keogh said. "Let it out, for the love of mike."

Father Lasques' voice was agonized. "I can't. It's all tangled up in the sack."

"Policia! Help, Policia! Help, a thief!"

Doña Florencia's cry seemed to wing round the plaza. The door of Porfirio's bar was wrenched inward. The light fell out, bathing the priests. In it Father Keogh had time to see the blazing eyes of a frightened white cat. Overcoming its fear, it kept low on the ground towards the saucer of spilling milk. Father Keogh was still on all fours. The fish head he managed to cram in his pocket. Father Lasques, his normally smooth hair on end, presented a woebegone picture of clerical guilt. His long face was pale and startled in the sudden shower of light. He still held the sack in his hand. Inside it the frantic bird plunged about. Porfirio and Vito seized Father Keogh and pulled him to his feet. Pablo and the Jeep held Father Lasques.

Father Keogh was struggling for breath. "This," he told Vito, "is not quite what it seems." He was aware as he said it that there could have been no more inept remark.

Two agentes came running across the plaza. They were Carranza and Beltran. They carried their pistols ready to shoot.

Vito's voice was reproachful and Porfirio's shocked.

"To steal from a poor woman who works so hard—you must know what a struggle she has to live."

"I have lost all my faith in you, Father," said Vito.

The plaza was dancing with squares of light. The thin-pillared bandstand sent a pattern across the ground and an American field gun, a relic of a bygone revolt, stood a rusting sentinel, gaunt in its outline. There had seldom been such an efficiently lit occasion. Heads bobbed in windows and figures appeared upon balconies as if a fiesta were taking place. Neighbors called out from house to house:

"They have caught the priests stealing a chicken!"

"*Now* what can you say for the church?"

"Beltran," Father Keogh told the taller agente, "I can easily explain all this."

Father Lasques appeared unable to speak. The chicken still set up a screech from its sack. Carranza took possession of it. Doña Florencia arrived out of breath. A blanket was covering her night clothes and her unbraided hair tossed about in the wind.

"It is mine, I can prove it. It is my best laying hen. If you call it by name it will answer. Papina! Papina!" she shouted at the sack. "She is white with just a small little piece of red brown on her back. That fool of a man I have let them get out. Jesús María José! The priests!"

"Doña Florencia," Father Keogh began, "if we could have a word with you in private—"

"No words in private," Vito warned. "This is something the Jefe should hear about. There are five of us here to witness what we found."

Father Lasques found his voice. "Can you deny that you've been luring a cat to these premises with the sole purpose of fostering superstition?"

"Certainly, Padre. The cat comes to us of its own accord. Myself, I should never encourage it, but Maria believes it is one that Anacleto used to look after at times, so now and again she gives food to it. But it's still strange, I think, Father, to mistake a cat for a chicken when the whole town knows you go short of food."

Doña Florencia attempted to help. Great blue circles sat round her eyes and the flesh was unfirm round her chin. She held the blanket close up to her throat. "If the padres are hungry it's possible that I could find a slightly older bird, but I should like to have Papina back. There was never a hen to lay like this."

Carranza turned eagerly to ask her, "Then the Señora will not wish to make a charge?"

"No indeed, I would not think of such a thing when it's priests that have stolen the bird."

Edmundo had followed her out. White cotton trousers were sucked back from his thin legs by the breeze. He was bare from the waist up but had put on his hat. He had intended to put on his serape as well. But he had passed his leg through the hole in the blanket instead of his head. Too stupefied to disentangle himself, he was obliged to gather it up as best he could. It dragged after him, tripping him up.

"I charge them, I charge them!" he shouted. "I am the master, my wife is no good. When I think what they

158

charged me for marrying her, most certainly I am accusing the priests."

Laughter ran round the small crowd that had gathered.

Doña Florencia rounded on him. "Silence, old fool, you've a head full of pulque and you're not nice to be seen in the streets. If the bird is set free there'll be nothing more said."

Carranza was about to open the sack when Edmundo lurched towards him. "No! I say no! Take that bird to the Chief of Police!"

"That is right," Vito said. "It is evidence. The Jefe has always been searching for that."

Father Keogh said, "Carranza, will the Jefe have left the office yet?"

"No, Father, he is working there well after midnight."

"Then take us to see him at once, please."

"And we will come with you," Vito said. "The Jefe will need a few witnesses."

Many people had ventured out by then and the crowd which followed the priests was considerable. Arrieta was left behind taxiing sideways, waving his arms about, shouting abuse.

"There is the church for you! There is the church!" He was fat and above the tight band of his trousers his stomach protruded. It glowed faintly in the light of the torches. "What a fine bird she was! What a fine bird! After this she will never lay again. Such a shock to the system is bound to be great. Twenty eggs we could get from that bird in one week. I tell you, that's eighty a month. In a year we shall lose nine hundred and sixty and she would have lived for another ten. That is nine thousand and six hundred eggs they have stolen from us."

The crowd took up his grievances under its breath.

"When you think how they are over *our* little sins."

"Six Hail Mary's, the Long One once gave me just for slapping my wife's mother's face."

It seemed to the Jefe that half the town had walked into his room. He was feeding the hummingbird. It hung in the air above a spoonful of honey, fluttering minute wings. A bottle of mezcal stood on the table upon which papers were stacked in neat piles. The Jefe was at work on the Victorino case. For a minute a hope flickered over his face when he saw the bandits come in with the agentes. Then he saw that it was the priests who were being escorted.

Edmundo made a way to the Jefe by clearing a path for himself with his fists. He stood shouting and thumped his bare chest. "It is me, Arrieta, who is making this charge, a good citizen dragged from his bed. They have stolen nine thousand six hundred eggs."

The Jefe sat down and picked up a cigar. When he lit it his eyes traveled over Edmundo above the flame. They came to rest on the white cotton trousers and there a few seconds his gaze remained. The trousers, worn thin from many washes, were covered with faded brown spots.

"Ten years did I say she would live? More likely it's twenty. That is nineteen thousand and two hundred eggs they have stolen from a poor man like me who must work with his hands."

Doña Florencia spoke from behind him. "The only part of him that does work is his throat. Jefe, the poor priests were hungry and they thought of this bird. But she does not belong to this fool that I married, she is mine and it isn't my wish that they pay for their sins."

Carranza spoke quietly; his tone was embarrassed.

"The bird was not pleased and the noise was great. We were running towards it before we were called."

Beltran plunged a hand in the sack. He brought the bird up by its legs. The flap of its wings blew the papers about on the Jefe's well-ordered table.

Doña Florencia joined in its squawks. "Not that way up, turkey brain—she will die from the blood in her head." She snatched the bird and placed it beneath her blanket, where it peeped from the crook of her arm.

The Jefe addressed the roomful. His voice and his face were expressionless. "Who can witness that this theft took place?"

Several eyes turned towards Vito.

He stepped forward with Porfirio, Pablo, and the Jeep. Vito removed his black felt hat and held it respectfully against his chest. His voice carried an unctious courtesy and he made little short bows as he spoke.

"We caught the priests in the act, Jefe. You won't find *us* holding back information. We know that a good citizen must always co-operate with the police."

"Yes, indeed," said the Jeep. "One must help to keep law and order."

"Personally," Porfirio said, "I shall hold nothing back, and it's not for the reward I get, either. It's only right to support the police."

"A fine body," Pablo agreed.

"There *is* a reward, isn't there, Jefe? For those who are willing to come forward and truthfully tell what they've seen of a crime."

The Jefe snapped, "Yes, there is."

Vito turned round towards the rest of the room. "Now, let others come forward to help the Jefe. Who else saw the priests steal the chicken?"

The response was reluctant at first. Then a number of hands were held up. The Jefe chose the nearest to him. It belonged to Alfonso Herrera the tailor.

"Well, Roncho, how much of this were you able to see?"

Alfonso's weight shifted uneasily onto another foot. "It was dark outside, Jefe, but when the door opened a little I saw these two padres go down on the ground. Then together it seemed that they made a little pounce. It was then that the bird was displeased and the noise broke out."

A voice at the back took the story up.

"And then when the full light came on them there they were with this bird in the sack."

The Jefe turned round to Father Keogh. "Do you agree that this is what these people could have seen?"

"They've described it with commendable accuracy but they have misjudged our motives."

The Jefe said, "Very well. Beltran, pay the informers five pesos each. Then get them all out of the room with the exception of the accused and the drunkard who is making this charge."

Arrieta had slid down the wall and was soundly asleep with his head on one side.

Thirteen people collected the sum, including Vito, Porfirio, Pablo, and the Jeep. Vito tossed up the coins in the palm of his hand. His teeth made a white curving moon in his face as the thin lips rolled back in a grin.

"Surely for those who catch the thief and keep a hold of him for the police the sum should be more than the ordinary informers get?"

The Jefe was writing. He did not look up. "If there is a conviction the sum is ten pesos each."

"That is most generous." Vito beamed. "I shall buy

162

my old mother a handsome new fan. One is usually too poor to go making such gifts."

"And I," said the Jeep, "some little trifle for my aunt in Oaxaca. That old girl thinks the world of me."

"I shall buy candles," Porfirio said, "and light them for my soul on the altar."

"I shall give mine to a beggar," said Pablo. "The best things in life come from doing good deeds."

When the room cleared the Jefe ordered, "Get Arrieta on his feet and bring him here."

The agentes lifted Edmundo up.

He was drowsy and muttering, "A million eggs! I have been robbed of a million eggs."

The Jefe snapped questions at him. "How long did it take you to get on the scene?"

"Why, I was there in a few little moments. As soon as I heard that poor bird call for help. I ran straight out from my bed."

"Why do you sleep in your daytime trousers?"

Edmundo opened his mouth and then closed it again. When he spoke he chose words with a drunkard's precision. "I am not a rich man. I have only one sleeping suit. I like to save that for my feast day. These are an old pair of trousers that I use up for the nights."

"Very well," the Jefe said. And he told the agentes, "Lock him up in a cell. Charge him with being drunk and disturbing the peace and bring me his trousers."

The agentes jerked Edmundo out.

"Burro," he screamed, "you'll be sorry for this. I will tell the whole world how you stood by the priests."

The Jefe held up a sheet of paper. The ink was still wet on the page. "Your charge has been entered against the padres. They will come up before the Juez de Primera

163

Instancia at noon tomorrow. As you will be required to state your case against them I should advise you to sleep yourself sober."

Father Lasques dabbed a handkerchief over his forehead. Father Keogh sat wearily down on a chair. The Jefe blotted the charge and filed it.

He said, "I have come to believe in the power of prayer. More practical methods having failed, I tried out a prayer myself today." The Jefe folded his hands together. "Please God, I pray, that the next crime committed in this town will be visible to at least half the population and that they will find it in their hearts to report it to me in the name of the Father, the Son, and the Holy Ghost, Amen."

Father Keogh achieved a shamefaced smile. "You can imagine how we feel, Jefe. We were after that nagual, of course. We wanted to catch it and prove that it wasn't a supernatural cat."

Father Lasques went up to the desk. His tall figure seemed bent with anxiety.

"How will you get out of it, Jefe? You told him you would send us before the Juez."

"I shall not get out of it," the Jefe said. "You'll go before the Juez."

Father Keogh's dark eyebrows shot up. "But, Jefe, you know perfectly well that we're innocent."

"The perfection of my opinion is extraneous to the case. I am a policeman, Father, not a judge."

"But—but—supposing the Juez won't accept our story," Father Lasques said. "Think how it will look to the town."

Father Keogh asked, "Surely you could accept our word?"

The Jefe relit his cigar. His voice was dry and brusque.

"If I accept that, I might just as well announce to this town that its police are corrupt. I have spent my entire period of office in Quantana trying to persuade these people by alternate encouragement and threats, that it is their duty to come forward and give an honest account of any crime they may have witnessed. If on the first occasion that they prove willing to do so I discount the word of thirteen people in favor of an explanation from two who are known to be my friends—I might just as well go out of business."

"That's carrying a sense of justice too far," Father Lasques objected.

"What your motive may have been is for the Juez to decide."

"But you *know* we weren't stealing her chicken," Father Lasques appealed. "You know we should never do such a thing."

"That you must prove to the Juez. Have you any means of doing it?"

"Yes," said Father Keogh. "Catch!" And he threw the fish head across to the Jefe. "We should hardly have set out to trap a chicken with that."

The Jefe examined it with distaste. "Good. I hope it is useful to you. I will state that you showed it to me at the time you were charged. We might find that will influence the Juez."

There was an edge to Father Keogh's voice. "It is pleasant to know that at least we have your good wishes, Jefe."

"As a man with a sense of duty yourself, Father, you should appreciate mine. I cannot let friendship prejudice it."

"It's a pity this town isn't quite so public-spirited when it comes to denouncing Vito and his accomplices," Father Lasques said.

"There I agree with you, Father." The Jefe leaned forward, his head on one side. "And I feel I must tell you that if I am obliged to pay out forty pesos to the joint proprietors of Porfirio's bar I shall never be able to find it in my heart to forgive either of you."

The corporal brought in Edmundo's trousers. The Jefe spread them out. "I am interested in these. A man doesn't usually sleep in his daytime trousers. If he wanted to get extra use out of them he would wear them for work. That is, unless by any chance he feels that the night is the only safe time to wear them." The Jefe examined the stains. "They might, of course, be coffee or chocolate. On the other hand they might be blood."

"You're thinking of Victorino," Father Lasques said.

The Jefe tested the material, tugging it crossways between his hands. "They're only worn out round the stains. The other parts haven't been subjected to the same amount of scrubbing."

Father Keogh felt one of the trouser legs. "They're certainly not worn to the same extent all round."

"But he had an alibi, hadn't he?" Father Lasques asked.

"Of course," said the Jefe. "Of course. These marks are splash marks. If he had been the one to waylay Victorino he would have been in the right position to have been sprinkled with blood. He would have been smeared with it in a different manner if he had handled the body or been actually concerned in the killing himself. He could have got these marks if Victorino fell towards him. He

166

would never have run out in these trousers tonight if he hadn't been so full of pulque."

"But what could his motive have been in killing a friend—bribery, I suppose?" Father Keogh put his right hand in his pocket to take the weight off the arm.

"He may have been employed to distract Victorino's attention away from the killers. He may not even have known what he was doing it for. He wouldn't ask any questions if a few extra glasses of pulque were at stake." He folded the garment and laid it on the desk. "We will send off these marks to be analyzed. Well, gentlemen, I wish you luck with the Juez tomorrow."

Father Keogh made a polite little bow from the head.

"That's really most good of you, Jefe. I hope you've a comfortable cell for us."

"May we go in together?" Father Lasques asked. "I've heard you go mad in solitary confinement."

"Don Pedro is more likely to fine men of your calling."

"Unfortunately," Father Keogh said, "we are not in a position to pay up."

The Jefe picked up his fountain pen. "I'll detain you no longer," he said.

Chapter 17 〜〜〜〜〜〜〜〜〜〜〜〜

CHELA WAS WAITING UP FOR THE PRIESTS. SHE HAD ALREADY heard the news. "There you are! What did I tell you? Such a little time you have known that Candalaria and already you pick up her ways. Where is the chicken?"

"We've given it back, of course."

"Santa María Purísima! Given it back! Am I to suffer all this shame and there is no chicken to make up for it in the end?"

Father Lasques demanded wearily, "Surely you of all people can believe in our innocence, Chela?"

She started to speak but the words were tailed off in a terrified whine. "Now see what has followed you back to the house! They say that this is the nagual that contains Anacleto's spirit. We shall all wake up dead in our beds."

A small white cat crouched in the doorway. It mewed up at Father Keogh and came timidly into the room. "What an extraordinary thing for it to follow us all this way," Father Lasques said.

Father Keogh remembered the fish head. He put his hand in his pocket and brought it out. "It probably got the smell of this during the rough and tumble and decided to keep an eye on it." He threw the fish head towards the hungry cat, which carried it into a corner.

"The evidence!" Father Lasques wailed.

"Oh, good Lord, I forgot," said Father Keogh. "Never

mind, the Jefe has seen it and the cat's need is greater than ours."

"What does it matter what the Jefe has seen?" Chela snapped. "The whole town will think I am starving you, stealing a chicken like that."

Father Keogh bent down to examine the cat with interest.

"It looks to me as if the spirit of Anacleto is about to become a mother in the near future. I don't expect they had bargained for that."

"Would it help to break down the superstition?" Father Lasques asked.

"It might," Father Keogh said. "It's not a very supernatural thing to do."

"It might make things worse," Father Lasques pointed out. "They'll probably be just as frightened of a nagual's offspring; in which case all we shall have done is to have added to the numbers."

"It depends whether the nagual's power is inheritable," Father Keogh smiled.

Chela leaned cautiously over the animal. "It is the sorceress who usually sends out the nagual at night. It is possible to choose any small creature you like, and it is told to look for somebody special and carry him illness and harm. It is most probably true that it is Anacleto. To turn into some little creature like this is quite easy. All the biza must be willing to do is jump four different times in the air and curse first himself, then his mother and father—which is not a nice thing. Then he must wear the skin of the animal he wishes to become."

"But it's still wearing its own skin," Father Keogh pointed out.

Chela was lost in the ritual. "The sunlight is bad for the nagual but the moon is good and a dog will always bark at them twice as loud as at anything else."

"Well, there wasn't a peep out of any dog," Father Keogh said. "And we passed quite enough on the way."

"That is a good sign," Chela told him. "So perhaps it is not a nagual but just Anacleto walking about. A white cat is what he might choose for he could turn into these in his lifetime." She caught Father Keogh's eye and made instant amends. "Although, of course, that is only something bad Catholics believe."

Father Keogh turned smiling to Father Lasques. "It's something to hear her admitting that. Well, look, Chela, I want this poor little thing taken care of, not only for its own sake but for ours. I'm still banking on the fact that they'll be persuaded that such a very masculine spirit as Anacleto would never have chosen a female form." Glancing again at Father Lasques, Father Keogh suddenly frowned. He asked anxiously, "Aren't you well?"

Father Lasques had his hands to his head. His sallow face looked pinched and his eyes seemed unable to focus. "It's nothing at all, Father, really. I think I'm a little tired."

Chela stepped backwards, her mouth open. She pointed at the cat in the corner crunching its way through the fish head. Her voice was no more than a whisper. "The nagual! It's brought illness upon him already. That is the chief thing they bring."

"That is nonsense for children," Father Lasques snapped. "I've an attack of migraine coming on, that's all. I hope I'll be all right for the Juez tomorrow."

"Never mind the Juez," said Father Keogh. "It's probably worrying about him that brought it on in the first place—that, and tonight's little do." He took the younger priest's arm to help him upstairs. Father Lasques stumbled, his vision impaired. "Never mind," Father Keogh comforted. "A good night's rest will put you right, and if necessary I'll get permission to appear for us both tomorrow."

Chela, soft-footed, padded behind them. "Father, I am a good Catholic, I live in your house—but quite nice people believe in such things, such as the second cousin of my sister's husband whose money is good every week. It's not wise to put the Long Father into his own bed. Let him go to the house of a friend. In that way the nagual might not find him again."

"Chela, I want you to run up to the doctor first thing in the morning. Ask him to give you some pills for migraine. I know there used to be something my sister took which helped her a little at any rate."

"It would be better to go for the curandera, Father, because she would tell us the reason the spell has been set, then maybe we could ask her to take the mischief away."

"Go to the doctor," Father Keogh repeated.

Chela left the house at eight in the morning. She was not back with the prescription until well after nine. Father Keogh reproached her severely. "You know perfectly well Father Lasques wanted something to make his head better in time for the court today."

She sulked, saying that the doctor had kept her waiting. But he knew that she had stopped to tell the tale of the nagual to everyone she met on the way and possibly called upon friends for that purpose. He took the prescription to be made up, himself. The sun laid a hard white glare across the town. His appearance caused a stir in Quantana. The suspicions of Chela proved correct. Everyone had heard of the nagual who had paid the priests' house a visit the night before. Dark eyes followed his quick, long strides and whispers broke out when he passed.

"He is going to Anastacio Carillo who makes up the medicines the doctor writes out."

"Myself, I am not one to believe in these writings. When a little something was stuck in my stomach once, he gave me a medicine which made me vomit. When I told him I would not pay for such a terrible thing he said the medicine was meant to do this! I ask you, to make someone vomit!"

"He is going very fast to fetch these medicines. The Long Father must be bad."

Anastacio Carillo was broad-shouldered and fat. In his tiny dark shop which the blinds kept cool he sold refrescos as well as patent medicines. Drinks made from fruit juices, seeds, and flowers stood round his shelves in glass jars. Clay containers were upturned beside them to serve the drinks cool in lieu of ice. Vito was inside the shop when Father Keogh entered. He said quickly on sight of the priest, "Another Coca-Cola, Anastacio, please."

The little chemist seemed bewildered and opened his mouth several times. "*Another* Coca-Cola, Señor Castillo? But you have not had—"

Vito's voice was emphatic. "Another one, fool. I can buy two, can't I? Or do you think that my money's not good?"

Father Keogh wondered why Vito should come to the chemist to buy Coca-Cola when Porfirio's bar was stocked with it, but he was more anxious about Anastacio himself. He knew that the chemist took drugs. The little man seemed half-witted. He padded round the front of the counter. His feet were encased in solid sandals cut out of motorcar tires. The leather thong cramped his toes and his instep shone with perspiration. His face had a porcelain gleam from it. His hand shook when he reached for the bottle and two clay containers fell down and broke.

Vito raised his drink to the priest. "Success to you, Padre, in court today." Father Keogh inclined his head. "I'm afraid that things will not go well for you; the facts are a little black. But I shall be pleased to pay your fines for you, out of my reward."

"That's very good of you, Vito. A kindly action never comes amiss." He handed the slip of paper to Anastacio Carillo. "Could you make this up for me as quickly as possible, please? I would be grateful if you could do it while I wait." Anastacio seemed unable to hold the paper. The prescription crackled in his hand as he tried to keep it steady enough to read. His lashes fluttered against his glasses. His lips moved forming the words.

"What sort of a chemist are you?" Vito inquired. "Can you or can't you make it up for the padre?"

"Is it a difficult one, Anastacio?" Father Keogh asked.

"No—it is—well, there are two things here. The pills are not something I have in my shop, but I could send to the nearest big place. Milpahuaca might have them in, but that will take days. The other is only a tonic."

"Then could you make that up? It might be better than nothing."

Anastacio met Vito's eyes. He seemed hypnotized by them. Vito leaned over the counter. "Answer him, turkey wit."

Anastacio stuttered, "Well, it's just if I—it's just if I have the right stuff."

"There's a fine chemist," Vito sneered. "It would be quicker to send it away. In Xicanatlan I have a friend who does this work. I could write to him if you like."

"I don't expect that will be necessary," Father Keogh said.

Vito again caught Anastacio's eyes. "Well, can you make it up?"

Anastacio took off his glasses. He wiped them free of sweat. "It will not take many moments." He went into his dispensary and they heard the clink of glass. Vito pushed his sombrero onto the back of his neck. "Ola! Father, once again good luck." He laughed as he walked out of the shop.

When Anastacio came back with the bottle of medicine Father Keogh said, "You were very afraid of Vito. Had he been making threats?"

Anastacio's eyes bulged. "No, no, of course not. Most certainly not."

"Was he trying to get you to pay illegal taxes?"

"No, Father, he just came to buy from the shop."

"You're lying, Anastacio. That's not the way to get help. If you told me what Vito had done to you I could inform the police."

Anastacio's tongue wet his lips. His voice held a note of hysteria. "I'm a good Catholic, I never tell lies."

Father Lasques insisted upon accompanying Father Keogh to court. He took a dose of the tonic and tried not to wince at the pain he experienced in moving his head. It even seemed hurtful to talk. "Do you think the Juez will be influenced at all by our cloth?"

"Don Pedro," Father Keogh answered him, "is a notorious sitter-on-the-fence."

The courtroom was tightly filled. Necks craned and feet shuffled in order to gain a better view of the priests.

"Santa Madre de Dios! The Long One looks close to his death."

174

"They say that the nagual found him first at the time he was stealing the chicken."

Cigar smoke rose, fouling the air. Women carried babies slung in rebozos. Children pattered barefoot across the floor. Men lounged in the doorways, their hats tipped to the back of their necks.

The case took twenty minutes. Don Pedro's questions were clear and precise. Edmundo was sober and solemn-voiced. He no longer talked of a million eggs. It was a pathetic story that he told of the chicken which laid to augment his income. The witnesses spoke in alphabetical order and of them all Vito, Porfirio, Pablo, and the Jeep were the most impressive. They made no exaggerations. They made no accusations. They stated simply and quietly what they had seen. The only touch of fantasy was provided by the defense.

A thin black frown sat across Don Pedro's forehead when the priests told their tale in turn.

"You are asking me to accept in your favor that you were engaged in trapping the spirit of a dead man with a fish head?"

"Well, put like that—" Father Keogh began.

Don Pedro interrupted him. "That is how you put it to me. You intended to catch the spirit of Anacleto Comachi Alvarez in a sack?"

"Well, we—" Father Lasques began.

"Answer me 'yes' or 'no' please."

Father Lasques was obliged to say, "Yes."

"As representatives of the priesthood do you believe in such superstitious rubbish?"

"No," Father Keogh said.

"Then do you expect me to believe it?"

"No, but—"

"Answer 'yes' or 'no' please."

"No."

"You are, I believe, short of food."

"Yes."

"You tell me that having caught this spirit, you intended to give it the freedom of your home in order to prove that it didn't exist?"

Father Keogh's temper was roused by the cold sarcasm in the magistrate's voice. "Don Pedro, you are presenting only half the picture."

"It is not my picture," Don Pedro snapped. "Kindly supply the other half."

"We believe," Father Keogh told him, "that certain people are using the supposed return of Anacleto's spirit in order to gain mastery over this town."

"Who are these people?"

"We would rather not say until we have proof."

"When you have I suggest that you charge them. In the meantime I consider you guilty of endeavoring to remove edible property which did not belong to you." Father Keogh saw the Jefe's shoulders droop. "It is reprehensible in view of your cloth that you should have seen fit to set such an example. However, in view of your circumstances and a petition for clemency on your behalf which has been made by Señor Vito Castillo Rivera and signed by the witnesses who felt obliged to give evidence against you, I will impose a fine of no more than five pesos apiece. I understand that Señor Castillo Rivera has undertaken to pay both these sums out of the award he is to receive from the police." Vito stepped forward and paid the fines. Don Pedro snapped, "Next case."

The oficial called, "Señor Fernandez Arrieta."

Edmundo stepped forward and stood shamefaced. Don Pedro fined him ten pesos for disturbing the peace.

Few people waited to hear Edmundo's case. They were too anxious to carry the news of the priests' conviction to the rest of the town. Quantana rumbled with indignation.

"If you ask me they have stolen that fish head as well."

"You have never heard such a foolish defense. Everyone knows that to catch a nagual one must pin its shadow with a needle or something else sharp and then wait until it howls to be free. The absurdity, taking a sack!"

"Yes, but you have to say that it was a nice thing for Vito Castillo to do to come forward and pay those fines like that."

"It shows that the boy has some good in him still."

On the way home Father Lasques was obliged to stop and vomit. He was suffering from stomach pains. He arrived at the house yellow-faced. Chela was waiting for them. Her eyes were round with fright. "I came back by the short cut to make you a little something warm to drink after the disgrace and I found this was pushed under the door." She presented them with a sheet of paper covered with muddy dots.

"What is it?" Father Lasques asked.

Father Keogh took the paper. "Oh, it's one of these handwriting dodges again. It looks as though they have printed out some kind of message with mud on the end of a stick." He helped Father Lasques onto the couch, put a blanket across him and felt his head. "You've got a touch of fever. I'd better get the doctor to have a look at you although it sounds to me like a thoroughly nervous upset all round."

Father Lasques was deciphering the mud dots. He read out, " 'You suffer from the espanto.' That means fright, doesn't it?"

Chela came forward with a cup of hot coffee. "It is a black-magic disease," she explained.

"But Father Lasques hasn't been frightened," Father Keogh pointed out.

"It comes when you look upon something horrible such as the face of Anacleto when you opened up his grave. It will be his ghost who is causing these things."

Father Keogh turned to Chela. "What are the symptoms of this dread disease?"

Chela looked grave. "For myself, as you know, I do not believe in these things. It is the Indios who think up these fancies. But they say that the espanto takes away the will to eat, makes one so tired that the desire to work is gone, and destroys the nerves so that in the end the afflicted one dries up and dies."

Father Lasques laughed. The sound struck Father Keogh as poignant. It was not often the young priest laughed. "What is the remedy, Chela?" he asked.

"The ghost must be begged not to haunt you. Sometimes it is done by taking flowers to the grave."

"Oh well, we'll pop up with a posy in the morning," Father Keogh said. Then he told Chela, "Go up to Doctor Juarez and if he's not in, leave a message. Say that I shall be glad if he will take a look at Father Lasques—and, Chela! Save the symptoms for the doctor or his Señora, please. The rest of the town will know about them soon enough."

Father Lasques sat up. "That Juez deliberately twisted everything we said until he left us no choice between sounding lunatics or frauds."

178

"He picked out what he wanted and used it, that's all."

"But why? Surely he doesn't want to be dominated by Vito for the rest of his life. He must know that today's verdict encouraged him."

"If he looked too closely into our case he might have found something to disturb his peace and quiet. He was determined not to look. He simply took the surface view."

Sam pushed the door open. "Did you two guys go crazy, Mac? I have a swell boss in Papa Martinez. He has enough stuff going to waste in the kitchen at the de la Costa to feed an army. Why didn't you tell me your bellies were touching?"

"Sam," Father Keogh informed him, "we were innocent."

Sam grinned. "Yeah, so was Cleopatra."

When he had gone Father Lasques said sadly, "If he doesn't believe us who will?"

"No one," Father Keogh assured him, "except perhaps the Jefe and the Juez!"

"We should never have allowed Vito to pay our fine. It'll raise him in the estimation of the town."

"We had no option, Don Pedro accepted it." Father Keogh opened an empty cigarette case and snapped it fast. "I made one of the most inexcusable mistakes in my life when I underestimated Vito. I should have remembered that he was trained by Anacleto."

Chela called, "The Señora Dyke Brown has come to see the Padre Keogh."

Father Keogh and Father Lasques looked at one another. "I hope it's to tell you she's come to her senses."

"My goodness, I hope so," Father Keogh said. He helped Father Lasques upstairs and looked back from the

179

door to say, "I let you in for this chicken fiasco. It was all my idea in the first place."

"It was my fault for missing the cat."

"By the way, where is it?"

"In the kitchen I believe. Chela said you had asked her to find a box for it."

"Yes, I must see that it's properly fed."

He could not bring himself to hurry down the steep flight of stairs. When he stopped to pick up the remains of a two-inch-long flying cockroach he knew that he was deliberately delaying the interview. He stood crackling the insect between his fingers. He was about to take it downstairs with him and throw it into the patio but he realized the uselessness of such a gesture. The house was littered with dried-up carcasses which crackled underfoot. It was pointless to wage a sudden war against dead cockroaches. And it was pointless to put off the interview any longer.

The small whitewashed room trapped the smell of the kerosene lamps and held it all day long. Locha had chosen her dress to match her eyes. Her hair sat so smoothly round her head that it looked like a close-fitting cap. She wore no make-up and no jewelry. She looked as pale and as fragile as one of the sweet-scented nardos that grew in the riverside fields. She was carrying a chicken newly plucked and trussed. "Mother sent you this. Why didn't you *tell* us you were short of food? I can't *bear* to think of you going hungry and I could *kill* Father for not letting you off. He ought to support his own class."

There were so many things which should have been contradicted in her hurried flow of words that he was at a loss to know which to center upon: the innocence of himself and Father Lasques, the fact that a Juez should certainly not reserve justice for those of his own class, or upon the fact that it was highly unlikely that Don Pedro would consider a Keogh the equal of a de Cortinez. Instead he accepted the chicken. It would supply Father Lasques with a light and yet nourishing diet and the skin would provide titbits for the cat. "It's very kind of Doña Marian, Locha," he said. "I wonder if I shall ever be able to convince Chela that this isn't the one we pinched?"

"She tells me the other priest's got espanto. The whole of the town is full of it." She offered Father Keogh a cigarette and put one in a holder for herself.

When he gave her a light she looked up at him over the flame. The cigarette trembled a little and her voice was unsteady when she blew out the smoke. "I wish I was that silly old Chela of yours. Then I'd be able to see you every day."

Father Keogh laughed. "I think you'd find she'd be delighted to change with you now. It's lowered her prestige considerably to keep house for a couple of poultry thieves."

"Father, you're not looking too good."

"Well, I've had a rather trying morning," he admitted.

She twisted the diamond that shone next to her wedding ring. She avoided his eyes when she warned him, "I'm afraid I'm going to make it worse." He sat opposite, inhaling deeply. "It's—it's Dyke. He saw you, didn't he?"

"Yes, he paid a call."

"Did he tell you what he was going to do?" When Father Keogh nodded she burst out, "I'm scared—I'm scared he might go through with it."

"I'm not entirely unwindy myself."

"Would they be very angry with you if he took you to court?"

181

"Who's 'they'?"

"Well, Bishops and things."

"I couldn't expect a congratulatory postcard from the Bishop and the 'things' might be pardoned if they were not overdelighted."

"Oh, why can't you all leave me in peace? Nag! Nag! Nag! Nag! Nag! I'm not the only person who can't make a go of their marriage. Dozens and dozens of people get divorced but they don't get badgered from pillar to post by husbands and mothers and priests. They're just left to do what they like with their lives."

"What are you planning to do with yours?"

She turned her head away, speaking so softly that he was forced to lean forward to hear. "What I always wanted to do with it, Father, just live somewhere quietly, not—not too terribly far away from you, and make no nuisance of myself to anyone."

"That doesn't sound very exciting. Don't you think it might pall in time?"

"Please don't make fun of me."

"You rather invite it, Locha. Don't you think it's time you pulled yourself together? I want you to do it before you realize what a fool you're making of yourself. That can be quite painful enough but it hurts twice as much when you find out that everyone else has made the same discovery a long time before you."

"Thank you, but I don't care about other people's opinions."

"Does mine interest you at all?" When she was silent he told her, "I'm losing my respect for you, Locha."

"But, Father, I can't *help* loving you!"

"Nonsense!"

"I can't—I've tried, I really have. I'm not asking you to do anything about it—I'm not asking anyone to do anything."

"But you are. You're asking Dyke to suffer."

"I couldn't go back to him now. I *hate* him for saying he'd do that to you. I avoid him at home. I'm never going to speak to him again."

Father Keogh kept steady eyes upon her. "Perhaps you should know that even if I were not a priest and you were not married to somebody else it would still make no difference to me."

"Am I all that unattractive?"

"I should prefer somebody older and a little more sensible."

She was silent a moment and then she said, "That's cruel. You need never have hurt me like that."

"I intended to help you. I want you to realize how stupid it is to risk ruining your happiness by hankering after someone you could never have had in any case." He looked away while she battled with tears. He found the sharp little struggle pathetic to watch.

"My feelings would be just the same, Father."

"Very well, if you can't think of yourself and you won't think of Dyke, think of me. You're making my life very difficult." He took immediate advantage of her dismay. "Gossip and scandal are rife in this town. It's quite bad enough to be labeled a thief, I can't afford to be known as a libertine as well."

"But you're not to blame. How could you be?"

"Chivalry prevents me from making that point public."

"You mean people are actually *talking* about it?"

"People are reveling in it!"

183

Her eyes opened. "Then—then even by coming here today I may have embarrassed you?"

"Acutely."

She would have run out of the room but she collided with Candalaria. The girl made a curtsy to Locha. "Señora!" Then she said, "Father, I have come to tell you that I shall have to miss our time together today. I was at the courthouse to hear your case this morning and the Señor Dentist cannot allow me to be away so much all at once."

Locha turned round from the doorway. "You must accept my apologies, Father. I quite see that it's only possible for you to receive persons of *exemplary* character."

Chapter 18 ~~~~~~~~~~~~~~~~~~~~~~~~

THEY HEARD HER RUNNING ACROSS THE PATIO. "WHAT IS the joke?" Candalaria asked. "I know there is one for your eyes are smiling. Ah, I can guess what it is. You are laughing because of the chicken. You think that I'll remember it when you're telling me it is wrong to steal!"

"Candalaria, you must try to believe that we were not stealing."

"Yes, Father." She lowered her eyes dutifully. "I have just seen that nice old Chela in the market. She told me that there are times when she had no more than a handful of beans to cook for the three of you. I cried and cried and cried."

Father Keogh was gratified that he had induced in her a more Christian spirit towards Chela. He was beginning to despair of making any progress with her. She met Chela on her way out of the room. The old woman patted her cheek. "We shall see you tomorrow then, Chata?"

Candalaria bobbed. "Yes, Mother Chela, good dreams to your sleep."

Chela sent a smile towards Father Keogh which showed up three gold teeth. "The doctor will come when he can, and that dear little Chata is not such a terrible child."

Father Keogh picked up his breviary. "You two seem to have come round to one another."

"Yes, well, we met in the market—and when she saw what a little I had to spend, she wept such nice tears for our plight." Chela unwound her rebozo. Out of it she took vegetables, spiced meats, a pumpkin, four bottles of Coca-Cola, and a pair of braces. "The Long Father will need these for the feeding him up."

"Not the braces, I hope."

"Those are for you, Father. Your old ones are not to be trusted any more. It is not a nice thing for the trousers of a priest to come down in the streets."

"But, Chela, how did you manage to afford all these things?"

Her smile broke out again. "It is presents from people, Father, now they know we are so short of food."

"If you tell me who they are I'll go round and thank them."

Chela shook her head. "That would not be wise. It might do them some harm with el Lobo. I have already made your thanks." She carried her treasures off to the kitchen, singing as he had not heard her sing for months.

185

The Jefe sent for Father Keogh. When he arrived he was asked, "Why is it that the worst heathen is always the first to shout for a priest?"

"Perhaps because he's the most in need of one, Jefe. Is it you who require my services?"

The Jefe came near to a smile. "No, I'm sorry to disappoint you, Father, but it's Arrieta who wants to confess."

"Edmundo! Has he been taken ill?"

"No, he's been charged. Those stains on his trousers were blood. He'll come before the Juez in three days' time."

The corporal brought Arrieta in. He went down on his knees when he saw Father Keogh. "The priest! The priest! Thank God, the priest! He will tell you I have not been lying. He will know that I'm telling the truth."

The corporal jerked him onto his feet and propelled him across to the desk. Father Keogh, watching the man, found in him an illustration of the answer he had made to the Jefe. Edmundo the faithless could only place his confidence in a representative of the faith.

"Edmundo Arrieta," the Jefe ordered, "tell the padre the story you have just told to me."

Edmundo was eager. "Well, Father, it happened like this: Victorino was a friend of mine, I loved him—yes truly I did. But, Father, I am sinful and the pulque is something I cannot resist. Well, on the night that this dreadful thing happened I went down to the witch as is always my way. I go to her every night. For a few centavos she makes me a small little mixture to take the pulque away from my breath. In this way it is sometimes possible to deceive the poor nose of my wife. The witch said to me, 'If you go to the grotto at half past ten, twenty pesos will fall in your lap.' Well, Father, I went to the grotto at just the time she said. Then I saw this friend of mine, Victorino. He had come from seeing the gringo Cooper in Salvadore's shadow show. I raised my arm and I called, 'Oye! Victorino!' He turned and he fell forward at me as if he was trying to bring me down. I was wet from his blood all down my trousers. His poor head came as close as all that."

"Who struck him?" the Jefe asked.

Edmundo still addressed the priest. "Three persons, Father, came out from the grotto. But it was dark and they had their faces covered right up to their eyes in scarves. They had rocks in their hands and they killed him—oh, you wouldn't have done it to pigs—his head fell between my feet. Then one of these rough ones came over to me and I thought he would go for me too, but he said, 'It is you who have killed this man.' I wasn't as drunk as all that. I said, 'Evil One! *You* have killed Victorino.' He said to me, 'You'll have a hard job to prove that unless you can tell them the palé has done it.' And he threw me the pesos straight into my lap. I was so scared by this horrible thing I had seen, that I drank until the pulque had taken my tongue and my eyes and my ears away."

"Do you know that it is a serious offense to withhold information from the police, Arrieta?"

"Yes, Jefe, but I thought you'd be sure to think that I had killed him." The man hung his head, his cheeks sagging.

"Take him to a cell," the Jefe ordered the corporal.

"I'll be with you in a minute to hear your confession, Edmundo," Father Keogh promised.

The Jefe said, "If he had made such a story up he would have used his native words, nagual or biza. He would never have chosen palé."

"It means the same thing, doesn't it?"

"Yes, it is a supernatural animal, but it varies from

187

district to district. It is in the Milpahuaca country that they talk of a palé."

"I see. So you think that these people could have been strangers from Milpahuaca?"

"Yes, employed by Castillo for the job. They could have ridden down off the Huapan road without anybody seeing them. They would have been warned that Victorino would pass the grotto at a certain time. Edmundo, as I thought, was used as a decoy, and possibly as a well-known drunk. If it had not been for his use of the word palé I might not have believed his story. Castillo must have contacted them by letter or message. Neither he nor the others have left the town themselves."

"It's something to know where the men come from," Father Keogh said. "That narrows it down a bit."

"It narrows it down to this extent: Castillo presumably knew where to find roughnecks and my colleague in Milpahuaca will know where to find them. But to identify them is another matter. It was dark, they were masked, and Edmundo was pickled in pulque. What chance is there even if I do take him round that he'll be able to recognize anyone? Men wearing scarves round their faces look much the same. There is a chance in a million that he might tell the voice—but to do that I must get the whole of Milpahuaca and the surrounding districts to say the word palé."

"It sounds pretty hopeless put like that."

"It is hopeless," the Jefe sighed. "We can only pray that having got away with it once, they will be unwise enough to try it again. Then we shall be waiting for them. That's the only way to work in Quantana. One can never get people the first time. But I think it might be advisable if you and I paid a call on the witch."

"Yes, I was wondering about that rather uncanny forecast of hers."

"She may be directly in their pay or they could be using her as a clearinghouse for information. One thing is certain, Father, no one does more business through Anacleto's spirit than the bruja. She must be making a fortune from keeping the evil eye away. She has probably sold half a ton of tronadora alone."

"Oh yes," Father Keogh smiled, "the herb which you rub on your forehead. I've come across that one before."

They waited to call on her until after dark. They did not wish Vito to know of the visit. The Jefe put on civilian clothes and Father Keogh wound a scarf round his Roman collar. The little adobe hut crouched as if cowering at the end of the river road. The walls showed mud scars in the light of the Jefe's torch. He said, "By the way, Father, we've come for a spell."

Father Keogh asked suspiciously, "Might I ask which one of us is in need of the witch's aid?"

"You are the one to need her, Father. You desire that the love of the Señora Dyke Brown shall be transferred to her own husband again."

Father Keogh came to a halt. "My dear Jefe, you know perfectly well that in my position I couldn't be involved in a thing like that. I won't have any part of it."

"You haven't any part of it. *I* am asking the aid of the bruja on the part of a friend unable to plead for himself."

"But she'd know perfectly well that you'd be the last person to believe in such nonsense."

"Every phony believes in themselves to a certain extent."

189

"But it'll get round the whole town," Father Keogh protested, "that a priest has gone to the bruja for a love spell."

"It'll do your reputation nothing but good. The whole town will hear that the padre is willing to try anything to rid himself of so embarrassing an affection."

"Chivalry might be already dead but it would turn in its grave at that."

"And Victorino would turn in his grave, Father, if he thought that a man of God was not willing to make a small sacrifice to bring his murderers to justice and possibly save others from his fate."

Father Keogh could feel his temper rising. "I should be willing to make a sacrifice but not in open mockery of my faith. I have been at considerable pains to convince these people that a visit to a witch is bound to prove unprofitable."

"I don't think the spell is very likely to work if that's what is worrying you, Father. We're fairly safe in predicting a failure. You'll be able to prove your words."

Father Keogh laughed in spite of himself. "I'm not at all certain that you're not the biggest rogue in the whole of Quantana."

The Jefe's reply was reproachful. "If you knew how considerate to your position I have been in this matter, you would be sorry for that remark. The most sensible spell to have asked would have been the withdrawal of the nagual from Father Lasques. But in view of the fact that Juarez is an excellent doctor and will probably make him well I thought it better not to give the witch an opportunity of claiming a cure."

"I'm sorry, Jefe, I can't do what you ask."

"I'm not asking you to say anything in front of the

witch but what you've just been saying. Repeat every word if you like."

Father Keogh breathed deeply, compressing his lips. "Very well, be it on your own head."

The Jefe pushed open the door. There was only one room in the hut and there were only two sources of light in it, the fading glow of cooling embers on the hearth and the end of the witch's cigar. The Jefe stepped into the room. "Mother, I am your attentive and dutiful son who kisses your hand. I bring with me one who cannot believe in your powers."

There was silence. Then the bruja replied, "Enter, my sons."

Father Keogh stepped in behind the Jefe. The stale air seemed to cling like a shroud about them. It smelt sour with decaying flesh and sweat. There was a rustle as somebody passed them. They saw the cracked outline of the wrinkled old face dark against the faint light of the fire. But before the witch straightened up with a burning candle she said, "Be seated, Padre, be seated, Jefe."

Father Keogh was startled. The witch had identified him before setting eyes on him and he had spoken not a word. He lowered himself onto a dirt-laden reed mat and wished heartily that he had sprinkled some of Chela's disinfectant over himself. He would certainly not leave without his complement of fleas. The room danced a soft jig in the candlelight. Dried bats and mice hung down from the walls; their shadows made ghoulish patterns. Dried hummingbirds were strung across the ceiling and the skin of an alligator took up the most prominent position by the side of a picture of the President. On the metete, a three-legged stone with its mano for the grinding of corn, there perched the least prepossessing stuffed owl Father Keogh had ever encountered. A squirrel skin hung down beside it. Four blackened pots were emitting a sickly sweet scent from the hearth and on the wide shelf that ran across one side of the room there were bundles of herbs two and three feet deep. On an upturned box at the side of the witch there were separate heaps of red and black beans and an outsize topaz. The witch herself was sunk into the corner as if she were part of the mud wall behind her. Only her eyes seemed alive. The hair plastered down on each side of her head smelt of a rancid goose grease. The brown of her chin and the brown of the blanket were indistinguishable in the dimness, as were the brittle-boned hands in her lap. But the lines of her face were visible. They made an intricate tracery blackened by years of filth. Father Keogh could imagine her spreading but never curing a disease.

The Jefe sat cross-legged. "Mother, the one I bring to you is cursed with a lady's love."

"I'm 'cursed' with nothing of the sort," Father Keogh said. The witch's eyes seemed to creep towards him. He could not picture them moving fast.

"The love is not of the choosing of the one I bring to you, Mother, and he would like the heart of the lady to return to her husband."

"I should perhaps make it clear—" Father Keogh began.

"I'm about to make it clear," the Jefe snapped. He resumed his solicitous tone. "Because of his cloth, Mother, the padre cannot believe in such things."

"*Does* not believe in them," Father Keogh corrected.

The Jefe ignored him. "So that I as his cuate must plead with you for him."

Mother Montezera kept her eyes on the priest. "It is not easy for those ones who do not believe."

The Jefe's hand went to his pocket. A faint rattle of pesos was heard in the room. The witch's eyes slowly left the priest and came to rest on the pocket. "I believe, Mother," the Jefe said. "Not as a policeman when I sit at my desk but as your dutiful son who kisses your hand."

"I am a good curandera," the witch admitted. "I am a white witch. I do not make black spells."

The Jefe leaned forward earnestly. "Mother, tell the padre if these things are true. Is it true that you cast a spell to bring Coyotito the little Maria of the Seven Eyes for his bride?"

The witch acknowledged the achievement with a nod of the head. The cigar flashed a tiny red signal into the room as she drew the smoke into her lungs.

"Is it true that out of your great goodness you cast a spell to bring new hairs to the head of the Señor Presidente Municipal?"

"It is true," she said.

"Is it right that you sent a word to the padres that someone would die if we opened the Bad One's grave?"

"It is right," said the witch.

"And is it correct that you warned the Long Father Lasques that soon he will dry up and die of espanto?"

"He will dry up and die," said the witch.

"And you told Arrieta to go up a hill and twenty pesos would fall in his lap?"

"All this is so," said the witch.

The Jefe emptied a handful of coins at her feet. "Mother, if it's in your heart, do what you can for this cuate of mine."

Mother Montezera nodded her head. Then she beckoned to Father Keogh. "The Long Father will die when he leaves this town."

"But a short time ago you said he'd die in it!"

"Of it," the witch corrected him. "He will die when he leaves this town." She seemed puzzled herself. Her eyes creased, staring at something that neither man could see. She had fallen asleep when they left her.

The Jefe said, "Don't let it worry you, Father. Even I could make that kind of prophecy. He could die at a hundred and two in Mexico City but it would still be after he left this town!"

"I'm not worried," Father Keogh laughed. "And I only hope you got something out of it. Personally I could have done without two million fleabites. How did she know who I was? She couldn't have seen me in that light."

"She smelled you," the Jefe replied.

"She *smelled* me! In all that filth?"

"They can always smell a foreigner." The Jefe scratched at a shoulder vigorously. "Yes, yes, it was worth it to me. She is not paid directly by them but they work through her just the same. They use her as a loud-speaker for the voice of Comachi's spirit."

"She took credit for everything," Father Keogh said.

"She will claim the Presidente's wig first thing in the morning. She hadn't thought of that before. But she proved her innocence to me when she admitted foretelling the peso business. She wouldn't have done that if she had known that the killing was connected with it. Don't you see how it's easy to work through her? They send someone down for a love charm or something and he lets her know what he wants passed on. Somebody told her that twenty pesos would fall in Arrieta's lap so she passes it on from herself. They are safe enough with her. She's the last one to admit that her sorcery has come from a human source."

194

"So she does know that she's a phony, then."

"She knows she cheats a little but she believes in herself well enough or if she doesn't she soon will. Her witchcraft proves right so often. The doctor does her cures for her and Castillo works her curses out!"

Chapter 19 ~~~~~~~~~~~~~~~~~~~~

THE DOCTOR EXAMINED FATHER LASQUES. FATHER KEOGH was waiting to hear his report. "He's had stomach trouble before," the doctor said. "Apparently there was some question of a suspected gastric ulcer a year or two back."

"I didn't know that."

"Well, they found no trace of it at the hospital and he was treated for nervous dyspepsia. I don't imagine conditions have helped him here. He's undernourished and he's been overdoing it. He's the kind who takes life twice as hard as anyone else. He's very run down. See that he keeps on with the tonic and I'll give him some powders to take after meals. He tells me the vomiting only seems to occur after food and the pains at about the same time. He says his appetite's affected and he's depressed."

"Yes, that does seem to be the case."

"He wouldn't take this espanto nonsense seriously, would he?"

"Good heavens no." Father Keogh laughed.

"Remember Doña Florencia and the cat! The power

of suggestion is formidable. That's how these spells work when they work at all." They walked to the doctor's car together. "There's just one other thing," the doctor said. "I'd rather you didn't mention it to him or to anyone else for that matter, but in a place like Quantana one has to consider all possibilities. Can you trust Chela?"

"Most certainly. She's a funny old thing but she's very devoted."

"Does anyone else have a hand in the preparation of your food?"

"No, no one but Chela."

"Nobody comes to the house?"

"We are not very popular socially. Sam Frankenson calls and the little Fernandez girl comes every day."

"Candalaria! Isn't she Castillo's piece?"

"One of them, I'm afraid. But she spends her time either with Father Lasques or myself. Why, surely you weren't thinking of—"

"It crossed my mind. As I say, these things do that in a place like this. The symptoms are not unlike those which can occur in chronic arsenical poisoning."

"But—but he'd die, wouldn't he?"

"He would if it was a case of acute arsenical poisoning. But his symptoms are not acute. A minute dose deposited in food can be tasteless and if it's administered at intervals it can produce much the same effects as you've seen in the padre. It's very difficult sometimes to distinguish from disease. However, if you say you're sure of Chela—"

"As sure as I am of myself, and anyway I eat the same food."

"Oh, well, then, we can dismiss the thought, but I'm afraid we can't entirely dismiss the possibility of a gastric ulcer, especially as there have already been suspicions in that direction. But we'll see how he goes. How's the arm?"

"Much better, thank you, although I still feel it a bit at times."

"You had a lucky escape there. Let's see your tongue."

Father Keogh put it out at him.

"All right. Pulse."

Father Keogh held up his wrist.

"You're a fine pair, aren't you? Haven't they got anyone whole to send?"

"We were both more or less in one piece when we came here," Father Keogh smiled.

"Oh, sure, this town could break anyone up. I should know, I was born in it." He waved as he climbed into his car.

Father Keogh watched its jolting progress up the cobbled street. Then he went in search of the nagual.

Chela was still gloating over her treasures. She had piled them on the kitchen table and sat fingering them.

"Chela, where's the cat?"

"Tonight we will have the leaves of the nopal cooked with chili. Tomorrow we will have mole de pepita, which is a nice thing, Father, for the gravy is made out of pumpkin seeds. And on Thursday—"

"Chela, where is the cat?"

"And on Thursday we will have mole de guajolote, for I hear there's a turkey to come. The cat is gone, Father."

"Gone?"

"It was while you went up for this morning's disgrace."

"Did you drive it out of the house?"

197

"Father, most certainly not!" She turned a bland and an innocent face towards him.

Father Keogh had learned that in the matter of lie detecting it was important to strike the right word. "Then did you *roll, push* or *carry* it out of the house?"

Chela survived the first two accusations but her expression gave her away on the third.

Father Keogh said angrily, "Chela, why will you believe these ridiculous things? It was even more important than ever to keep that nagual in the house. Now when Father Lasques gets better they will think it's because it's gone whereas if it were here all the time, when he gets well they would realize that it couldn't have had anything to do with his illness."

"*When* he gets better," Chela said.

Father Keogh became a prey to an unpleasant suspicion. He took a quick step towards the old blackened clay pots that boiled on the hearth. He took off all the lids.

Chela padded up to him anxiously. "Father, there is nothing in there that should not be. I tell you it's presents from people."

Father Keogh turned round severely. "I want the truth from you, if you please, Chela. Have you cooked that cat?"

He fancied for a moment that she looked relieved as if she were expecting a worse accusation. Her superstitious horror at the thought of consuming a nagual was genuine enough to convince him of her innocence.

"I gave it to el Choco, the organito, Father. That one's too silly to know any fear. He took it right out of the town, and up to the Huapan road. If you will not hide the Long Father from the nagual then the nagual must be taken away from him and confused."

Chela's gloomy prophecies and her lack of tact were a source of continual irritation to Father Keogh. When the young priest found it impossible to face either mole de guajolote or plain boiled chicken she shook her head in his presence and said, "Unless we call in the curandera, the Long Father will not last."

Even her more outrageous remedies and methods of diagnosis failed to amuse him in time. He was deeply concerned for Father Lasques.

"An egg should be rolled all over the body, but this must be done in the shell. Then when every small part of the body is cleansed, the egg should be broken into a plate and the pattern it makes will show where the pain is lying."

"He *knows* where the pain is," Father Keogh snapped. "He doesn't need an egg on his stomach as well."

The pains and the vomiting continued. The digestive powders were effective inasmuch as they lengthened the period of relief after a meal. But it was difficult to induce Father Lasques to eat at all. He had no appetite for what was put in front of him and was subject to fits of exhaustion and depression. He never complained of it but it showed in his eyes and in the corners of his mouth. It could be seen in his every movement.

Quantana was aware of every symptom. Chela supplied the details in spite of Father Keogh's repeated instructions not to gossip. Father Lasques was finding it increasingly difficult to digest anything solid. His thinness alarmed Father Keogh. He sat by the younger priest, trying to encourage him to finish a bowl of watery soup.

"There's nothing in sopa aguada to harm a newborn babe. Did you take that bismuth stuff after your lunch?"

199

Father Lasques nodded. He finished the soup and an hour and a half afterwards was subject to an attack of abdominal pains and nausea which left his forehead wet. He was hard put to it to find sufficient energy to accomplish his daily tasks. Father Keogh took over every possible duty from him but the young priest was stubborn and loath to give in.

He leaned back on the old horsehair sofa. Father Keogh was shocked by the angular line of his jaw.

"It's a curious thing, isn't it, that my symptoms should be following the exact course of the illness of the evil eye?"

"Espanto? No, it's not curious at all. Chela supplied the town with the description of the illness before you got the mud letter. They fitted the spell to the symptoms, that's all."

Father Lasques quoted Chela: "Takes away the will to eat, makes one so tired that the desire to work is gone— the desire is still there, Father, but I am worn out after an hour on my feet."

Father Keogh answered cheerfully, "So would I be if I lived on sopa aguada." But his eyes could not hide his concern.

In the quiet of private houses shuttered against the night, round the three-stoned Indian hearths, in the pulqueria, by the fountain and in the market place Father Lasques' disease was discussed.

"When the Ingles-Irlandes was saying Mass at the church the Long One was going from door to door to try to get more people to hear it and I tell you from the way he was walking I thought he would fall."

"It is certainly espanto he is suffering from. There is no doubt he will dry up and die."

The Jefe sent a message to ask Father Keogh to call.

"How is Father Lasques?" he wanted to know. "Still vomiting after eating and drinking?"

"Yes."

"What does the doctor think is the matter with him?"

"I rather think he suspects a gastric ulcer."

"Has he considered poison at all?"

"Yes, he did wonder about that but we discarded the theory because Chela buys and prepares all the food herself. She's absolutely above suspicion and anyway I eat it too."

"You drink from the same cup of coffee? Of chocolate? You eat from a communal plate?"

"No, of course not, but I tell you there's no question of Chela being suspect."

"No one is above suspicion in Quantana. He never touches anything outside?"

"No, but we have been getting presents lately."

"Of food?"

"Yes."

"Who from?"

"I don't know. They're anonymous gifts."

"Eat nothing that comes from an unknown source and do all your shopping yourself. When you were dying Chela called in the curandera. Has she done this for Father Lasques?"

"No, but only because I've stopped her."

"They may be working on her through the witch. When is he due his next meal?"

"Tonight."

"See that he takes nothing till I arrive and do not tell Chela I'm coming."

He reached the house at half past seven. He brought the doctor with him.

Chela carried in two bowls of soup. She was flustered at the sight of the Jefe. "I did not know there were people calling. I have only sufficient for two."

The Jefe asked, "Which is which?"

"Well, the little blue bowl is the Padre Keogh's. The Long Father's isn't so rich."

The Jefe put both bowls on the table. Neither priest cared to speak. Father Keogh was watching Chela's face. She kept startled eyes on the Jefe and her voice seemed to stop in her throat.

"If it's something the Señor Doctor does not approve of I could make the Long Father something else."

She put quick hands out to take back the soup. The Jefe removed the bowl.

"What did you make it with, Chela?" Doctor Juarez inquired.

She stepped backwards, her eyes going from one to the other. "There is nothing in there that should not be, just small little remnants and leftover things. Nothing's been brought from outside."

Father Keogh, watching her, turned his head away. There was a damaging fear in her eyes.

The Jefe carried the bowl to her. "Would you drink this yourself?"

The whole room was silent until she echoed him, "Drink it myself?" She wheeled suddenly round and sank down beside Father Keogh. Her bony hands pulled at his sleeve. The hair had turned grey at her parting. The tears, rolling fast, lodged before they dropped in her deeply creased cheeks. He could feel their soft warmth through the cloth on his knees. He felt not unnear tears himself.

He looked down at her sadly. "Chela, Chela!"

"Padre, I'm not a bad woman. You tell them you know that."

The Jefe came after her holding the bowl. "Get up and drink this soup."

Father Keogh said, "No, Chela, if there's something in this soup which there ought not to be tell us what it is but don't drink it yourself."

She turned her wet, pleading face to the Jefe. "Bones, I say, bones—just a few poor old bones." Her voice quickened eagerly, stressing her point. "From the chicken the Señora Dyke Brown brought." She pulled at Father Keogh's sleeve again, demanding confirmation. "There was this chicken, wasn't there? There was a bird that the Señora brought?"

The Jefe asked her steadily, "If you won't drink this soup yourself, is it because there is poison in it?" She seemed slow to grasp the implication at first but when she had done so Father Keogh thought he observed on her face the same look of relief which he had noticed when she had found herself able to deny having cooked the nagual, as if she had been dreading a worse accusation. She stood slowly up, held out her hands for the bowl and drank the soup. Her gulps sounded loud in the room. She returned the bowl to the Jefe, drew the back of her hand across her lips, wiped it on her skirt and shouted at him, "Meddling old burro! Coming here frightening an old woman to death. What sort of a Jefe is that? They could find work for you at Porfirio's bar. Vito Castillo has need of such men. And now what's to be done for the padre's supper when you've made me drink up all his soup?"

Father Keogh's relief could be heard in his voice. "You see, Jefe."

"Yes," said the Jefe, "I see. But that woman has been

203

up to something. That much is certainly clear. Well, Mother Chela, let us look in your kitchen."

She snapped at him, "Mother to you indeed! I would have said 'No' to your father, be sure of that, if I thought he would make me a mother to you."

She was anxious again as she led the way. Her eyes were uncertain and sly. Father Keogh and the doctor accompanied the Jefe. The kitchen was dark and stained with smoke but it was very well stocked with food. The Jefe fingered pumpkins, ran rice through his fingers, sniffed cheeses, and looked into the old blackened clay pots.

"Where did this come from? And this? And these?"

To each question Chela answered, "A small little gift, Jefe, a present, Jefe, from someone who cares for the padres."

The Jefe was examining a pestle and mortar in which Chela had been pounding chilis. He turned to her. "What are these people's names?"

"They have no names, Jefe, they're sent without names."

The Jefe put out a hand and took down a basket. Into it he swept everything edible within sight.

"Thief!" Chela screamed at him. "Thief!"

The Jefe put the handle of the basket over his arm and led the way out of the kitchen. In the small whitewashed room he lit up a cigar. "Well, it was not the soup."

"I should have been very surprised if Chela had been guilty," Father Lasques told him.

"I should have been brokenhearted," Father Keogh admitted.

"I am still more inclined to suspect a gastric ulcer," said Doctor Juarez. "We'd better get an X-ray. But that means Milpahuaca." He turned to Father Lasques. "In the

204

meantime I want you to leave off the medicine and all solid foods. I'm going to try you out on a milk diet for forty-eight hours. Is it possible for you to fetch it yourself and administer it yourself?" he asked Father Keogh.

"Certainly. I'll take the jug up to Alejo myself and never take my eyes off it."

Chapter 20 ~~~~~~~~~~~~~~~~

FATHER LASQUES SPENT THE FORTY-EIGHT HOURS IN BED. During the first ten he suffered intermittently but within fourteen hours he had visibly improved. The milk seemed to cause him no discomfort. Father Keogh collected it and heated it in a special container which he kept hidden in his room.

The improvement convinced the Jefe of poisoning and the doctor that his suspicions of a gastric ulcer were correct. It was the doctor who supplied the first steps towards a more solid diet. He brought in a piece of white fish which his wife had steamed herself.

"All you need do is to heat it, give him a dose of the bismuth powders and let me know how he is within one hour of consuming the meal."

Within two hours of eating the fish Father Lasques was subject to violent internal spasms again and an exhausting bout of nausea.

The Jefe asked, "How much do you pay Juarez?"

Father Keogh said, "Nothing. He treats the church free."

"Then he would have no motive for poisoning the patient."

It was the first time that Father Keogh had laughed for many days. "Jefe, you really are insufferable. I believe you could even suspect Juarez."

The Jefe lifted heavy eyes. "I merely remain unsuspicious of myself because I happen to be a personal witness to the fact that I am not corrupt. I should take no one else's word for it in Quantana. Continue to cook the padre's meals yourself and refuse to touch anything anyone brings to the house."

Chela resented Father Keogh's intrusion upon her kitchen. "If you are to cook for the Long Father think what nice little pieces of poison I shall have left over to put into *your* soup!"

He smiled at her. "Sorry, Chela, doctor's orders."

"Doctor's orders!" Chela sniffed. "If you ask me it's the stuff that he puts in the medicine that is poisoning the Long Father's stomach. It was the same with my sister's husband once." She broke off under Father Keogh's thoughtful stare. "I did not mean that he did it on purpose, Father, this Señor Doctor is not a bad man, he is just someone who cannot make medicines. It is the curandera who does most of his work for him."

"Chela," said Father Keogh, "see that the padre is not disturbed while I am out." Into a wickerwork basket he put the remains of the tonic, and the digestive powders. He covered them with a napkin and hurried towards the Jefe's office. In his mind he was memorizing the details of the day he had taken the first prescription to Anastacio, the chemist. He recalled the sharp shadow of Vito as he entered the shop, the tongue-tied nervousness of the per-spiring chemist, his reluctance to make up the prescription, and the biting persuasion of Vito. He remembered that at the time he had thought it unlikely that Vito had gone in to buy Coca-Cola. He had suspected some kind of black-mail.

The Jefe fingered the bottle of tonic and the six diges-tive powders. He made a scathing reproach on himself. "I, who tell you that I suspect everyone in Quantana, trusted a chemist to be a chemist."

Father Keogh said, "I should have thought of it first but it struck me that Vito might just be extracting his taxes and I knew Anastacio drugged. I dismissed the whole thing from my mind, but how do you account for the fact that we were warned that he was suffering from espanto before Anastacio had time to make up the prescriptions?"

"That's easily accounted for. Your Chela could have chattered to a dozen people in Castillo's pay. We know he uses the witch as a mouthpiece, so he gets the news to her and she cashes in with the espanto. All Castillo had to do after that to keep the Comachi myth alive was to see that the threat of espanto was carried out. He knows that there's no one but Anastacio Carillo to make up the medicines. So he gets to work on him. Carillo made the tonic up at once and the padre had a dose of it before he came in front of the Juez."

"Yes, and was ill about an hour or so afterwards on the way home."

"That's it. They got the witch to make a forecast and then they proved her right. How's that for Comachi's spirit?"

The Jefe sent for the doctor. "Now, this is how I see it. When he took neither food nor medicine he was better.

When he took food again he took the powders and he was worse. Your wife prepared the fish herself so that one supposes that the fish was all right."

"One would be correct in that supposition," the doctor said.

"Then we're left with the powders and the tonic. The pills came from Milpahuaca?"

"Yes."

"It can't be the powders," Father Keogh said. "They helped him. We noticed that they kept the pains off."

"Arsenic," the doctor told him, "is absorbed into the system. The symptoms in small dosages take time to materialize. The powders you thought were keeping the pains at bay might well have been the poison having a delayed effect. You've cause to suspect Carillo?"

"We've no cause not to," the Jefe snapped. "He has the knowledge and he has the materials. He'd be able to judge the dose. If Carillo ground white arsenic into these powders or dissolved it in the tonic such a minute quantity would have to be used that a taste would be most unlikely."

"Most unlikely," the doctor said.

The Jefe questioned him again. "You say that there was already a history of stomach trouble?"

"Yes, but no evidence was found of an ulcer. However, the fact that it was suspected at all, and in view of the present symptoms, serious consideration should be given to it. It's impossible to be certain without a chemical analysis of these medicines." He turned to Father Keogh. "The padre must be sent to Milpahuaca for an X-ray. I'll give him a note to Guillermo Sanchez. How soon can you get him off?"

"As soon as we can get the Bishop's permission. If he answers at once Father Lasques could catch the Sunday bus. That would get him into Huapan on Monday morning and give him time to rest a bit with Father Lopez until his train goes."

"In that case he can take the stuff in to the Forensic Laboratory himself," said the Jefe. "You can't always trust the posts around here and I can't spare a man." He gave Father Keogh a letter addressed to the Departamento de Medicina Legal de la Procuradaria de Justicia Milpahuaca. "Tell him to hand this in with the powders and the tonic and for God's sake don't tell that Chela of yours."

The bus was due to leave at eight A.M. on Sunday morning. Father Lasques went up to the church at half past six to say Mass at seven o'clock. No more than a handful of people were present to mark the beginning of Holy Week. Only five of the townsfolk witnessed the blessing of palms in the church.

When Father Lasques returned he sought out Chela. The interview seemed to leave her in great distress. Father Keogh supposed the farewell had upset her. It was as much to reassure himself as to comfort Chela that he told her, "Father Lasques is not going away for good. He'll only be gone about a fortnight and then, providing they don't keep him in hospital, he'll be back."

Father Lasques seemed distrait himself. He sat with his suitcase across his knees, determined not to let it out of his sight. It contained the tonic and the digestive powders and the Jefe's letter for the Forensic Laboratory. He clutched his black hat and his breviary and Father Keogh noticed that he only held one glove.

"Where's the other? I'll fetch it for you."

Father Lasques said hastily, "No! I mean thank you, but I'll get it myself."

He went to put down the suitcase but Father Keogh stopped him.

"You sit still. You've got a journey ahead of you." He called to Chela and when she came he asked, "Could you find the padre's other glove—it's the right, isn't it? He's probably left it upstairs."

He was taken aback by what happened. She covered her face with her hands. Father Lasques seemed to choose his words carefully.

"It doesn't matter, Chela, if you've already thrown it away by mistake."

"Thrown it away!" Father Keogh said.

Father Lasques answered, his eyes upon Chela, "It got itself mixed with some rubbish."

Chela went out of the room.

Father Keogh was puzzled. "What rubbish?" he asked.

"Just rubbish," Father Lasques replied. His voice put an end to the conversation.

Roberto appeared at the door. "We cannot leave until this evening, Padres. We shall make the journey overnight. Something has gone wrong with the engine. I have had her pulled into the garage. Domingo-of-the-Hired-Car is putting her right and Mateo will work on it too but they will be at it the whole of the day. We will let you know when we are ready to go."

"Well, it'll give you more time to rest," Father Keogh told Father Lasques. "I think you'd better get straight up to bed."

"I should prefer to stay here," the young priest said.

Father Keogh had not realized until he was about to be deprived of it how appreciative he was of the younger priest's company. Although they had nothing in common and neither of them had succeeded in influencing the other, it was pleasant to be able to discuss difficulties and share hopes.

Father Lasques' wrists and his ankles were pathetically thin. His neck and his jaw line were equally thin. Father Keogh was conscious that the soft, melancholy eyes were very fine and that the long face had a strength in it, in spite of its pallor, which would always remain in his mind. It would be no fault of Father Lasques if he did not return to the town which had done its best to destroy him. His voice was worried when he said, "There's one thing I'm frightened of, Father. When I go, their enmity will be directed against you alone. I have been no help to you. I realize that, but at least I have felt that while I have been here it has diluted the danger so to speak and there have been two of us to hit at instead of one."

"That's not the only help you've been to me or to the whole of Quantana," Father Keogh said.

"I'm afraid I have done very little personal good in this town. They dislike me for myself as well as what I stand for."

Father Keogh said, "It's always been a slow fight in Quantana, but your work will bear fruit, you'll see." He leaned forward, anxious to impress on the boy that his efforts had not been in vain. "It may not be yet—but it will come later. All those pamphlets you wrote, all the visits you've made, the prayers you've said and your personal courage—all those are going to inspire many people some-day just as they've already inspired and benefited me."

The ill-at-ease smile of Father Lasques spread to his eyes. The smile did not show personal gratification. It was not one of pride or even of pleasure, it was one of relief.

On the way to the bus stop Father Keogh was troubled

by the weakness still apparent in the young Spaniard's step. He made slow progress up the cobblestone streets. His height seemed to add to his frailty. The town was comparatively deserted but as they left the river road behind them shutters were opened and heads appeared. A curious noise broke out. It was hard to identify at first. It ran up the street like a sighing wind. It burst out in the plaza and doubled back again down the Avenida de Cortinez. It started softly, apprehensively almost, then it gathered a full-throated strength as if encouraged by sister sounds. It was cheering.

Father Lasques stopped to listen. "You see, they are glad that I am going away."

Father Keogh silenced him. "Just a minute."

A second sound went with the first. Hundreds of pairs of hands were clapping, from windows and balconies, doorways and patios, and from dark hidden corners in narrow back streets. It fell over the town like raindrops pattering upon a tin roof.

"Yes, they are glad," said Father Keogh. "But not for the reason you think. This is their way of wishing you luck. They are telling you that they're happy for you because you are escaping the nagual. And that should tell you something else. Your work has already had good effect. They are daring to raise a common voice. In wishing you well they're defying Castillo."

There were six people waiting for the bus. Alfonso Hererra the tailor, Alfredo Gonzales the mozo from the Casa Grande, Domingo's mechanic Mateo Garcia, Doña Florencia, Salvadore of the cinema, and old Saturnino the grocer. Domingo was still examining the engine.

"What was wrong with it?" Father Keogh said.

Domingo closed the hood. "That's a question you

might ask the saints for me, Father. Somebody took it to pieces."

"Oh," said Father Keogh, "you mean it was done deliberately?"

Domingo nodded. "I went to the Jefe. I said, 'Someone has been at this bus.' "

Father Keogh's frown was anxious. "What did he say when you told him that?"

"He said that he thought what might have happened was that someone was trying to stop the Long Father from getting away from the town."

"Is everything all right now?"

"Oh yes, but in case something else should go wrong with it the Jefe has made me send Mateo along. It is bad to break down on those roads in the night."

Roberto blew his horn. "No Me Olvides" was ready to start. The six passengers climbed aboard. There was the usual assortment of baggage and livestock. Alfredo the mozo had five hummingbirds fluttering about in a wicker-work cage. They looked like colored beads. Father Lasques was the last to climb aboard. He looked a sad-eyed and overgrown schoolboy, reluctant to go and yet anxious to put an end to farewells. He stood holding his one glove and his breviary. He extended a thin hand to Father Keogh. Father Keogh shook it. He felt a quick little stab of pain at the lack of strength with which his grip was returned. He found it suddenly difficult himself to find a way of saying good-by to "Marcelino the Merry." Roberto blew his horn again.

"Well, send me a postcard of Milpahuaca. You'll never see a more terrible church."

"I've heard that it's not in the best architectural taste," Father Lasques smiled.

213

The bus jerked forward, stalled, restarted and finally swung round the edge of the plaza. Father Keogh stood watching the lights of it climbing steadily out of the town. He heard the gears change on the hill by the church and saw "No Me Olvides" lost in the treacherous Huapan road that curled like a black arm round the side of the mountain.

He took a longer route home, passing the Hotel Martinez. He had no wish to hurry back to the little white-washed room. He realized that it had been an extraordinary solace to return to it certain of meeting with Father Lasques' avid interest in the least important incident connected with the town. It was not only because he had felt himself less alone in the day-to-day struggle for Quantana's salvation but that he had come to feel his love for it equally shared. He was no longer the proud parent trying to impress the outsider with family snapshots. Father Lasques had helped to complete the album. Every soul in Quantana had come to have as great a personal meaning for him as for Father Keogh. They had endured disappointments and spent long consoling hours together making the most of a hope. Father Keogh had always been sensitive to the pressure of personality which a room newly vacated by its usual inhabitant could convey. Once as a young seminarian he had stayed out after hours. He stood in great awe of the kindly old rector, before whom he was instructed to appear the following morning. The appointment was for half past eleven. By half past twelve the rector had not appeared and Father Keogh was informed that he might consider himself free to go with the misdemeanor pardoned. It was never referred to again, but Father Keogh had sat for an hour amongst well-thumbed books which he had seen the rector handle a hundred times, amongst personal papers and pipes and a pair of old carpet slippers half-concealed under a chair. Their joint accusations were more effective than any words the rector might have chosen to speak. It was not until later in life that Father Keogh recognized the wisdom of the silent remonstrations which had made him reproach himself. Father Lasques would have left behind him the challenging memory of a companionship which had not always been sufficiently appreciated.

Father Keogh was not looking forward to the empty whitewashed room. He glanced apprehensively up at the Hotel Martinez. All the lights were ablaze in the suite which Vito occupied. There appeared to be some form of entertainment in progress. But the laughter and the voices seemed unnatural and overloud. A polite clapping broke out from the long room above.

Someone was deliberately shouting, "Bravo, Señor Castillo, that's a very fine speech you have made."

And someone else roared agreement. "Yes, indeed it is, Señor Castillo. A very fine speech indeed."

Then there followed an outbreak of laughter which struck Father Keogh as regimented and false.

The Jeep's stunted figure appeared at the window. "Eh! Vito! It's a long time since I have heard such a good speech."

Father Keogh left the hotel behind him. He thought no more about it than that there was fear amongst Vito's guests. He doubted that they were enjoying themselves. He was glad beyond all proportion to find Sam stretched out on the old horsehair sofa at home.

Sam said, "I thought you might feel lonesome without the boy friend, although he's not the type I'd pay to have around to cheer me up."

"He used to cheer *me* up," Father Keogh answered.

215

Then he exclaimed, "He's forgotten his watch!" It was lying on Father Keogh's typewriter, carefully kept in place by the strap.

Sam turned his head round, grunting. "Chela came in and fixed it there. She said the boy friend told her to."

Father Keogh sent for her. Her eyes were half-closed with tears.

"The husband of my sister had just such a stomach. He was all right when they left it alone, but as soon as they sent him to hospital he never came out again."

"Chela, your sister's husband has been overtaken by more appalling catastrophes than anyone else in the world. To my knowledge he's died six times."

"It is not always the same sister's husband, Father. The Long Father said you would know what to do with his watch."

"What to do with it? Does he mean that he wants it repaired or something? It seems to be going all right."

Sam suggested, "Perhaps he wants it hocked."

Father Keogh unstrapped the watch and locked it away in a drawer. "It's an odd thing to do," he said. "But perhaps he didn't think it was safe to travel with it again. He had it stolen coming up."

The Jefe walked into the room. Sam rolled over to greet him.

"Hi there. Here's the third social outcast. I guess we're the only three in Quantana who didn't get asked to el Lobo's banquet."

"Oh, it's a banquet, is it?" Father Keogh asked. "I heard something going on when I passed." He was still standing by the desk. He could not take his mind off the watch.

"Sure, and it's very select. You wouldn't get Vito asking tramps. Gold-edged invites went out. Papa Martinez was honored. I put it up in the the bar just to show we're in right."

The Jefe sat down. "Who else was asked?"

"Search me," Sam replied. "The Presidente maybe and his little Señora Hotpants. They usually go."

The Jefe said to Father Keogh, "I took Anastacio in for questioning this afternoon and I found he already knew we were suspicious of him and that the other padre is taking the stuff to Milpahuaca for analysis. Maybe that's why they tried to hold back the bus. That woman of yours must have talked."

"She couldn't. She didn't know anything about it."

"Well, somebody's talked."

"Anastacio denied it, of course?"

"Of course. But he is guilty, all right. He won't squeal on Castillo until I have proof and I charge him with it. Then he'll be too scared not to squeal."

"Hell, do you have to wait for proof?" Sam asked.

"Yes," said the Jefe, "I do. I cannot charge a man with my own suspicions. Padre Lasques could still have an ulcer. Those medicines may *not* have been fixed. We must wait for Anastacio to squeal."

"There's too much waiting around here," complained Sam. "Look, Jefe, how's this for a line? You cook up some kind of charge against them and put them in jail for 'questioning.' Keep on forgetting what it was you wanted to ask them—keep them in for as long as you can. Then you let them out and say you're sorry you made a mistake, and you have a red face about it but what the hell, everyone makes a mistake sometime. Then while they're inside Mac here shins into the pulpit and gives the town the

217

works. 'So what?' he says. 'What's Pussyfoot's spirit going to do about it? Not a darned thing. No one's going to get hurt on account of it never was Pussyfoot playing around. It was these guys all the time, see? And when they're out of the way nothing happens!' Well, that's proof that it's *Vito's* spirit?" He made a thumbs-up sign with a half-smoked cigar.

The Jefe said, "Señor Frankenson, I am not Vito Castillo. No matter how much I should like to see these men in prison I cannot 'cook up' a charge."

"Oh, for chrissake!" Sam turned eagerly round upon Father Keogh. "How about all this bell, book and candle stuff, Mac? If this flock of yours takes the bogy stuff all that seriously couldn't you do your mumbo jumbo and get rid of the evil spirit?"

"If you mean exorcism," Father Keogh said, "I could if I were sincerely convinced that there was an evil spirit, but as I'm not I should be simply convincing other people that there was."

Sam slapped his hand against his forehead. "You two are in with Pussyfoot's ghost. The *three* of you give me the creeps!"

Chapter 21 〰〰〰〰〰〰〰〰〰〰〰

THE SIX GUESTS WHO HAD BEEN INVITED TO DINE WITH VITO
sat round a big table, their foreheads wet and their eyes
wary. Few of them had much appetite for the food that was
put before them.

Señor Martinez accepted, with a smile that might have
been fixed to a spring in the sides of his mouth, the com-
pliments of his fellow guests to the staff and chef of his
own hotel. Beside him his hard-mouthed Señora sat. Her
face was as pale as the doeskin gloves that reached her
elbows. She had no need of the great silver fan that she
carried. Señora Martinez was cold with fright. She sat in
strange company according to her own social lights. Certainly there was the Señor Presidente Municipal and Doña
Arcelia but there was also Domingo-of-the-Hired-Car and
Gerardo Hernandez who worked for the grocer. Señor
Castillo was democratic. His invitations were never reserved for the elite of Quantana alone.

The six round the table attempted to eat. They fell
repeatedly into a chilled silence but orders came from
each end of the room.

"Laugh! Clap as if you were applauding a speech that
Señor Castillo is making. He is telling you wonderful
things. He is starting a fund for a hospital. He will con-
tribute quite largely himself. He has asked the Señor
Presidente Municipal to form a committee for just this

219

thing. Clap, if you please, Señores and Señoras. We are in need of a hospital here. The funds ran out last time we tried."

Six pairs of hands were obedient.

"Now laugh again. Talk loudly. Somebody mention his name—again please and again. Loud enough for someone passing in the street to be able to hear. You are supposed to be enjoying the company as well as the hospitality of Señor Castillo."

Vito himself was not present, and Pablo was also absent. The Jeep sat perched on the back of a leather sofa. The light caught the silver down the seams of his trousers. His dwarfed legs looked absurd in the charro boots. He kept a gun trained upon the guests.

Porfirio lounged at the other end of the room, one leg thrown over the arm of a chair. He played with his pistol, balancing it over his knuckles and letting it slip to catch it again and toss it up like a coin in the air. He pointed it, closing one eye down the barrel as if to get the sight between the plump white shoulders of Doña Arcelia. The sweat gathered under the Presidente's wig. It ran into his ears and lodged in his eyebrows. It sent an acrid odor into the room whenever he made a movement. He dabbed at his neck with his napkin.

He said to Porfirio, "Señor, if that gun were to explode by mistake—"

"If it explodes," said Porfirio, "it will not be by mistake."

"Have the goodness, Señor, to direct it at me and not at the back of my wife."

Porfirio made no attempt to change.

The Presidente seemed short of breath. "Señor, we are perfectly able to understand what is required of us tonight.

We are to say that we have enjoyed a most pleasant evening in the *company* of Señor Castillo Rivera."

Domingo, owl-faced, nodded. "Yes, that's what we have to say, that Señor Castillo is here with us now."

"And you are to say that Pablo was also present."

The men nodded, the women were silent. Frightened eyes kept on their plates.

"And what would be likely to happen, Gerardo?" Porfirio inquired of the boy. "If you were to forget some of these details."

Gerardo stammered, his fingers dissecting a chocolate butterfly in the center of his plate. He did not raise his eyes. He appeared to be quoting someone. "The Señor Castillo Rivera would feel sorry for us."

Porfirio clapped with his gun in his hand. "Fine, that is fine. You have learned your piece well. And we have to remember that if Vito feels sorry for someone there must be a lot to be sorry about."

"Yes indeed," giggled the Jeep. "Sometimes I wonder what he has in the place of a heart, that boy."

"He has five extra eyes, six tongues, and at least a dozen ears to make up for the gap in his heart. So if anyone did forget something he would certainly know who that person was."

"There's not much to remember," the Jeep said. "Vito and Pablo could not possibly have been anywhere else in the world tonight because they were here. That is all."

In the morning Vito was asleep when the Jefe and Father Keogh appeared in his bedroom. He sat up and yawned. The Jefe pushed open the shutters. The sun, thought Father Keogh, seemed in love with Vito. It made a glad rush for the boy in the bed. It seemed to fondle his

221

hair and to bring out loving lights in the pale olive skin. The great black eyes were narrowed in its glare.

"I am sorry not to have been up to receive you, but my guests stayed late last night."

"I have already interviewed them," the Jefe said. "You appear to have made an impressive speech. Every one of them referred to it. You have promised to build them a hospital, I hear."

Vito yawned. "Have you come to make contributions to my hospital? Is that why you're making this call?"

"Vito," Father Keogh said gently, "Anastacio is dead."

Vito was silent a moment. Then he leaned back on his pillow. "Anastacio Carillo the chemist? How did he die?"

"He appears to have taken an overdose of sleeping pills."

"Well, that's not surprising."

"You were expecting it?"

"It is only astonishing that he has not killed off half the town. A drug fiend should not be in charge of drugs."

Vito leaned out of bed. He picked up a woman's nightdress which lay on the floor and stowed it carefully under his pillow.

"You feel," asked the Jefe, "that he might have tampered with medical prescriptions?"

"Half the time he couldn't see straight. If I ever wanted a medicine myself or for someone I knew I wrote to a friend in Xicanatlan. That way I was sure I would get the right thing. Did the fool mean it or did he make a mistake?"

"We aren't certain," the Jefe replied. "He may have been worried about something or frightened of someone."

It was Father Keogh who said to Vito, "If you got

your medical supplies from Xicanatlan what were you doing in his shop the day I brought in my prescription?"

Vito frowned as if trying to remember. Then he answered, "I was thirsty. I was buying a coke."

"When you supply it yourself in Porfirio's bar?"

"My dear Jefe, the bar and the chemists are at opposite ends of the town. I was thirsty the chemist's end."

"He struck me as being very frightened," Father Keogh said.

"He was very frightened," Vito agreed. "I tell you, he would not have made up your prescription if it had not been for me, my friend. But I did offer to write to Xicanatlan."

"What was he afraid of?" the Jefe asked.

"The padre."

"The *padre?*"

Vito laughed. "This poor Anastacio was not very bright. He did not need dope to soften his brain. A cat seems to have followed you home, Father, on the night that you stole the chicken. Anastacio and many others like him believed it was Anacleto's spirit and he was scared to have anything to do with you. You saw what he was like for yourself." Vito put a fist in his pillow and eased it under his neck. "But the world isn't short of fools. There are many to fill Anastacio's shoes. Well, gentlemen, is that all?"

"That's all," the Jefe said.

When they left him he curled down as if he intended to sleep again but he shouted for Pablo as soon as they had gone. The big man came shambling in.

Vito snapped at him, "That goose brain of a chemist has killed himself."

"In that case," said Pablo, "he has saved you some

223

trouble. He might have talked. We should have had to fix him in time."

"Yes, but if I had known he was going to do me this favor so soon, we could have saved ourselves another kind of trouble last night, my friend."

Pablo sat heavily down on the bed. He stretched his arms above his head. The hairs on them, wiry and black, looked alive. He showed rotting teeth when he yawned. Big Pablo was afraid of the dentist. He went to the witch when a tooth ached. "You could not let a priest take a parcel of poison to Milpahuaca."

"What good would those bottles have done them? They could never have traced them to me now that Anastacio's dead. I have taken a risk which I need not have taken. Anacleto would never do that."

The death of the chemist put a chill on the town. Father Keogh could feel it even through the strengthening rays of the sun. It was a silent and thoughtful day in Quantana and it was one which was not forgotten. "The-Monday-of-Anastacio's-killing-himself" was spent in discussion. By Tuesday morning the most generally accepted opinion was that far from poisoning the priest, Anastacio had incurred the displeasure of Anacleto's spirit by attempting to cure him. Of the few who had kept up their church attendance not even Chela was left. She received the Sacraments in the house again. Father Keogh was alone in the church for the six o'clock Mass.

Chela was mournful and frightened. "Something is bringing bad luck, Father. First it's the Long Father's stomach, poor thing, and then it's the whole of Anastacio. There must be something to say for these naguals."

Father Keogh sat down, exasperated. He hammered his fists on his knees. "My good Chela, surely you *must* see that there's nothing supernatural in this? We think Father Lasques was poisoned. We believe Anastacio did it and that's why he took his own life. We are sure that Vito Castillo put him up to it, but now that he's dead we can't prove it."

"No, well then, where is the truth in it?"

Chapter 22 〰〰〰〰〰〰〰〰〰〰

"AND THAT," SAID THE JEFE TO FATHER KEOGH, "IS THE answer we'll get from everyone. I can even imagine the Juez saying the same thing in court. It's not hard to believe in Comachi's spirit. It serves Castillo well enough."

They were waiting on the plaza for the return of the bus. They saw the vultures rise from the old white wall and they saw the engine snort as it rounded the corner. "No Me Olvides" was bottle-shaped. The sun catching the windows was carried into the town.

"She's two hours late," the Jefe said. "They must have had trouble somewhere."

Domingo stood apart from them. He had come to meet his mechanic. He avoided the Jefe and Father Keogh but the Jefe chaffed him, calling out, "Well, Father, we're in high company. Domingo was a guest at a banquet."

Father Keogh smiled at the boy. He knew that most people received an invitation at some time or other to dine at Vito's table. It was considered unwise to refuse.

225

The bus drew up to a rattling stop and cast a violent black shadow across the three men. Seven faces turned to look out of the window. Seven pairs of eyes seemed alarmed at the sight of the Chief of Police. No one seemed anxious to make the first move.

"Hello," said the Jefe. "Something is wrong." He walked up to the bus and called up to the driver, "Roberto Ibarra, have you had trouble?"

Roberto answered, "The engine was fine."

Father Keogh joined the Jefe. "Roberto, how did the padre stand up to the journey? Was he very tired when he arrived?"

Roberto climbed down from the driving seat. He might not have heard the priest. He went off with his hands in his pockets. Domingo claimed Mateo's attention. Alfredo the mozo was the first to get out of the bus. Father Keogh put the same question to him.

"I could not say how he was, Father. I was not the one to sit next to him."

And Alfredo pushed his way through the Indian laurels and went up the hill at a run. Father Keogh tried old Saturnino.

"I was asleep all the while," he replied. They had none of them met the priest's eyes.

Alfonso Herrera came next. The Jefe shot out an arm and detained him.

"You! How did the other priest take the journey? How was his health when he reached Huapan?"

Alfonso's eyes leaped up to Father Keogh's and returned to stare at the ground so quickly that hidden weights might have pulled them down. He spoke in no more than a whisper.

"Doña Florencia has something for you."

Then he wriggled himself free of the Jefe's hand. Behind him Salvadore had made his escape. His white shirt and trousers trapped the sun as he hurried across the plaza.

Doña Florencia was slow climbing down. "We should have an airport," she said, "not buses. It's a terrible way to travel. But I suppose here there is nowhere to land." She addressed the remark to no one in particular and handed Father Keogh an envelope as she passed. It bore his own name upon it in the small scratched writing of Father Lopez. Father Keogh stood holding it, his eyes on the Jefe's face.

The Jefe said, "Give it to me."

He opened it up with his thumbnail and read the short note through. He returned it, took a whistle from the flap of his tunic pocket, and when an agente answered it, ordered, "Get hold of Roberto Ibarra, get hold of Mateo Garcia, Alfredo Gonzalez, Salvadore, Roncho Herrera, Saturnino, and Doña Florencia. I want to see them all in my office at once." He turned to Father Keogh. "I want to see you there, too." And he walked off and left him to read the note. It was still several seconds before he could do so. It was not easy to decipher at first in Father Lopez's tiny heaped-up hand.

I could extract no information from any of these people concerning Father Lasques. I can only hope that his decision not to undertake the journey after all is due to an improvement in his health.

> *Yours in Christ,*
> Eucario Lopez Benitez

Father Keogh closed his eyes. Then he went to the Jefe's office. The passengers and Roberto were already inside. The oficial pushed forward a chair for the priest.

"This looks a bad business, Father."

"Yes, Ernesto, I fear it does."

The Jefe addressed Father Keogh. "It strikes me as curious, Padre, that someone traveling on a bus which only goes to Huapan should not reach his destination. I thought these good people could tell us what happened."

Father Keogh could hear his own heart in the silence that followed.

"Well," said the Jefe, "will somebody speak?"

A worried conference of eyes took place. In the end it was Roberto who shuffled forward.

"The padre got off the bus."

Father Keogh stood up. "Got off it? But why? Where did he get off, and when?"

"It was by his own wish," Roberto said.

Doña Florencia supported him. She seemed surprised at being able to do so with any degree of truth. "Yes, certainly by his own wish."

Father Keogh was battling with bewildering possibilities. In the few minutes between reading the note and taking a seat in the Jefe's office he had cause to remember that he was not yet a fit man himself. He felt a limpness all over the body and a curious sense of suffocation right at the back of the heart. He found himself breathing heavily and the sweat which oozed from his palms was cold from shock. He managed to ask in his normal voice, "For what reason, Roberto, did the padre get off the bus?"

They looked at each other and shuffled their feet.

"He gave no reason, Father."

The Jefe bent forward. "Unless a man wishes to relieve himself, in which case he will ask you to wait while he does so, it is not usual for him to get off a bus in the middle of the night and sit himself down on a mountain-side."

Mateo corrected the Jefe. "He did not seat himself, Jefe, he walked."

The Jefe asked the question slowly. "The suitcase he was carrying, did he take it or leave it behind?"

"He took it with him," Alfonso Herrera replied.

"You knew he was ill," Father Keogh said. "Didn't you try to persuade him to come back? Didn't you ask him why he wanted to go off into the night like that?"

There was silence until the Jefe inquired, "Which way did he walk, towards here or towards Huapan?"

"He went into the mountain, in the part by the Bad One's grave."

The Jefe turned to Father Keogh. "Could he have gone out of his head? That would take him into the Arenales country and only a madman would go into that."

"That is where he went," said Roberto. "The Great Green Walk of the Wandering Dead."

"He was in his right mind when he left," said Father Keogh.

The Jefe took time off to light a cigar. Father Keogh sat with his eyes closed. In his head he was trying to form a prayer. But he could think of nothing but Father Lasques' watch. "He said you would know what to do with it." If Father Lasques had known he was going to die, he might then have wished the watch to be sent to his mother.

The Jefe boomed a question. "Were you so afraid of Comachi's spirit that you turned that priest out of the bus?"

Their protests seemed genuine enough. "As if we should do such a thing, Jefe, to someone as sick as all that."

"Why, the poor boy could hardly sit up, Jefe. Doña

229

Florencia was nursing his head from the back in the bad bits."

"It was the bumps that disturbed him so much, but Roberto went slowly for him so as to shake him no more than he must."

The Jefe turned round to the room again. "In that case did anyone hold the bus up? Did anyone demand Father Lasques' suitcase, and when he refused to part with it did anyone force him off?" Every head shook in meticulous unison. "Did you look for him on the way back?"

"Yes, Jefe, that's why we were late. Everyone got out and searched."

"So you did think it a strange thing to happen, then?"

"Yes, Jefe, we thought it was strange."

"Would he have had any food with him?"

"A little," Father Keogh replied.

"He took none of it with him," Mateo said. "He left it behind on the seat."

"All right," said the Jefe, "clear them out."

The oficial emptied the room. The Jefe opened a drawer and took out a bottle of mezcal. He poured a glass for Father Keogh and pushed it across the desk.

Father Keogh asked him, "Do you think they were telling the truth?"

"One would think not," the Jefe answered. "They very rarely are. Now, Father, how sick was this boy? He was in a highly nervous and poor state of health. Is it possible that espanto or a possibility of poisoning might have preyed on his mind? If he did get off that bus by himself and wander about in that stretch of the country—well, you know what that country is like. Do you think he could have been driven to taking his own life?"

Father Keogh said, "Emphatically not. He was certainly talking of espanto before he left. He said it was strange that its symptoms were so closely related to his own." Father Keogh stood up. He felt pain in his right arm from the shoulder to the wrist. "But no, certainly not. He could not be affected by that sort of thing. In any case he would never have forgotten the importance of taking those bottles to Milpahuaca."

"Then he's been kidnaped," the Jefe said. "You realize there will be nothing to go on? Normally one would take statements and piece the information together but here one can only take statements and unravel the lies. Castillo was giving a banquet so that lets him out. Apparently all his minions were there. But he may of course have made use of our Milpahuaca friends again. We will try to make a search in the forest—but it's like looking for a pin in a maize field. We shall need an Indian guide. Coyotito would be best."

"There's—there's not much hope of finding him, is there?"

"No," said the Jefe, "there's not much hope."

Father Keogh sent a cable to the Bishop to inform him that the young priest was lost. Then he went home to fetch the holy oils. He was placing the ampules in a small leather bag when he felt someone standing beside him. He had not heard Chela come into the room. One hand was hidden behind her back. She drew it out slowly. He watched the action with the same cold sense of reluctance he had felt in opening Father Lopez's note.

Over her palm an object lay. It was a roughly constructed cross. Nailed to it through the feet and the hands was a doll. Attached to it, held in place by coarse thread, was a plain black glove. The doll was roughly yet skillfully made. It was not more than three or four inches long. Its

231

rag body was clothed in a miniature cassock and round its neck a tiny Roman collar sat. Its head and its face were beeswax. The crude features bore a compelling likeness to the Spanish priest.

Father Keogh waited for Chela to speak.

"It was found on the morning of the Long Father's going. Up in the church when he went to say Mass. He gave it to me to put on the fire but it was something I did not dare do, Father, it might have made the black magic come worse. When you asked me to find it, he thought I had made a mistake and destroyed the glove as well, and later I did tell him the whole thing was burned to stop him from wearing this terrible curse."

"How did they get hold of his glove in the first place?"

"That I don't know, Father, no one can tell."

"Why didn't he tell me about it?"

"He said it was nonsense to worry you with it and that anyhow such things were too stupid to take any notice of."

"Did he know what it means?"

"Yes, for I told him. I said, 'This is the spell to bring death. When a doll is made up to look like someone, and something of theirs is tied onto it, then this doll has been tortured to make sure he will die.'"

"Do you think that's the reason he left me his watch —because he thought there might be a chance of being killed?"

"It is possible, Father. When he brought it back first he just laughed but when he saw I was crying he said to me, 'If this is the way they intend me to die, Chela, they could do me no greater kindness. It would be a privilege to die with the mark of the nails.'"

Father Keogh put the figure on the Jefe's desk. The Jefe turned it over in clumsy hands. "Well," he said, "a pretty toy. Comachi himself might have thought this one up. Castillo has certainly inherited his touch." He opened a drawer and dropped in the figure. He told Father Keogh cheerfully, "It's probably only a symbolic threat. It would amuse them to compare him with Christ. It doesn't mean we shall necessarily discover him nailed to a cross."

Father Keogh answered, "There are many ways to crucify a man."

"The young fool should have brought it to me at once. It's quite likely that it was only intended to scare him off leaving the town. They might have thought they could stop him from taking the bottles. When he didn't change his plans they decided to fix the bus. Well, if you're ready we might as well start."

Outside there were two cars and a jeep. Father Keogh, Roberto, and the oficial were to travel in the first car. The Jefe was driving it himself. The doctor followed with Coyotito, and six agentes were packed into the jeep. They were already in summer khaki. They carried ropes, acetylene lamps, and guns. The plaza was crowded and silent. There must have been over a hundred people to watch the search party drive off.

Tongues were loosened when it had gone. "Victorino was the first, and Anastacio the second. And now it has taken the priest. They are not so unwise, those people who believe in the Bad One's spirit."

"I should have liked to have said a prayer for him but one feels that it's asking for trouble."

Chapter 23 〜〜〜〜〜〜〜〜〜〜〜〜

IT TOOK THE SEARCH PARTY TWO AND A HALF HOURS TO reach the slow start of the Great Green Walk of the Wandering Dead. The cars and the jeep drew up in the road.

"Here," Roberto told them, "is where the Long Father got off the bus."

The doctor walked over to Father Keogh. "It would be better if you stayed behind. You must not put too much strain on that wound of yours."

"I'll go carefully," Father Keogh promised.

"Carefully!" The doctor laughed. "A snake could trip over those roots in there."

Roberto was sullen at first but under the Jefe's questioning he began to grow hysterical.

"What way did he go? How can I tell you? You don't drive a bus with your eyes looking round. Besides I went fast when I left him behind. I have never been faster before. I can tell you—I needed my eyes on that road."

The Jefe asked, "What made you go faster than usual, Roberto? What were you running away from?"

Roberto was waving his arms about. "Questions and questions, all the time questions! Why should I answer? I'm not a bad man."

Father Keogh spoke quietly to him. "Roberto, the Long Father was terribly sick. If you could give us some idea we might be in time to save him. If you do know I'm sure that you'll tell us, for you certainly aren't a bad man."

Roberto turned his head away. "It is just how I told you this morning. The bus stopped by the Bad One's grave. It was too dark to look back at the Father. We left him here at the side of the road."

Coyotito was barefoot. His black felt hat shaded his eyes. "If we go far into the Green Walk, Jefe, it is dangerous for someone to go out of the line, for it takes only a few little moments to get lost in this terrible place." He carried a knife for the marking of tree bark. Everyone was supplied with water and food.

The going was not hard at first. Thorny bushes and stumpy acacias covered the ground. Laurels and verbena grew amongst creepers and ferns, and a few boulders had rolled down the mountainside to wink granite sparks in the sun.

Coyotito called back to Father Keogh, "Take care not to come near to the leaves of the 'Bad Woman.'"

The "Mala Mujer" did not grow high, but it stung like a nettle.

On the medium slopes of the mountain the tall liquidamber trees grew. In sharp black lines against their brilliant foliage stood the cross that marked Malo's grave.

Father Keogh alone walked towards it. The other twelve waited behind. He stood with his head bent beside it, saying a silent prayer. He prayed that the God who forgave all sinners would prevent a further crime in a penitent's name: that the evil one man had done living and repented of dying should not constantly spring from his grave.

He felt a jagged shot of pain through his right arm as he made the sign of the cross. He was about to ease the

235

weight of the arm in his pocket when the wind played a trick on his eyes. A few yards to the left down the hillside there had been a small flutter of white. In the hard sunlight it looked as if a dove had landed, spreading out quick plump wings. There was no sign of it when he looked again, then the wind stirred a similar flurry. It was the pages of a book that it turned. Father Keogh ran towards it. He bent down on one knee to stare at it. It was Father Lasques' breviary. The Jefe reached his side. He called Coyotito and the search party spread out. Coyotito was chewing a sugar cane. The doctor was puffing, his breath short. A jilguero sang up from the valley and its voice had incredible volume over the silent hills. They were an hour and a half searching the slopes.

Coyotito walked with his young body bent. His sharp Indian eyes searched the ground. A pile of horse dung was dismissed as a clue—"No, Jefe, this is not right for our time, this dung has laid many days in the sun. No horses were this way last night." Then he went down on one knee like a sprinter awaiting the signal to start. He ran forward several yards and shouted, "Someone in boots has passed this way. Someone went into the forest but people have also come back." He pointed to the grasses trodden down in two different directions. The outgoing signs led back to the road again.

"Well, that won't help us," the Jefe said. "Footsteps don't show up on the road. The wind wipes them out in the dust."

They took the sharp descent towards the forest of Arenales. From a distance it did not look green. In the morning heat haze the countryside stretched like blue gauze. The evergreen oaks threw mauve patches of shade over the descending slopes. Their trunks wore a colorful garland; orchids and begonias twisted round them, battling to reach the sunlight with climbing plants, creepers, and tenacious convolvulus.

It was Coyotito who found the black glove on the verge. He handed it silently to Father Keogh. The Jefe said, "Quite a trail."

They had come within penetrable distance of the Great Green Walk of Death. The oficial found the handkerchief. It was sodden from morning dew. Father Keogh recognized it at once as belonging to Father Lasques. The Jefe was thoughtful, his heavy brows drawn.

"There are things I don't like about this. Someone has made it too easy for us."

"Could he have laid a trail himself," the oficial asked, "to guide us to where he was taken?"

"He would never," Father Keogh told him, "have thrown his breviary down like that, whatever danger he might have been in."

Coyotito marked the trunk of a great red cedar with a quick twisting flash of his knife.

Coyotito headed the file. The Jefe, the oficial, and the doctor followed. Father Keogh came next, then Roberto and the six agentes. Father Keogh carried the small leather case with the holy oils inside. They started forward and after fifteen yards it seemed that the sunlight had been switched off, so suddenly the close darkness fell. Parrots shrieked, sending darts of bright plumage high above to catch the high rays of the sun which now and again pushed a pale way through as if determined to see what was going on.

The trees seemed to grow in a dense conspiracy. Mahoganies tangled their branches with aloes and ebonies. Rubber trees grew in between, and far above the heads of

237

the searchers the tall chirimoyo dangled its out-of-reach fruits.

Coyotito kept both his ears and his eyes alert to the dangers. The deer snake and the deadly nauyaca might be surprised in the undergrowth. He pointed without comment to a butterfly. It was black and its giant wings hung downward from an overhanging branch. It was supposed to bring ill luck.

When they discovered Father Lasques' hat the Jefe said, "This is deliberate, all right, and it could have been done for two reasons. To lead us off the track or to put us on it. It could be they want us to find him." He glanced casually towards Father Keogh. "It might be wise to prepare ourselves, Padre, to find the threat of the doll carried out after all."

In Father Keogh's chest a slow pain started up. It hammered persistently, gaining in strength. At ten-minute intervals the procession stopped. The Jefe put a megaphone up to his lips. The name he called rang out hollowly, dancing back in the echoes with frivolous mockery. "Las-ques! Las-ques!" It seemed to Father Keogh that the name itself held trapped in it a melancholy note of despair. He was wondering about the young priest's preparedness for death. Father Lasques would be well acquainted with it. Even in his short experience he would have witnessed it many times. The contact could have been salutary or otherwise. Sometimes in youth the experience could bring a hardening, not towards the dying themselves but in the attitude towards death of the observer. It became a familiar thing. Awe was removed from it, and the familiarity with it could become dangerous insomuch as it could foster a false sense of exemption. Father Keogh himself had experienced it not long after his own ordination. The first few contacts with it had produced in him a sensation of "This could be happening to me" which had awakened his senses and reminded him forcibly that his time in the service of his Master was only lent. As a result he became the more careful in his use of it. But later, although he was unaware of it, he became a victim of the reverse emotion—"This could not happen to me." He became accustomed to the call of the sick and the dying. Unconsciously he saw himself in the role of the perpetual caller, always the visitor to the bed of death, never the occupant. When he realized it he realized also the risk he was running of being found unprepared for death. From then on he kept it to the foremost of his mind. He woke reminding himself that it might be the last time he woke, that his day must be spent in awe of this possibility; that he must give to his next Mass and thanksgiving what he would give to them if he knew them to be his last chance of giving. He failed frequently to bring conviction to it but in his repeated attempts he felt a protection against carelessness.

He knew little enough of Father Lasques other than in an official capacity. Their communal table and their common difficulties had resulted in closer appreciation of each other but had never brought with it that intimate friendship where one may say of another, "I know this man." But he did not doubt the young priest's fervency. It was a blessing that he should be taken in youth with the fervency undiminished; the world had made no claims as yet upon the heart of Father Lasques. There was a comfort bordering upon peace to be felt in that certain knowledge of a brother priest. It was a comfort which could lessen the horrors of the tangled green maze and even the horrors of what might yet be to come. He prayed that Father Lasques might have made in his short lifetime a study of the preparedness for death.

It was not cool in the forest of Arenales. The heat crept about in the undergrowth. It gripped already-sweating feet, it rose steadily, menacingly, up to the knees, and it put added strain on the arms hacking away with knives and machetes at the cloying foliage that sprang back in the face. After the place where the hat had fallen Coyotito could trace no more signs of penetration.

The Jefe stopped the line and shouted. They had reached a baldness in the forest. The sun pounced on it, blinding in its unaccustomed glare. It was a patch of deep grasses that ran towards a ravine. On either side of it the forest gathered again as black-stemmed and closely packed as ever. The Jefe was looking through field glasses. He passed them to Father Keogh and pointed. Far down the ravine which curled, a grey molten crack, round the edge of the grasses, vultures hovered. They circled and dropped. They hovered, tattered black scraps in the idle blue sky, then sank towards the river below. The party moved quickly towards the edge along which the mangroves grew. It was on the nearside bank of the river below that the vultures covered their prey like black ants on a lump of sugar. The pain in Father Keogh's chest impeded his breathing and he was conscious of every bone in his body.

The Jefe ordered his men: "Collect boulders. Throw them as near as you can to the birds. If you can scare them I might have a chance to see." He raised his heavy field glasses and trained them on the spot. It seemed to Father Keogh that centuries were passing before the vultures rose, frightened off by the stones. The Jefe put down his glasses. He said, "No, it was only a goat."

Father Keogh never knew how he completed the journey home. It was not unconnected with obstinacy. He was aware of the doctor's sour eyes on his back. It was dark when they reached the edge of the forest again and made for the Huapan road. Their lamps danced at their sides and their torches flashed. Coyotito had once missed the marks on the trees. A chill had run up the line of the party which not a soul expressed. They knew that to lose the way once could be to lose it forever in the Great Green Walk of Death. But Coyotito had halted the line and advanced step by step by himself. He found the marked tree and called to them.

Quantana was anxious for news. The evening parade came to a halt on the plaza and the town clustered round the search party.

The doctor helped Father Keogh out of the Jefe's car into his own.

"I'll drop you and come back later. I want to give you a good look-over but I've one or two calls to make first."

Vito put his head through the window. Behind him stood Porfirio, Pablo, and the Jeep. His eyes met for several seconds the exhausted and despairing eyes of the priest. His voice was quietly solicitous. His troubled inquiry seemed genuine.

"No news at all of him, Father?"

Father Keogh felt again the quick temptation to accept Vito as he presented himself. There was a perpetual trap in the boy's superbly affected innocence. "There's no news," Father Keogh replied.

"Would you like us to search for him, Father?"

The doctor spared Father Keogh an answer. He put

the car into gear and drove off. Vito was forced to leap backwards.

"Sadistic young skunk," the doctor said. "I've no doubt that he is behind it."

"I'm afraid so," Father Keogh agreed.

Chapter 24 ~~~~~~~~~~~~~~~~

THE TOWN WAS DEPRESSED AND SILENT, SECRET WITH MANY thoughts. No one believed that Father Lasques was alive. Father Keogh, in the back of the doctor's car, was fighting exhaustion and grief. He grieved not only for a brother priest but for the whole of the town. Easter was only a few days off and Father Keogh could sense defeat. It was already the Wednesday of Holy Week; the church bell would be silent until the Saturday when it tolled to declare the end of Lent. But who would answer it when it rang? Its tongue might be silent forever for all Quantana cared. On Maundy Thursday and on Good Friday there would be no outdoor passion plays performed by the townsfolk with skill and a deep sincerity in portraying the crucifixion of Christ. Other towns and other villages would be free to give expression to their faith and rejoice. Only Quantana would lack the spirit of fiesta, fettered by superstitious fear. Anywhere else in Mexico the streets would have been decked throughout the week. Great papier-mâché figures to represent Judas packed with small portions of gun-

powder would have hung from the lamp poles and balconies, and on strings from house to house. They could
vary from ten inches to ten feet in height. At ten o'clock on
the morning of Sábado de Gloria, the Judas Day longed
for by children, the figures would all be set alight. Joyous
explosions would burst round the towns. At the same hour
the church bells would send out their call and the children
would flourish their wooden rattles.

Father Keogh had seen such days in Quantana. The
streets had been crowded with the figures of Judas. Although ostensibly meant to represent the betrayer of
Christ, they had been known to carry a striking resemblance to unpopular politicians and townsfolk. Father
Keogh had once been considerably embarrassed to recognize a likeness to the Presidente Municipal. Don Timoteo,
who made every figure, starting as early as February or
March, denied the resemblance. Father Keogh remembered
his guileless reply. "It's a trick of your eyesight, Padre,
although I won't say that the persons who ordered these
figures were friends of the one whom you name."

He smiled in the car at the memories of those far-
off happy days. Then he saddened again. Sábado de Gloria
in this year would bring the children of Quantana no fun.

The town in itself was resentful and thought nothing
of blaming Father Keogh.

"What we want is a priest who does not make trouble.
It's foolish to stir up unrest."

"He has put the Bad One's spirit against us, that's
certain."

"Yes, for it's taken the Long Father now."

In the house of Roberto Ibarra the six passengers who
had ridden on the bus had gathered together to comfort
and bolster each other up.

"Well, we have done nothing that's wrong." Less confidence showed in the eyes than the voices. "No, it's not our fault what happened."

"How could we talk to the Jefe with Vito Castillo about?"

"We cannot say a word to him, Mateo. It would be as much as our lives would be worth."

"Besides, we cannot be sure who it was in the dark."

"We have told him no lies," said Alfonso Herrera.

"And I showed him the place," Roberto reminded them, "where the Long Father got off the bus. You couldn't do much more than that."

"I told him the truth," insisted Doña Florencia, "when I said he got off at his wish."

"Oh yes, that little bit was the truth."

In the town a few righteous heads were shaken. "The seven-sinful-ones-of-the-bus have not told all they know. They could say, if they wished, what became of the padre."

"Those seven are not the only sinful ones. There are others who should tell what they know."

In the pale pink-washed house of the Presidente Municipal, Doña Arcelia was having one of her many hysterical outbreaks since the night of the Martinez banquet. Don Agapito administered brandy from Veracruz and sat smoothing his wife's black hair. His own thick wig shone in the lamplight. "But, my treasure, my sweetling, my heart's love, no one will talk. We are sure to be safe if only you will not open your pretty pink mouth."

"Agapito, you should go to the Jefe. You should tell him that Vito Castillo and Pablo were not there at the dinner that night—you should tell him and save your own face."

"But, my angel, I should never have gone to the din-

ner if it had not been for you. I'm not afraid of Castillo
myself. It's for your sake I try not to offend him. He
would be too cruel to take his revenge on me. That boy
was not Malo's disciple for nothing—it's you he would try
to hurt. In that way he knows he could injure me most."

"The Jefe will find out," she wailed at him. "And
then when he finds you were lying you will be Presidente
no more." She sat up, suddenly vicious, and spat at him,
"And why else do you think that I married you? Silly
bald old fool!"

In a room at the Casa Grande, Dyke Brown also drank
brandy from Veracruz. He sat in Locha's bedroom that
was somber with Spanish furniture. His hair was ruffled.
He had run his hands through it several times. "I don't
get it—I just don't get the tears. That Dago priest didn't
mean a darned thing to you. So what, if he's lost in a
forest?"

"He's been up to hear my confession and he brought
me the Sacraments here to the house."

"That didn't stop you from saying he looked like a
Mickey Mouse on stilts."

"Oh, don't you see, Dyke, don't you see?" Locha
slid off the great canopied bed. A mosquito net wound
round the posts. "If this has happened to Father Lasques,
it could also have happened to *him*." She rolled over on
the bed again, her face in the crook of her arm.

Dyke Brown walked across to her, his glass in his
hand. "So now we're back on *him*."

"It was *always* him."

The boy sat wearily down beside her. "I don't get
this Keogh either—this—this goddam priestly Paddy. He
doesn't look that good to me."

"Men can't tell."

"There's nothing unusual about him. He doesn't have a thing a dozen other guys haven't got except that collar round his neck, and I've seen dandier setups in those. What's more, he must be as old as God's uncle."

She raised her head. "He's *not* old. He's not even nearly fifty yet."

"Anyone over forty is nearly fifty."

"Then anyone over twenty is nearly thirty. So what about you?"

Dyke Brown went back to the brandy bottle. He returned with two glasses filled. He passed one to Locha. "Then just what *is* so wonderful about him? Supposing *you* tell *me!*"

She sat up to sip at her brandy. "Nothing. He may be perfectly ordinary to other eyes but he's just—just the only man for me."

"He is *not* the man for you!" Dyke shouted at her. "He may be the man for his Bishop or his Pope or his God Almighty, but he is *not* the man for you."

Locha took hold of his hand and held it to her. "Dyke, I should never have married you. But I did so hope I could make it work. I promise I tried, but when he was so ill, it just seemed to—well, it all seemed to boil up again. But you do know, don't you, that next to him I love you more than anyone else in the world?"

Dyke bowed from the head and waist. "Honey, you couldn't possibly have paid me a sweeter compliment."

"I sit here trying to will myself out of it, but I can't. Everything I see, everything I touch, reminds me of him."

"What, in the bedroom?"

"No, silly, everywhere. All over the place. It's so

lonely. It's the most terrible thing to be shut in a room without someone you're longing for."

"What do you think our apartment was like after you ran out on me?"

"Oh, darling, I'm sorry. It must have been horrible for you. It's the worst kind of prison there is; even the furniture's your enemy. It's a depression you can't describe. It's the moping about that's so awful. When you wake up in the morning full of a cold kind of despair and your whole day is made up of 'will you catch a sight of him or won't you, and if you do, will he be nice'—and then when you do see him you spoil it by thinking, In ten minutes, in five minutes, in three, he'll be gone, and you've got the rest of the horrible day left to face."

"I itch to get my hands on him, too, but I guess it doesn't come from the same emotion."

"You feel so lonely when your world is made up of someone and everything to do with them, and they're somewhere else and they don't even care. But at times I don't think it's possible to suffer so much by yourself without the other person joining in."

Dyke stood up. "He's going to join you, honey, he's going to suffer all right. I didn't change my mind about that court case. I'm going to go through with it. Look, Locha, I'm clearing out. You don't have very long to make up your mind. Either you come with me for good or—well, you know what. That guy's month is up."

He went out quietly, closing the door behind him.

In the little adobe house on the lower road the witch sat beside her cooking pots. No one had told her that Father Lasques would meet with disaster if he left the town. No one had told her that he would meet with dis-

247

aster at all. Yet she had warned him herself. She was trying to remember how she could have come by such an accurate premonition. She believed it had come in a dream. Mother Montezera was alternately proud and afraid of herself.

The only signs of revelry were coming from Father Keogh's house.

Chapter 25

WHEN THE DOCTOR PUT HIM DOWN AND DROVE OFF IN HIS car Father Keogh stood several moments listening to the noise which came out of his house. A woman was squealing with laughter and a girl's voice whooped in delight. A chair crashed and the lamplight shivered. Chela's voice, odd and unfamiliar, cried out, "Ola! Señor Frankenson, there are many who would pay to have this little girl on their knees."

Father Keogh reached the tiny strip of hall. He pushed open the door of his living room and stood still. Sam held a chair in front of him. Chela lay stretched on the old horsehair sofa. A cigar jogged up and down in her mouth as she laughed. Her eyes seemed unable to focus. She lay wheezing with merriment. Candalaria, hair falling loose over polished shoulders, was stalking Sam. It was Sam who saw Father Keogh first. "Mac! Mac, for Pete's sake take care of this kid. She has a skinful you could keep the bar open on for a week."

On Father Keogh's desk four pulque bottles stood.

He asked severely of Sam, "Have you been giving these women alcohol?"

Sam's wail of resentment pierced his head. "Me, been giving them pulque! They've been giving me hell! Honest to God, Mac, I never touched a drop. Look, it was this way. I called around for news of the boy friend and I find a party going on. So I think they have something to celebrate but it seems they were drowning their sorrows."

Candalaria crept after Sam again. She moved like an Indian dancer stalking a foe on the stage. "The poor Señor Frankenson, his voice is so big in the town about the women he has and the ones he will have—but look how he is when you try to go up to him—see how he runs away then."

Sam squeaked, "Mac! For Pete's sake, Mac—this kid could eat a man."

Father Keogh said, "Candalaria, behave yourself at once. And as you seem at least able to stand on your feet kindly make Chela some coffee." She dropped her pursuit of Sam and danced her way out of the room.

Sam put down his chair. "Gracias, pal!" Then he said, "Hey, Mac! You look like you had a hard day at the office. You could do with a mouthful of pulque yourself." His voice dropped. "Did you locate the boy friend?" Father Keogh shook his head. "That's too bad."

Father Keogh stood over Chela, his hands on his hips. On the sofa she screwed her eyes tightly in her head. She seemed to feel that by not looking at him herself, she could prevent him from seeing her. "Chela, where did you get that pulque?"

She whimpered softly, "Presents, Father."

"From whom?"

Sam picked up one of the bottles and smelled it. "This

is real pulque of Apan. Porfirio has a monopoly on that around here. This must have come from his bar."

"Chela," said Father Keogh, "no one from that place would make us a present."

Sam inquired, "How about little Miss Light Fingers, isn't she persona grata up there?"

Father Keogh had no need to question Candalaria. When she came in with the coffee, he gathered the truth from her face. The pulque had taken command of her. The impertinence was gone. She cried inwardly, making no sound. Her lips and her shoulders and the coffee cup shook. She made an unsteady approach towards Chela. It was Sam who came forward to rescue the cup. He held it to Chela's mouth. "Well, I reckon this is a real cosy home-coming, Mac."

Father Keogh said, "Candalaria, did you steal or were you given that pulque?" She stood with her head down, picking at strands in her dress. Chela gulped down the coffee, her eyes still shut. Father Keogh said quietly, "Those other 'presents,' which were supposed to have come from anonymous people who wished us well—you stole them, didn't you, Candalaria, encouraged by Chela? The pumpkins, the meats, the vegetables, even the braces? That's why Chela was so alarmed by the Jefe when he came and looked into the cooking pots. She thought he had found you both out. You've been stealing from stalls in the market, and shops. Well, Candalaria, isn't that so?" There was no expression on his face when her answer burst out. It neither confirmed nor denied his suggestion. She had something else to tell him.

"It was not my parents who sent me to see you, Father, it was el Lobo who made me come down to your house for the talks. It was when you went to my mother

250

and father and asked them to see to my soul. They told him about it and he made them send me down to you."

"Why did Vito think it a good idea for you to undergo a course of religious instruction?"

She put the back of her hand up to clear the tears from her eyes. "He has spies in the whole of Quantana, Father, but he had nobody right in the house of the priests."

He asked of her gently, "Have you been spying on us, Candalaria?" Candalaria nodded her head.

Chela rolled off the sofa, shaking both fists. She scrambled forward to claw Candalaria's skirt. "Burra! Burra! May the devil devour her. I will go to the bruja—I'll burn herbs to destroy her. I'll put in a topaz to make the spell worse. Her eyes will fall out and her flesh will fall off." Father Keogh bent down to hold back the old woman but she fought him to free herself. "Father, I knew nothing of this, I will swear it. I am not a bad woman, I took what she stole for your sake and to help build the poor Long Father up. If I knew she was telling el Lobo about us I would have taken her neck like a chicken's neck—"

Father Keogh interrupted. "Be quiet." Sam helped put Chela back on the sofa. Candalaria's voice was toneless. "It is quite right that the old one knows nothing. She talked foolishly sometimes because we were friends—but she did not know that I carried the tales."

"Did you make friends with her for that purpose and was that Vito's idea as well?"

"Yes, Father, the stealings were all done to please her so that she'd be my friend."

"And you passed on everything you heard about our movements?"

251

"Yes, Father, and then when you and the Long Father were out in the town or the church and the old one was busy cooking the stealings, I used to read letters and things you had written."

"Then you read our reports to the Bishop and his replies to us, and you told Vito everything you found out?"

"Yes, Father."

Sam said, "How's that for a pint-sized bitch?"

Candalaria put a timid hand out to take a pinch of Father Keogh's sleeve. "I did mean to be good from the talkings with you and the other poor priest but el Lobo is someone to make you love him even when you hate." She sat back on her heels to look up at him. Sam's eyes strayed to her legs when she settled her skirts. "But I liked what you said in the talkings. I did listen to some things you said. I did say the prayers and I did read those nice little lives of the saints."

"Burra!" Chela screamed at her. "Burra!"

"Oh, save your breath, grandma," Sam advised.

Candalaria pulled on Father Keogh's sleeve. "When the talking had been going on for a bit I had nothing to do with el Lobo."

Father Keogh looked steadily down at her. "You still see him at Porfirio's bar or the Hotel Martinez every night."

"Yes, but only because I'm afraid to stay back now."

"I thought you weren't frightened of Vito."

"I wasn't afraid when I let him make love to me, then I could do what I liked with him. But now he is angry because I say 'No.' And I say that because of what you and the Long Father said in the talks."

"Do you know what has happened to Father Lasques?"

She shook her head decisively. "No. If I did I would speak out at once. El Lobo has left off trusting me since you and the Long Father have made me take away the love."

"Was it you who passed on the information that Father Lasques was taking his medicine to be analyzed in Milpahuaca?"

"Yes, Father, I passed on things like that."

Father Keogh put the question slowly: "And did you steal his glove?"

She lowered her head when she answered him. "Yes, Father, last Saturday, when the old one was busy I looked round the house."

"Was that at Vito's orders too?"

"No, Father, this didn't come from el Lobo. It came from the witch."

"From the witch? Do you realize what use she made of that glove?"

"I know that it was put on the killing doll, Father, but this wasn't done by the witch. She is a good curandera, she doesn't make bad spells. She was not pleased when she heard of this doll."

"Then how do you account for her wanting the glove?"

"The witch received a letter, Father, made of the writings of many people so that no one could tell whose it was. The letter was teasing and made her feel cross. It called her a silly old woman and said that she could not make her magic spells work."

"Well, it had something there," said Sam.

Father Keogh told him, "She might be right yet about Father Lasques. She said he would die of this town. What else was in the letter?"

"It called her names that a witch would not like, such as a silly old goose brain and rude things like that. It said she was not even clever enough to cast a spell on the Long Father to make him drop one of his gloves on the floor of the church at a certain time. It said that a true witch should be able to bring about something like this."

"He wouldn't wear gloves in church, would he, Mac?"

"No, but I hardly think that would stop them. Well, Candalaria, what happened then?"

"The witch was so wanting to prove herself, Father, she paid me to get hold of the Long Father's glove."

"And you dropped it on the floor of the church at the right time. Somebody picked it up. Sewed it to the doll, and put it back in the church for Father Lasques to find. Have you any idea who that might have been?"

"No, Father, I know nothing but what I have said."

"Has she still got that letter?"

"No, for it made her so cross that she burned it with some other strange things, to make a spell against those who had sent it. She said that would bring on their ruin."

"Oh, for chrissake!" Sam moaned. "She doesn't even have the brain of a goose."

"The Jefe always thought they worked through her," Father Keogh said. "This is an example of it. Castillo's behind it all right but how to prove it I'm sure I don't know."

Candalaria's tears fell again. "I did not know either what would be done with the glove, but the witch paid me well and it seemed such a small thing. I have not so much money now that I say 'No' all the time to el Lobo, and the Señor Dentist has turned sour with his pocket as well, but—" She wriggled closer, suddenly confident. "I

254

think I could find this thing out. It would be a happiness to do it, Father, to make up for the spying and the braces and the pulque. El Lobo is hungry for me—it's always like that when you keep saying 'No' if you don't say 'No' too long. I will go back to him, Father. He is someone who might tell his secrets in love."

Chela was instantly mollified. She sent Candalaria a smile full of pride. "Now that will come in the nature of a nice little sacrifice and make up for the rest of her sins."

"It would be in the nature of a nice little nothing of the sort," Father Keogh replied. "One sin cannot excuse another. You must never go back to him, Candalaria, now that you've make the break. The only way to make up for the thefts is to make restitution. Unfortunately that can't be done with most of the goods. You'll have to try to remember whom you robbed and each week out of what you earn at the dentist's you must try to pay them back. What you can't manage I'll try to make up when I can. But what's left of that pulque must go back tonight."

Candalaria put a quick hand to her mouth. "No, Father, no. I could never do that. Vito would never forgive me if he knew I had taken something from him to give to you."

"I haven't had it," Father Keogh pointed out. "You and Chela have."

Sam held up an empty bottle. "Yeah, and they didn't do too bad."

Chela moaned, holding her head, "It has set up the pains in me, Father. Mother of God, I shall die."

"Candalaria, if you won't take this pulque back, I must." She twisted suddenly round and ran out of the house. Father Keogh sighed, "So much for the 'talkings.' "

Sam said, "So much for her guts! If you have an apple

255

rotten to the core it doesn't matter how much you polish it, Mac."

"Oh, I don't know, it looks better with a bit of a shine on it." Father Keogh took a bottle of aspirin out of the cupboard, put two in his hand and gave them to Chela. She swallowed them down with the dregs of the coffee. "You'd better lie there and sleep until I get back."

Sam asked, "You're not really going up to the bar with that hooch?"

"Have you forgotten that I'm already a convicted thief myself? I can't afford to be known as a receiver of stolen goods as well."

He began to collect the bottles. Sam tried to remonstrate with him. "Listen, you're plain crazy, Mac. You're going to stick your neck out so far those bums will be able to saw through it in three places. What the hell good's it going to do you? Did you forget they may have murdered the boy friend?"

"All the more reason to give them back their pulque."

Sam was silent a moment, thoughtful. Then he gave his thigh a slap. "That's right, Mac, that's right! You have to set a good example around these parts." He held out his hands and flicked his fingers. "Come on, give poppa a couple of those babies. I guess I'll come along with you."

Father Keogh hesitated. "What are you up to, Sam?"

"Me? Why, what would I be up to? I just thought I'd come along."

Suspiciously Father Keogh passed him two bottles. Sam said, "Wow! They broke into another. No wonder the old girl's out cold."

"They've probably been at it most of the day."

It was dark in the street outside. Father Keogh's limbs were stiff and he found the going hard. Sam lagged

256

behind him frequently. Once, when he stopped, Father Keogh turned round. "I just have to tie up my shoelace," called Sam.

Pablo's guitar was playing in Porfirio's bar. It was empty except for the four men and Maria. Since the news that Father Lasques had not been discovered, nobody cared to come in. Vito and Porfirio were rolling dice. The Jeep sat perched on a stool, filing his bitten nails. Father Keogh addressed Porfirio, "These bottles were found in my house. They appear to have come from this place. Two are full, one's empty and the other's been broken into, I'm afraid. If you'll tell me what I owe you I'll pay you for what you've lost." He had with him the whole of the Bishop's allowance. He and Chela would live on a handful of beans all the week.

Vito collected the dice. He played with them, throwing them up in his hand. "And how did our pulque get into your house?"

"Candalaria," Maria supplied. She leaned plumply over the counter, a pleased smile breaking over her mouth.

"Well, well, well," said Vito. "What do you think of that? I have noticed your influence on her, Father, she has spoken so well of you of late. It's a fine thing when your best girl is stealing from you to give to another lover."

"A fine thing," Porfirio said.

Father Keogh placed his two full bottles down on the counter. He turned to take the other two from Sam. He took a startled step backwards involuntarily. There was a change in Sam. His eyes were half-closed and his lips hung loose. He tipped forward on the balls of his feet. His hat was worn rakishly and his tie was thrown over one

257

shoulder. Father Keogh went towards him. "Sam!" The bottles he took back were both empty. Someone had finished the other half.

Maria asked coldly of Vito, "What is 'best girl' about a slut who will rob you?"

"Only that she's young enough to be your daughter, Old Mother," Vito grinned. Then he said to Father Keogh, "You owe for *two* bottles of pulque."

Sam lurched towards him. "If I wasn't so goddam scared of you I'd knock your teeth so far down your throat they'd bite right through your tonsils, for making that dirty crack at Mac." He reeled backwards and Father Keogh caught him. "Unfortunately I'm scared." He rolled the words out, giggling. "Punk," he said. "Goddam punk."

Vito, Porfirio, Pablo, and the Jeep closed in on him. They made a tight little circle about him. Father Keogh could hear the punches fall. He tried to break into the ring. It was Porfirio's fist that struck into his chest. It sent him giddily backwards against the counter. He brought glasses and bottles and cigar boxes down. Sam yelped, "Mac, they're killing me. Call the police, Mac, call the police."

Father Keogh reached the door. His shouts brought Carranza, Beltran, the corporal, and finally the Jefe. Vito broke away to greet him. He ordered, "Arrest these two men."

The Jefe helped Father Keogh up. "Upon what grounds?" he asked.

Porfirio waved fat arms about. "What grounds? Take a look for yourself. They have come in here breaking the place up. This little gringo is drunk."

Sam emerged tattered and bruised from the circle.

258

Father Keogh stared at him. Apart from the disorder his clothes sustained and a cut across his eye, he looked normal and sedately sober. "Drunk," he inquired. "Who, me? I didn't have anything to drink since the Doomsday before last. These punks beat me up."

"This man is sober," the Jefe agreed.

"Arrest him," said Vito coldly, "if you know how to discharge your duty. He threatened me with violence."

"All I said was I was too scared to hit him. I wouldn't call that a violent threat."

"Look for yourself," Porfirio wailed. "You can see how they've broken the place up."

Maria spoke with her eyes upon Vito. They were bright with a cold revenge. She had been savagely nursing his insult. "The slut Candalaria stole some bottles. The Father was giving them back. The gringo is right, he's had nothing to drink. It was el Lobo, el Gordo, Porfirio, and the Jeep who broke the place up. They were punching the gringo's head."

The Jefe arrested the men. He detained them in jail for questioning. Father Keogh said, "But, Sam, if you didn't drink that pulque what did you do with it?"

Sam winked at him. "I tipped it out tying my shoe. The next time you want an angel in a nativity play, Mac, remember as an actor I have class!"

Chapter 26 ~~~~~~~~~~~~~~~~~~

THE DOCTOR SOON HEARD OF THE FIGHT. UNDER THE HARD lights of the Jefe's office he attended both Father Keogh and Sam. His voice was irritable when he examined the priest. "You're determined to induce a state of collapse. All you needed after today's exertions was to get yourself knocked about."

"He didn't pick the quarrel," Sam explained.

"Whose choice it may have been is immaterial. The result is the same." He said to Father Keogh, "I've warned you before not to aggravate those wounds. You have to take a rest. I don't like your tongue, I don't like your pulse, and I can't say I very much care for your heart."

"Isn't any of me popular?" Father Keogh inquired.

The Jefe was phrasing the charge. "Now, the Señor Frankenson will accuse the whole lot of assault."

Sam winked at Father Keogh. "Yeah! And I didn't cook up that bit either. Those punks really beat me up."

The Jefe ignored him. "Their defense will be that a man aping drunkenness deliberately provoked them. They may get away with that with the Juez. They will come up before him in three days' time."

"If Don Pedro has an ounce of sense he'll give them a life sentence," said Sam. "They couldn't disturb his peace of mind in jail. That's the best way to stop them taking up his reading time."

260

"Unfortunately he can't give a life sentence for an offense of this kind. If he could he would. Don Pedro cares for them no more than the rest of us but this offense will more likely result in a fine."

"Surely he'll be influenced by their past record," Father Keogh said.

"If they had a record we could prove they would already be in jail."

"Yeah, but the Juez knows it's vital to get them inside."

"He could give only a short sentence in a case like this, and when they came out they could gravely trouble his piece of mind. It is bound to be a fine."

"Christ, if I'd known that," Sam sighed, "I'd have drunk that goddam pulque."

"It's a great help," the Jefe told him, "to be able to extend the hospitality of the jail to them at all. I can detain them no longer than seventy-two hours before they are charged but they won't be lonely during that time. Either myself, the oficial, or the sarjento will keep them company. We shall grill them continually. Of course we shan't put it like that. We shall merely be asking a number of questions to see if they can help us in the disappearance of Father Lasques. If we are lucky we'll trip one of them up."

Father Keogh said, "Jefe, I feel I should like to continue the search."

"You would be no use, Father. My colleague from Milpahuaca and my colleague from Arenales are sending me reinforcements, and even they will be no good. If he is lost in that forest luck and not skill will find him. You could start at a hundred points with a hundred men and still miss him."

Sam shook Father Keogh's arm. "Go to it, Mac, we only have seventy-two hours. If you're going to convince this stinking dump it doesn't have to be scared of Pussy-foot's spirit when the hyenas are safely locked up, you have to look snappy about it. You shin up that pulpit and preach your guts out and I'll scoot around the town delivering angel food by hand. I'll bust open doors, I'll drag them out by the ears, I'll get them into that goddam church if I have to put a gun behind them."

Father Keogh took Sam's hand in both his own and shook it. "Gabriel himself couldn't get them into church but if you could drive a few up to the plaza in the morning I'd be grateful, and you have my word of honor I won't put you into the choir."

Sam grinned at him. "You must have heard me sing sometime."

Father Keogh went quickly back to the house. "Chela, I want you to come up to the plaza tomorrow and bring all your friends. What a shocking smell of soup!"

"Yes, well, it's lucky we have anything left with you stopping Chata from bringing us manna from Heaven."

"Manna from Heaven should be sent, not pinched." He turned and said brusquely as Chela groaned, "Surely you've got over your hang-over now?" He suspected her of making capital out of it.

"No, Father, I shall die of it yet. But it was all for the sake of the Long Father. If I had not been so sad for him I should not be so sour with the pulque."

Father Keogh suggested wickedly, "Couldn't one of your sister's husbands help you? One of them must have undergone a similar experience at some time or other."

Chela put a hand to her head. There was a hint of malevolence in her voice when she told him, "The Señora

Dyke Brown is here for you and she's been crying the whole of the time. It is shame when you think how sad someone can make a poor married lady's heart." She padded off into the kitchen.

Father Keogh called softly after her, "Chela, I'm afraid I can't see her now. Tell her I—"

Locha came out before the sentence was finished. She was demure in a pale shantung suit. The evidence of tears was not visible. She was wearing a pair of sunglasses. They looked extra dark in the lamplight.

"At the risk of jeopardizing your reputation, Father, I felt I must see you before I go."

"You're leaving Quantana?" Father Keogh inquired.

"I'm going home with Dyke."

"Congratulations, Locha," Father Keogh said. "I never really lost my faith in you. I knew you'd do the right thing."

"I am going," she told him quietly, "because I want to spare you from a court case."

Father Keogh put his hand to his head. "Great heavens! I'd forgotten about it. The month he allowed me must be up."

Her prim composure left her. She snatched the sunglasses off her face. Her eyes were resentful and hurt. *"Forgotten* it!" she said.

He knew he had offended her deeply. She had imagined him unable to concentrate upon any other problem but the one which connected him with herself. She still thought of herself as his foremost concern. His best means of assisting her would be to disillusion her. "I've had rather a lot on my hands," he explained.

She was coldly tight-lipped when she answered him. "The Candalaria girl for instance."

"For one instance. Vito Castillo could be classed as another."

"Well, I really mustn't keep you from two such admirable causes. Good-by, Father."

Her clattering heels as she ran up the street reminded him of other occasions when as an unruly, engaging child she had run away from him after defying him. He still found it hard to remember that Locha was in her late teens.

In the morning Sam rounded up the flock. There were few enough willing to gather on the plaza. He called out, "It was like I said, Mac, I had to drag them out by the ears. You get cracking and I'll go whip up a few more."

Father Keogh told them, "Castillo and his friends are in prison. They may remain there only a day or two because the charge against them isn't serious enough to warrant a longer sentence. Terrible things have occurred in this town for which these men are undoubtedly responsible. Worse crimes may be expected if they regain their freedom. You have a choice to make—between the freedom of murderers and thieves, and your own and your children's. It is within your power to rid yourselves forever of the evil which has silenced not only your tongues but the voice of your conscience. This is your chance to end the unofficial dictatorship of Vito Castillo Rivera. It may be your only opportunity. There are those amongst you here now who may have information and who could supply evidence which would remove for all time the fear that has stifled our town, which could make Quantana a proud and happy place again: somewhere no man need be ashamed or afraid to live. If you will tell what you know to the Jefe you need have no fear of Castillo's vengeance or that of his accomplices for if you tell what you know to the Jefe they will not come out of prison.

264

"You have not long to make up your minds. Sábado de Gloria is only seventy-two hours away from us, and on the morning of that day which should be so joyful, these men will be out again to darken our lives. If you hesitate you will have sold your children into a bondage which will affect not only their material but their spiritual rights, not only their earthly lives but their chances of heaven. Evil cannot be condoned without being absorbed. You will be mercilessly putting your children into the way of sin. You have now the opportunity to protect their faith.

"While these men are in prison no harm can come to you. We cannot eliminate coincidence but the so-called 'spirit' of Anacleto is unable to work without them. You will surely see that for yourselves. Test it over the next few days. You will suffer from no supernatural forces. Those forces have been carefully organized by Vito Castillo. It is he and his followers who have issued the threats and carried them out. It is he who has forecast disaster and brought it about. It is his influence and his alone which has sent people in fear of their lives. Anacleto Comachi can do you no further hurt. It is my belief that he died repentant, and I have absolved him. It is a double affront to our Blessed Lord in whose name he was forgiven his sins that they should be used by the living to perpetuate villainy. Will you be guilty of allowing this offense?

"Denounce these men, give them over to the punishment they deserve. Free yourselves, and on the morning of Sábado de Gloria link the terrors and the hardships you have known in this town to the passion and crucifixion of our Lord Jesus Christ, join your newly found faith, your joy and your freedom to the glory of His resurrection."

The crowd dispersed in silence. Father Keogh called on the Jefe. "Any news from the Milpahuaca search party or the Arenales men?"

The Jefe shook his head. "No, and I ought to warn you again, Father, that when there is it's not likely to be good."

It was impossible not to dwell on the fate of the young Spanish priest. Father Keogh alternated between artificially stimulated hope and despair. He walked slowly home. Even so, he was back in the house before Chela, who had stayed for a gossip en route. In his room he found a note. It had been written upon his own typewriter. *If anyone gives information against Vito Castillo, Candalaria Fernandez will suffer.*

Father Keogh went up to the Jefe again. He was greeted with the nearest resemblance to a grin he had ever seen on the Jefe's heavy face.

"Well, Father, I hear that the witch's spell has worked. The Señora Dyke Brown is going back to the States with her husband."

"News in this town," said Father Keogh, "travels faster than sound. I am afraid it didn't entirely work. Didn't you ask for the 'heart' of the Señora to return to her husband?"

The Jefe inquired politely, "Is she leaving it somewhere behind?"

"The whole thing is a little too noble for my liking. I'm not worried about her happiness, I'm sure of that ultimately, but I am concerned for his. If she goes back to him in that spirit I wonder how long he'll put up with her?"

"We must see what we can do," the Jefe said. "We must cast another spell."

"Never mind about spells, look at this." Father Keogh handed the note to the Jefe. "It was written on my own typewriter. I found it still in the machine. And I have no doubt whoever did it took the trouble to wipe off his fingerprints. Do you think we should send the girl to Huapan? Father Lopez would find someone to look after her."

The Jefe came slowly towards him. "Send her to Huapan! Over my dead body that girl goes to Huapan."

"But isn't it a risk to keep her here, when she's been threatened?"

The Jefe sat down again and leaned over the table. "My dear Father, have you no faith? Don't tell me you believe that Comachi's spirit can operate without Vito's support?"

"You said yourself that he might have Milpahuaca thugs in his employment. They could work without him."

"Wouldn't that threat apply to the rest of the town?"

"Of course, but we can't pack the whole of Quantana off to Huapan and Candalaria's been singled out."

The Jefe said, "She may be the means of bringing Castillo to justice at last. That girl is not leaving this town."

Father Keogh lit a cigarette. "I always said you'd be capable of baiting a trap with a baby if you thought it might bring you your precious proof."

The Jefe lit up a cigar. He spoke softly but there was no softness in his words. "This place has been my work, Father, just as much as it's been yours. It nearly cost you your life once, yet you don't want to leave it. You don't want to see it get the better of you and what you stand for. And my feelings are just the same. This place has cost me plenty—promotion, for instance. I could have had a transfer to Milpahuaca if I had got Quantana straightened out. First it was Comachi and now it's Castillo, but most of all it's the place. Everything I've got I've put into this town and it's tricked me every time. It won't help itself so it can't help me. It's drained me of feeling, it's deprived me of home life and hobbies. I'm a man with no time to spare. You are determined to bring this town back to its faith, I am determined to bring it to justice. What have I got out of it? About the same as you, Father—nothing but trouble and personal failure. When I retire those are the only recollections I shall have to lighten my twilight hours"—the Jefe brought his fist slowly down upon the table top and left it there—"unless I can take with me, finally, a certain amount of success. I wouldn't leave Quantana now if they offered me Mexico City itself. You could say I want my revenge."

"And to get it you're willing to risk a young girl's life?"

"I'd be willing to risk my own."

"That I've never doubted. But you'll be using this girl as a decoy. Don't forget that the last time they made a threat it was carried out. Victorino was killed."

The Jefe took up his memory pad. In the window his hummingbird shimmered against the light. "Nobody leaves or comes into this town without my permission during the next seventy-two hours. If they do they'll be shot. I'll get the search parties to reinforce us. I'll have the whole town circled. Then perhaps if the tiger comes after the smell of the little goat we might find it's the same one who killed Victorino and went off with the priest."

"Supposing it kills the little goat as well?"

The Jefe turned round to Father Keogh. He lifted his heavy shoulders and slowly let them fall. "How important is one little goat compared to the whole of the flock?"

"That isn't for us to say. It might be that one creature is more precious to the Shepherd than any other. It's not for us to select the sacrifice. God has His uses for the little goats of the world. He might choose to speak to us through humbler things than that."

"Shepherds!" The Jefe sighed. "Little goats!" He stretched out his hand for a bottle of mezcal. "Kindly remember you're talking to a heathen."

"I haven't forgotten," Father Keogh said. He stood for a moment or two considering. Then he asked casually, "What about me, Jefe? It might be awkward for me to be trapped in the town. Supposing I have to go to Tephuango or something?"

"I'll give you a pass. You can have my car if you want it, but you'll have to drive yourself. I can't spare a man off this job."

"Thank you," Father Keogh said. "Will you be telling the girl that her life is in danger?"

The Jefe shook his head. "I don't want her taking any precautions she wouldn't normally be likely to take."

"No, of course not. We don't want the target to hide itself."

"That's right," the Jefe said.

Father Keogh called upon Candalaria.

Chapter 27 ~~~~~~~~~~~~~~~~~~~~~~~~~~~~~~~

HE WENT TO THE DENTIST TO ASK FOR HER. SEÑOR CAMPOS was a sour man crabbed in mind, a drinker who never cared to toast a fellow's health. The dentist drank in secret. He could never forgive Father Keogh a religion which prevented him obtaining a divorce from his wife. He liked the priest even less now that his influence had caused Candalaria to reject his attentions. Father Keogh had never been easy about the dentist's hostility. He dreaded the signs of a toothache.

"May I speak to your receptionist, please?"

"No."

"I'm afraid I insist."

"She's busy. How would you like me to come and disturb you when you're practicing that black magic of yours at the altar?"

"If I were practicing black magic I should welcome the interruption. Excuse me, I'm going to shout." He raised his voice and called into the musty interior, "Candalaria, I've something to say to you."

There was no answer but a door squeaked open. He guessed that she was afraid to come to him in case he had something further to say to her on the matter of pulque. He called, "I'm not going to scold you. I want you to call at my house as soon as it's dark tonight. Good-by, Señor Campos. It's good of you to have been so amicable."

He asked for the Jefe's car at seven thirty. He said that he wished to visit Tephuango. He often went to the Indian settlement. Candalaria arrived at the house at eight. She was sullen and ill at ease. Because she had done him an ill turn she resented him for it. It was the age-old pattern, Father Keogh thought. "I'm going to take you out to Coyotito. You can stay with him and his wife until it looks safe for you to return. You must lie on the floor of the car under a rug and there mustn't be a squeak out of you. I'll let your parents know you're in good hands but I shan't tell them whose. With any luck during these vital hours someone will come forward to speak against Vito. Then we might have enough evidence to keep him out of harm's way for a good long while. Are you willing to go?"

"Yes, Father."

She wore Vito's big amethyst ring on her finger. Father Keogh glanced at it. "Were you *given* that?"

"Yes, Father." He could sense when she was lying by now.

"If you stole it, wouldn't you like me to give it back to Vito for you?" When she answered, "I was given it, Father," he sighed. It was impossible to teach her, impossible to make her alter her ways. He said, "Very well. Be careful Chela doesn't see you come out."

He had not driven for many months. He felt acute strain on his aching right arm. The headlights lit cobblestones ahead of them and were lost in a haze at the start of the river road. Candalaria curled up in a ball on the back seat. Father Keogh draped the blanket over her, arranging it carelessly. "Don't forget, not a squeak, or I'll end up with Vito in jail." They were stopped at the climb to the Huapan ledge. Five agentes were blocking the way.

They were strangers to Father Keogh. They were Arenales men. He handed out his pass. They checked it in the light of acetylene lamps and waved him on. A soft noise disturbed Father Keogh. Candalaria was crying. He called over his shoulder to her, "Don't be frightened, I think that's the last lot we'll meet."

The wind blew a cool breath through the car windows. When they passed the cross which marked Malo's grave Father Keogh's thoughts traveled beyond it. They tramped wearily through the Green Walk of Death again. He sent his mind searching for Father Lasques. His body felt weary and short of breath. He was not unalarmed by the doctor's words. He felt an almost hourly loss of strength as if his energy were leaking away. He had never felt conscious of nerves before. But he felt victimized by them now. They shot pains of apprehension through the pit of his stomach. They pierced his head and made clumsy fools of his fingers. They caused him to jump when Chela came round a door. They made him lose track of his thoughts and he could not collect them. They blunted his appetite and set him craving to smoke. They wasted invaluable time. Where once he could have planned to the hour the order of his day, he was left juggling with unaccustomed inefficiencies until he feared that midnight would be upon him before he had said his Prime, and also, no matter how he might try to stifle it, there was the thought of the miniature crucifix and the little wax-faced doll.

He glanced swiftly towards the perilous stretch of the country that spread to the foothills of Arenales. The forest was full of the shrieking sounds of night. It was easy to imagine them the cries of lost souls in the Great Green Walk of Death. He felt an absurd irritation with it for the

272

fact that it never looked green. It was grey under cloud at daybreak, blue in the heat of the morning, plum-colored in sunset, and black by the light of the moon.

He stopped the car short of Tephuango. "Come along," he said, "we'll walk. We don't want the whole community turning out."

She rose under the rug like a small patched mountain. She was still quietly sobbing as she walked by his side.

"What's the matter? Are you frightened?" She shook her head. "Coyotito and his little Maria will look after you. They're both of them friends of mine."

Low fires flicked softly through the doorways of huts. The great organ-cactus fences wheezed in the wind. The dirt track was soft under foot. They made no sound but a dog howled. The cenzontle was singing a long way off. The night throbbed with the bird's varied notes. Coyotito's was the third hut in the line. Father Keogh whispered his name through the doorway. He came silently forward, machete in hand. Father Keogh pushed Candalaria inside. "Hide her until I come back for her."

Candalaria seemed unable to thank him. Her voice was small when she said, "My mother and father would not have taken the trouble to save such a very bad girl. They're not so foolish as you."

The lights were all out on the plaza when Father Keogh returned to the town. The Jefe asked, "Any trouble?"

"Money for jam," Father Keogh replied.

"I've been waiting for you," the Jefe said. "I've failed to break down Castillo and the others remain as dumb, but Roberto Ibarra and Doña Florencia have something to tell us at last."

He called in Roberto and Doña Florencia. They

were nervous and twisted their hands. "It's not that we told you a lie, Jefe. It's just that we left out some truth."

"Kindly leave nothing out, this time. Remember that Edmundo Arrieta is serving a three months' sentence for withholding information from the police."

It was Roberto who started the story. He used many gestures and made many excuses before he arrived at the point. "It was just where I took you to, Jefe, that I picked up two men in my lights."

"What men?"

"That was not possible to tell. They wore masks and a handkerchief round their heads. But I saw they had guns and the bus had to stop."

"It was terrible, Jefe," Doña Florencia said. "Myself, I thought I would have another heart attack. One of these men came and called to Roberto."

"Did you think he might have come from Milpahuaca by the way he spoke?"

Roberto answered, "No, Jefe. It was somebody using a rough made-up voice, like you might do when you play on the stage. But you could tell that he came from these parts. He said that if the Long Father didn't come down in the road with his bag they would shoot every soul in the bus."

"That's when the Long Father made it his wish," Doña Florencia said.

"And you drove off and left him? You gave no sort of help?"

"Well, Father, I thought that we must drive on. They would most certainly have shot the whole lot."

"Why didn't you tell us these details before?"

"Well, because, Jefe, they said we should all die if so much as one of us opened our mouths."

"And what makes you take the risk now?"

"Because Vito Castillo is shut up in prison and the Father has told us no harm will come to us."

"You think it had something to do with Castillo, then?"

"Well, Jefe, it's true when we say in the darkness we could not make out these men, but one was a big man, a big man like Pablo, and the other was smaller like Vito might be."

The Jefe said to the corporal, "Cabo, fetch me the files on the Martinez dinner. I'll just take a look at those statements again." The corporal brought them and the Jefe ran through them. "Presidente! Doña Arcelia! Domingo, Señor Martinez, Señora Martinez, Gerardo Hernandez, the boy from the grocer's! Vito seems to have made a great impression on them all with his hospital speech. They seem to have learned exactly the same bits by heart."

Father Keogh said suddenly, "Jefe, when I went past the hotel that night I remember thinking the dinner party sounded forced."

" 'Forced'?"

"Well, organized. Nothing sounded quite spontaneous. I just put it down to the fact that nobody ever does enjoy themselves at these things much. But I heard them applauding Vito and saying what a good speech he had made and the Jeep came to the window and said the same."

"Two things are interesting about that," the Jefe said. "One is that these men who held up the bus are the same size as Pablo and Vito, and the other is that there was nothing good about this speech at all. It might be worth questioning these people again to find out why it stayed in their minds to such an extent that they have all memorized the same parts of it."

Chapter 28 ~~~~~~~~~~~~~~~~~~~~~~~

FATHER KEOGH RETURNED TO HIS HOUSE TO FIND A BUICK parked outside. Dyke Brown was behind the wheel. There was no malice in his smile or his voice. His greeting was overfriendly and his expression in the soft light of the dashboard struck Father Keogh as decidedly smug.

"Good evening, Padre. The Jefe gave us a pass to get out of this lousy dump at our own risk. We're heading for the States. It seems you're expecting some kind of trouble tonight. My wife said there was something she wanted to tell you before she left." He nodded towards the house.

Locha sat on the old horsehair sofa. She stood up when he came into the room. Her beauty was a wistful thing, that seemed to fall from her head to her feet in a gentle veil. He had always admired her composure. Even as a child she had been able to summon it. A tantrum could turn to a sudden calm as if she had put on a prim little bonnet and tied it firmly beneath her chin.

In her eyes there was the bewildered look of youth encountering its first disillusionment. He was taken aback by her opening remark: "Why didn't you tell me you hated me so much?" She gave him no chance to reply. "Oh! I knew you disapproved of me, I don't blame you for that, and I knew you couldn't really return my feelings, but I thought that at least you felt something towards me—just some sort of friendship perhaps." She hesitated, trying to martial her words into the stiff order she would have liked them to fall, but they betrayed her. "You couldn't have felt anything for me but sheer, ugly *hatred* to behave the way you did."

"What is it you think I've done, Locha? I never hated Anacleto and I don't even hate Vito Castillo. I should hardly begin with you."

She asked him politely, "Please don't hedge. You see, I've had it proved to me. It makes it so much worse if you hedge." She worked at the varnish on one long fingernail, violently chipping it off. Then, ashamed of the gesture, she covered it up, pushing it into her glove. "And please don't think I blame you. I quite understand. You thought I was going to save you—and why shouldn't you? The last time I saw you I promised I would. You must have been waiting and waiting to see whether I carried that promise out, and then when I didn't you got scared. Oh! I know it was terrible of me. I told you I'd go back to Dyke to save you from the court case but I found I couldn't make a sacrifice like that, not even for you. I loved you too much to go away from you and I told Dyke there was nothing I could do about it and I was through with him for good. I hadn't the courage to tell you. I knew I should have put you out of your misery at once and told you my nerve had failed me. You must have been waiting and watching and the suspense must have been awful, I quite realize that."

It would be impossible to tell her that in his black anxiety over Father Lasques he had not found the time to dwell either on the threat of the court case or the possibility of Locha's rescuing him from it. It had also seemed of singular unimportance compared with the fact that if Vito Castillo came out of jail a free man he would have proved the power of Anacleto's spirit beyond dispute to the greater portion of Quantana. Had he spent a little more time and thought upon Locha during her moments of indecision, he might have been able to influence her. It must have been she who had done all the waiting and watching. He wondered how many others might have been in need of his personal assistance if he had not allowed general disturbances to blind him to their need.

He said quietly to Locha, "You know it was always for your sake and not for mine that I wanted you to go back to Dyke. I've prayed that it wouldn't have to be in a spirit of sacrifice, that you'd want to be with him again. He told me just now that you were leaving with him tonight. What happened to change your mind?"

All efforts to control her voice failed her. "You minded so much about me loving you that you went to the *witch* to get rid of me. You! A priest! When you've told other people superstition's a sin! You go in for magic yourself—Oh! Don't dare deny it! I refused to believe it at first, but Dyke took me down to the filthy old woman and she told me herself it was true. I saw then how horribly wrong my love was, not just because what it made you do hurt me so terribly, but because it's endangered your soul!"

He found it hard to suppress a smile at first. Her tone had become shocked and quiet. Then for a moment he longed to retract the hurt both for her sake and his own. It cost him unexpected pain to force himself to leave her new opinion of him unchanged. But he realized he could assist her best by doing so. He did nothing to correct her false impression. He was rewarded when she said to him, "I *want* to go back to Dyke now, Father." She held out a piece of folded paper. "This is how I came to find out."

She went out of the room as he opened the note. He made no attempt to turn round. For a moment he felt

278

that she could not have left him. A trace of her perfume stayed behind on the air as if she were standing beside him still.

Outside in the street Dyke Brown gave three blasts on the horn of the Buick. The first two were short but the third, held for several seconds, spoke to Father Keogh as clearly as the young doctor had once spoken himself, "You lousy, goddam Turk!" Father Keogh stood listening to it. Then he went to the window to bless them both before he looked down at the note.

It was addressed to Locha and signed *A well-wisher.* It read: *The Reverend Michael Patrick Keogh was so anxious to be rid of you and your embarrassing affections that he visited the witch to ask for a spell to be concocted to make you return to your husband.*

Father Keogh drank a cup of coffee before he went up to ask the Jefe, "I wonder if you could identify some handwriting for me?"

"Is there anything to check it with?"

"Yes," said Father Keogh, "this." He leaned over the table, picked up the Jefe's writing pad and slapped it down again with the note beside it. The Jefe examined the two samples carefully. He twisted and turned them and held them both to the light. "Well, of course, I'm not an expert on this and it's really an expert's job, but on the face of it I think—yes, I think I should take the risk and say—yes, I should say it is mine!"

In the whole of their long acquaintanceship Father Keogh had never seen the Jefe laugh so heartily before. Every inch of his heavy body shook.

"I do believe," Father Keogh said, "that excluding Vito Castillo I've never come across a bigger villain than you."

279

The Jefe held his hands to his stomach. His dark eyes were alight with his tears. "Now, now, Father, you know someone always has to help the witch."

"What made you write Locha that note?"

"You complained that the first spell didn't entirely work. I thought this might insure that she took her 'heart' back to the States as well!"

He was still laughing when they heard the shot. The Jefe took up his pistol, all sign of merriment gone. "Now," he said, "what will we find?"

Father Keogh felt the new pain in the pit of his stomach. "Locha and Dyke would have got away, wouldn't they, by now?"

The Jefe replied, "Who knows?"

The oficial, the sarjento, and the cabo ran in. The Jefe gave out abrupt orders.

The plaza was filling with voices and lights. An elbowing crowd carried torches and lanterns, hysterically shouting the news. The lights lit only their faces and hands. It looked an eerie, disembodied crowd.

"They say it's a girl who's been killed."

"Alejo has witnessed this thing for himself. He came running back with the news to Gerardo."

"It is through the head that this poor little thing has been shot."

"No, the bullet has passed through the lungs and the heart."

"Alfonso Herrera has said it's the eye."

"—and this eye has rolled all down the face!"

When the Jefe's jeep sped through the crowded streets with the doctor and Father Keogh inside, it was the sight of the priest which inflamed the town. The whole of Quantana seemed rocked by the jeers.

"Vito Castillo could not have done this!"

"The Bad One himself never lied like this priest."

"Who was it said we should come to no harm?"

They ran by the jeep and called in their abuse.

They leaned out of windows to shout at him. They shook their fists from doors. He could disregard the insults but he could not ignore the fear. It was spreading like a flame in a driving wind. It caught all it touched in its race down the streets.

Down by the River of Small Receptions the jeep, braking, stirred up the dust. All three men ran down towards the river. An agente from Arenales came forward to meet them. He saluted the Jefe and said, "I had my orders to shoot if someone refused to stay still when I called out for a name."

"Yes, those were your orders," the Jefe said.

Three other agentes were grouped on the bank. They waved when they caught sight of the doctor. He and the Jefe reached the spot first. Father Keogh was stumbling after them. Behind him the crowd poured down from the river road in a stream of bobbing lights. The acetylene lamps of the three agentes sent a hard white circle over the girl on the ground. Father Keogh's first thought was that there could not be so much blood. It had soaked through the blouse and the bottle-green skirt and the hair at the nape of the neck. Candalaria lay on her face.

The doctor turned her over. He opened her blouse. The agente explained to the Jefe, "I could only see somebody moving. I did not know I was shooting a woman."

"You did right," the Jefe told him. "Now where was she going, this girl?"

Father Keogh was numbed into lack of feeling. His answer was almost casual. "She wasn't going anywhere. She was coming back. I took her up to Tephuango when I borrowed your car tonight." He had noticed tied up to a bush in the bank Coyotito's flat-bottomed canoe. She had braved the quick waters of the River of Small Receptions where so many children were drowned.

The Jefe told him quietly, "I ought to arrest you for that."

Father Keogh said, "Yes, you ought."

He went down on one knee beside her. The close lamplight felt warm on his skin. The doctor had wiped the face free from blood. Her name went singing backwards, tossed through the crowd like a sighing wind. "Candalaria! Candalaria! It's the little Candalaria killed."

The doctor said, "It's all right, there isn't much damage. It's quite a small wound in the hand. It's that which has spread all the blood about. She must have rolled over and over on it. She's fainted, she'll soon come round." As he dressed the hand she opened her eyes. They held an unfathomable blackness under the strong, white glare. She blinked several times and made a move to sit up but lay back again, bemused. Father Keogh put his hand out to pillow her head. "You're not badly hurt, Candalaria. It isn't a serious wound."

She twisted round at the sound of his voice. Once or twice her forehead creased. Then very slowly she smiled.

"It is not that I like to steal, Father, but my fingers think before my head."

They took Candalaria home in the jeep. The Fernandez were more put out than anxious. "Sick? But then where will she sleep? There is only one room with five boys in it. Her mother and I are already in with the other four."

Father Keogh snapped, "Where does she usually sleep?"

"She is not often here at the nighttime, Father. She's a bad girl. She's always been bad."

"Small wonder," Father Keogh said, "if this is the kind of encouragement she gets to come home."

The doctor carried her into the living room. "That is for feast days," the mother complained. Father Keogh looked with even more resentment at the luxuries supplied by Vito. A petate was reluctantly fetched from upstairs and Candalaria was rolled up on it behind the door. The doctor gave her an injection to aid her to sleep and they left her, her dark hair a shawl round her shoulders, the bandaged hand aggressively white against the dirt of the petate. The Jefe said to Father Keogh, "You've punished yourself more than I could. You've proved to them that Comachi's spirit is highly efficient without Castillo's help."

"Jefe, I feel quite badly enough on account of the girl herself. I shouldn't have done it, I realize that, but it seemed so callous to expose her to risk without lifting a finger to save her. I was afraid that you wouldn't protect her enough."

The Jefe snorted, "I shouldn't have protected her at all, but I should still have done a better job than you."

"She seemed anxious to go," Father Keogh said. "I can't think what on earth made her want to come back."

"You've done Castillo a favor, Father. You've released him from jail. No one will have the courage to talk against him now. Only one fact is going to impress them. The warning said 'Candalaria will suffer' and Candalaria has!"

283

"But surely even this town can recognize a perfectly ordinary accident."

"This town, Father, is divided into three parts: those who are superstitious and are frightened of Vito; those who are not superstitious and are frightened of Vito; and those who work for Vito. You can look forward to seeing him on Saturday." He left Father Keogh without saying good night. Such a discourtesy in a Mexican left Father Keogh more aware of the Jefe's displeasure than anything he had previously said.

The kerosene lamp had burned out in his room. Chela was hiding beneath her bed. She came down, candle in hand, when she heard his step. "Mother in Heaven, I thought you were dead. I would have gone down on my knees for you if it was not that I lay on my back. When I heard of the shooting I thought, There, they have got him again. That poor little Chata. It comes from so many bad sins. Father, someone has been in this house." She told him, relighting the lamp, "It was not long before the sound of the shooting. I was out in the kitchen stirring the pots and someone crept in through the patio. I heard them open the door and come into this room. I ran up the stairs and got under my bed. And there I have stayed until this moment."

"Is anything missing?" Father Keogh asked. He picked up the lamp to look round the room. On his desk something captured the light. It was Vito's big amethyst ring. Candalaria had made restitution at last. Father Keogh stood looking down at it. "There's no need to worry, Chela. Candalaria came to the house."

"What did the wicked one take, Father?"

"Nothing. She brought something back. She must

have managed to slip the agentes on her way into the town. She was shot trying to return to Tephuango again."

A knock at the door made Chela squeak.

"Mother of God, they have come for us. El Lobo is out of the jail."

"Vito is bound to stay there until he comes before the Juez. I'll go and see who it is. Get yourself out of the way, Chela." She scrambled up the stairway, her pigtail bobbing.

It was Sam who had knocked on the door. He looked strangely pale in the light of the lamp. His tie was neat and his hat sat straight. Father Keogh was several seconds before he realized that Sam was drunk. His small eyes were swollen and dull. There was no sign of the bellicose unsteadiness he had assumed in Porfirio's bar. He had a mummified composure as if his limbs were tightly bound. He walked stiffly past Father Keogh, his heels hitting hard on the tiles. A bottle of brandy stuck out of his pocket. Father Keogh followed him into the room.

Sam raised his right arm slowly. His whole body turned round when he pointed at the typewriter. He made his words overprecise. "I did it. So help me God, I did it. I wrote that goddam note. I came in here when you and that gasbag were up at the plaza and I wrote that goddam note." He put the bottle of brandy to his mouth and swallowed more than a quarter of the contents.

Father Keogh came slowly towards him. "What note are you talking of, Sam?"

"The one about the Fernandez kid. *I* sent it— I said, 'Candalaria will suffer,' and whadda ya know? She did. I'm a witch!"

Father Keogh pulled a chair from the desk. He

sat on it, forcing himself to keep calm. "You sent that warning note, Sam? But why?"

Sam came across to him pigeon-toed. "When I was a kid they said if you walk this way you got yourself beautiful legs. Why'd I send that note?" He made an effort to clear his speech. He sounded primly unfamiliar. "I'll tell you a joke. I guess it will slay you the way it slays me. We have a great sense of humor between us, Mac. I thought that note would *help!*" When Father Keogh was silent, he said, "I knew you'd laugh. I thought it would be a good thing if Pussyfoot's ghost made a threat so as you could prove he couldn't carry it out with Castillo in clink."

Father Keogh put his hands to his eyes. "Oh, Sam!" was all he could think of to say.

Sam suddenly flung the brandy bottle against the far end of the wall. "Now see what I did—I killed you! Jesus! I came off the wagon. Godalmighty, I broke my pact—I never thought of it till now." He came forward and clutched Father Keogh's lapels. He forced him to stand up and clung to them. His face creased like a frightened child's. "I killed you, Mac, I killed you." He fell forward against Father Keogh and sobbed. "My God, I broke my pact."

Father Keogh forced him away and supported him. "God is not Shylock, Sam. He's not likely to claim a pound of flesh in return for a bottle of brandy."

Sam was soothed for a moment, then suddenly howled. Father Keogh stepped backwards, wincing at the noise. "He's gonna die, the priest's gonna die." Sam turned round and reeled out of the house. Father Keogh attempted to follow him but Sam was soon lost in the darkness, staggering up the street. His bellowing roused the entire

286

town. "Jefe! Jefe! The priest's gonna die." His shouts gathered strength in the night.

In the morning Chela found Father Keogh fully dressed on the old horsehair sofa. He had been unable to find the energy to take himself to bed.

Chapter 29 ━━∿∿∿∿∿∿∿∿∿∿━━

IN THE MORNING THERE WAS A MESSAGE FROM THE WITCH. *You will die if you stay in Quantana.*

"That's our girl," the Jefe said. "Always the first with the news. Not that anyone could have missed it with that idiot screaming his head off last night. I arrested him. He's sleeping it off in a cell."

"Where did you pick him up?"

"In the bandstand, bawling his lungs out."

"May I see Vito Castillo?"

"Certainly, Father, if you promise not to smuggle him out to Tephuango." When Father Keogh reached the door he added, "By the way, the search is off." Father Keogh went silently out of the room.

It was ice-cool in Vito's cell. The sunlight stayed outside. The stone window was one foot thick. Vito stood up when the priest was shown in.

"You're not a holy ghost I hope, Father? From the racket I heard going on last night I thought you were breathing your last. If I may say so, you look dead already."

Father Keogh put the ring in his hand. Vito polished it up on his sleeve.

"That girl was always a bitch. You shouldn't have bothered with her, Father; I could have told you that. You'll never make her improve herself. What a strange way your God works. Such pointless interference in people's affairs. I gather she need not have been injured at all."

"How did *you* hear that?"

"Señor Frankenson's noisy conscience kept the whole jail from sleeping last night."

"It might be more accurate to say, 'What a strange way God's children work.' It was I who took her to Tephuango and Sam who wrote the note. It was pointless interference on *our* part."

Vito lounged easily against the cell wall. "Do you know what has happened to me, Father? I have come to believe in Anacleto's spirit. It is really too much of a coincidence the way these things come true."

Father Keogh answered him, "It's not always been coincidence, has it? It was you who had Victorino killed, you who drove Anastacio to suicide, and I fear that you have murdered Father Lasques."

Vito held up his hand to examine his ring. "That little bitchkin has scratched it. You would have a hard job in proving those things, Father."

"Don't you think it possible that someone might prove them for me? Can you rely on the people you know not to talk?"

"How could anyone tell what has never happened?"

"Even you must fail to comfort yourself with that." Father Keogh was sitting on the small wooden stool. He leaned forward to tell Vito gently, "There's a possibility

288

that you might have to face a lifetime in prison. You're young now, but twenty years makes a difference to feelings, not only figures and faces. If you had nothing to comfort you during that time what sort of man would you be when you came out? You'd be middle-aged and you'd have nothing to live for except the hope of a hopeless revenge. You offered me your protection once."

"You refused to accept it."

"The price was too high. But now I am offering you protection, not against coldly planned murder and tyranny but against wasteful bitterness and despair, and against the possibility of destroying yourself so that even a regained freedom could offer you nothing."

"Ah," Vito said, "you are offering me your God. Well, don't you think we'd better see first if I receive this unlikely sentence? It wouldn't do to worry Him too soon. You must understand, Father, that we expect to be with you again by Saturday. I am able to pay any fines."

"Aren't you ever troubled by the spirit of Anacleto, yourself?"

"Now don't tell me you believe it. That's not good for a man of the faith."

"Men of the faith believe in spirits although not in the same way as you. They are more often referred to as souls."

"That's right, you have preached he was penitent. You think that he's in purgatory trying to work himself up to a halo." Vito's amusement was genuine. "Really, Father, one ought to pity you, you cannot be sane. Do you truly believe that you could make a man of Anacleto's kind sorry for his sins?"

"No, I don't believe I could and I don't think I did but I believe that you and the Jeep and Porfirio did."

289

Father Keogh ignored Vito's laugh. "I think that possibly he was sorry for committing the sins when he was dying because he saw the cause that would live on in people like you. I think he might well have despised you. That could have made him despise himself. He might have seen himself very clearly in you. Father Lopez has always maintained that it was one of you who shot Anacleto, and deserted him when he was dying."

Vito's mouth closed and his eyes became hard. "That old fool! How could he prove such a thing?"

"He couldn't—only you would know whether it's true or not, you and Anacleto. That's why I asked you if you've never worried about the 'spirit' you've made such use of. It may be no more than a feeling on my part, and it's one which I cannot explain—but I think you'll receive that sentence, Vito, and I think Anacleto will give it to you."

The Jefe called out as he passed the office, "Castillo's guests are sticking to their stories, but that hospital speech still sounds rehearsed. It could just be that that alibi was fixed."

Father Keogh went to ask after Candalaria. She answered the door herself. The room was filled with flowers and fruits. Quantana, which had crossed its streets to avoid the girl before, had loaded her with gifts. "This one was nearly a poor little martyr and all for the sake of that priest."

She was dancing about with her news. "Father, the doctor has told me something—there will always be a slowness in these fingers." She held up the bandaged hand.

Father Keogh tried to console her. "The damage isn't permanent. You'll regain the use of them in time. You'll find you'll be able to type."

"Oh, yes, for the typing they'll be all right, but they

must work much faster than that for the stealings. They will *never* be quick enough for that again and this was the hand I used most." She asked him with her eyes wide, "Do you think it was our Lord's work, Father? I do not think I could have put an end to the stealings myself."

Father Keogh answered, "Yes, Candalaria, I think it was. I think it may have been His way of helping you because you couldn't help yourself. Not such 'pointless interference' in people's affairs after all!"

A crowd followed him all the way home. It was angry and murmuring threats. At the door of his house he turned to address them. "Remember what I told you on the plaza. Tomorrow is the day on which our Blessed Lord died. He gave His life for you to save His world from sin. At ten o'clock on Saturday morning I shall ring the church bell. When you hear its toll you will have only another two hours in which to save this town from sin. Vito Castillo comes before the Juez at noon. After that he will be free again. Your future is in your own hands."

Chapter 30 〜〜〜〜〜〜〜〜〜

ON GOOD FRIDAY HE FASTED. HE FOUND IN HIMSELF A spiritual paralysis, as if suddenly there had been withdrawn from him the power to concentrate in prayer.

He was aware that he lost it in striving for it; aware that to bring into himself the voice of God he should not be straining human ears. The voice of God to be heard was a state in itself, not a state which the mind could achieve. It was something that received the mind. It was a being, this hearing, an effortless, new being that could only be heard by the total suppression of self. He suffered keenly from the agonies of anchorage to self. Yet he had known freedom from it; not often, but sufficiently to envy the saints. Once achieved, it seemed so strikingly simple that it appeared there had been nothing to do to gain it. It brought a sadness sublimely beautiful which must have had in it the first seeds of happiness ever to have been felt on the earth. It was a stifling sadness sweet with the scents of a thousand far-off summers which had not yet been but which were there in suspended permanence if only he could reach up to take them. It brought not the promise of eternity but the certainty of it as if eternity were long since explained. When the body became the body again that precise understanding was gone.

There were material aids which he put into use. There were new disciplines which could be imposed upon the self. In providing himself with extra spiritual exercises and duties and laying additional claims on the flesh he could build up his ability to free himself of it. They seemed a mundane groundwork but they proved a constructive solace in the impatience of marking time. But in the long hours of that bitter Good Friday he felt himself unable to reach even the lower approaches of the longed-for elusive state. Doubt made its cowardly attack upon him. He had a fierce inborn hatred of doubt. It seemed a meager compromise between faith and disbelief; to rebel, to refute, or to be frankly incapable of acceptance seemed preferable to doubt. It was a niggardly, despicable thing, a mixture of bravado and timidity, a mental sitting on the fence.

Supposing he had not, after all, been able to induce in Malo a desire to repent? There had been no one but himself to help Malo, no one to struggle against him for the redemption of himself. If he had not been convincing, if his words had lacked weight, if his truths had not seemed strong enough, then he, as the spokesman for them, must have been lacking in strength. If he had let this man go to his grave in his sins there could be no self-forgiveness for Father Keogh.

He used every concentrative power of which he was capable to try to force his memory to relieve him of doubt. But it took him so far and no further. It played cruelly and tortuously with him. It hovered as a name can hang on the tip of a tongue almost present, yet totally absent. It could take him back to the Indian hut again. It could shoot pain through newly inflicted wounds. It could fade the sight from his darkening eyes once more. It could relive the moment of dying—Malo lay oddly straight before him in the dirt of the Indian floor. He could recall saying the Act of Contrition, he could hear his own voice begging Malo to follow his words, but he could never hear Malo's voice.

His body though physically weak was too strong for him. He was conscious of every ache and pain. His mind, darting and unrestrained, sped after a dozen earthly things. He felt powerless to pursue it. It played on the question of whether there had or had not been a veiling of Vito's eyes at the mention of Father Lasques. It probed the possibilities of the Jefe's being right in his suspicion that the banquet alibi might be false. It dwelt on the brightness of Candalaria's eyes when she told him she could no longer steal. It doubted whether anyone in Quantana would have the courage to give evidence against Vito Castillo. It wondered if Sam would be able to give up alcohol again, and it conjured up the memory of Locha's perfume as if once more a breath of her had suddenly filled the room. It remembered that there would be soft grey mists in Ireland sweet with the countryside's breath; there would be a soothing and sweet refreshment in the rains. And again and again his mind escaped him to the dimness of the Great Green Walk of Death. Unable to pray for himself, he prayed that a brother priest might never feel the agony of knowing himself out of touch with God.

In the Green Walk of Death a brother priest in the moments when the fever slackened could pray as he had never been able to pray before. It seemed as if the prayers were all that could live in him. They rose from his bone-thin body as if they and not it were the framework that kept his flesh alive. But in between he lay, his brain burning, talking aloud to the trees tangled so tightly above his head that even the wind could not free the clinging leaves. The forest had made of Father Lasques a creature unlike himself. It seemed as if it had magnified his every fault of feature. In the overlong face the cheekbones protruded and the lips had shrunk back in a permanent smile. The hard suffering of the blistered eyes made a cruel contrast with the steady grin. With a dark growth of beard he looked a stranger to God and to faith. He might have been a criminal crawling his way to an ill-gotten freedom. He had long since lost the power to support his own weight on his legs. He dragged his full length across the ground. Blood had dried on his face and his hands into a pattern of crisscross stars. Where the undergrowth had scourged him and clawed him afresh the new blood flowed to lodge in them. His suit was a collection of rags which somehow still

294

clung to his back and his limbs. His last hunk of bread was a moving and reddish-brown mass. He could conceal it nowhere about his person to protect it from the ants. It was the torture of the ants which forbade him to rest. Whether he lay in the pains of the fever or whether his brain was temporarily cleared, he fought with them continually to fend off the merciless regiments. They were nearly an inch in length and they bit with a strong pincer jaw. They swarmed up his sleeves and under his collar. They tried to force their way into his ears and his nostrils. There were times when he could not prevent them from entering his mouth.

When his mind was calm he prayed for strength to crawl within reach of Quantana again even if it meant only that his dead body could bear a silent witness. In his diary he had scratched out a note. *Vito and Pablo responsible for my death. Medicine undoubtedly poisoned.*

They had carried him into the forest. He seemed to have suffered interminable agonies as he hung over Pablo's back. They had taken his breviary, his hat, his handkerchief, and his glove. They had dropped them at intervals from Malo's grave to the edge of the forest. Then they had retraced their steps to the road. They were an hour and five minutes and ten miles farther on when they entered the Green Walk again. Big Pablo showed no signs of tiredness. They did not penerate far into the forest. Father Lasques was faint from the flow of blood to the head when they set him at last on his feet. At first he believed they were digging his grave. But it was only his suitcase they buried, with the bottles of medicine inside. They had given him water and bread and they had given him a choice. "We could shoot you immediately, Father, or we could leave you to find your way back. One is a clean and a quick way to die; the other—well, how long would the water last? How far could you get on that bread?"

"These people can live on their faith," Pablo laughed.

"How long will that last in a place of this kind? No one has ever come out of it, Father, who has not marked his way."

He chose the forest and felt a stinging agony seize the whole of his head. They had thrown pepper into his eyes. They turned him round, spinning his shoulders between them until he crashed giddily onto his back.

He wandered blindly for hour after hour and it was late in the following day before he could see again. By that time he was lost. The trees Vito had marked had disappeared and the forest seemed a twittering grave. He traveled a circle for nearly two days. Of the rations they had given him to lengthen his torture only the one hunk of bread was left. There was nothing inside the water jar. When the fever set in he called loudly to keep his purpose in mind. "Keogh—Quantana—Keogh."

Sometimes the face of Vito seemed right between his eyes but was only a trick of the shadows. Sometimes Pablo's great, bellowing laugh broke out but was only the clarion call of a night bird. Sometimes the lights of the bus that had sped off to leave him were only the palely inquisitive moon. But once he believed he saw lantern lights and once he thought someone had called out his name. He called back, straining his lungs and his stomach, but it was impossible to make his voice heard. He never knew night from day, never knew if the sun had really blackened or whether he himself had lost consciousness. But when the fever pitch dipped into milder attacks he tried to make use of his sense of direction. He worked out that Quantana must lie to the north, and he struggled to keep a straight course. But he was forced to make detours in search of water. He came once or twice upon boglike ground and scooped up sufficient moisture to ease swollen lips. Once he discovered a group of small boulders surrounding a stale pool that was left from the rains. It was thick with mosquito spawn. He used his hands to pull himself closer and pushed with his feet. In the heavy undergrowth he met a pair of eyes. He had no power to protect himself. He could only lie and wait. The nauyaca was two feet away from him. He could see the four "nostrils" plainly on the ugly upper lip of the snake. For a second or two they stared at one another, then the creature slid quietly away. He drank what he could from the scum-covered pool, filled up his flagon and forced himself on. At night the wind brought him the faint sounds of running water. It must come from high up on the mountainside where the stream fed the River of Small Receptions.

It was on the morning of Good Friday that he feared Vito was right. No one could leave the forest who had not marked his way.

It was on the afternoon of Good Friday that the deputation called upon Father Keogh: Mateo, Alejo the goatboy, Coyotito, and Roberto-of-the-Bus. They spoke on behalf of the town and assured him repeatedly that their words were not representative of their own sentiments. Nevertheless, they spoke strongly enough. "This poor little Candalaria's very near death was not at the hands of the Señor Castillo. Foolish ones think that it does not matter that a policia from Arenales shot her by mistake. They think you are taking good luck from this town. Some say the Bad One's spirit arranged it. These warnings have always been right before—Victorino and then the poor

297

Long Father. These things don't come about by themselves."

"They certainly don't," Father Keogh agreed. "It's easy enough to prophesy death if you're willing to murder to prove it. And that's what Castillo has done."

"These people would like you to go, Father, before something else comes about. There would perhaps be a priest who would not mind Vito so much, who would just marry and baptize and bury and nice things like that which Vito has said he would not wish to stop. It is better for all sakes to leave him in peace. If he's not troubled then no one gets hurt."

Coyotito stepped forward. "Father, I could show you a way round the mountain to pick up the bus out of sight. There are many who want you to go, Father, because you've a place in their hearts. It's well known that you too had a warning to say that you would not live."

"On the morning of Sábado de Gloria at nine I shall celebrate Mass in the church. Those who have faith will join me at ten o'clock when I ring the bell. After Mass I shall walk the way round the town so that any who see me will realize that I have come to no harm."

It was the Jefe who brought down the second note. "This time they've sent *me* the scare warning. You seem to have been given a time limit now. It may be nonsense and again it might not." He read out, " 'Death will occur after ten o'clock on the morning of Sábado de Gloria.' " The Jefe threw it down. "It may be the witch cashing in on a chance again or it may be to scare you. Or it might even be a genuine threat. If you go to that church you must go with an escort."

Father Keogh shook his head. "That would destroy the purpose."

"I haven't enough men to line your route. It's taking a risk to walk round this town at a moment when it's none too friendly towards you. I can guarantee that a policeman won't shoot you but I can't answer for anyone else. The people are scared of you now, they think you bring trouble. Some idiot may think it his duty to put you out of the way. Again someone working for Castillo might fix it."

"It's my fault if anything happens."

"Yes," said the Jefe, "it is."

The doctor and Sam added entreaties.

"Mac, this thing has me good and scared. I came off the wagon, remember? I broke my pact. You don't have to be too slaphappy about murder, Mac, they can fix it around these parts."

The doctor told him, "You'll never make it by the look of you now. You're just about played out. If you don't get to bed and stay there, even I wouldn't give you till Sábado de Gloria."

Father Keogh could hardly support his own weight on his knees. He was forced to hold onto a chair. Chela bombarded him with well-meant appeals. "What is the use of it, Father? You will never get back to this house. You will die if you walk round the town, then they will believe all the more in the Bad One, and what is more so shall I."

As he knelt, a devouring weariness seemed to cleave a way into what strength he had left. It was as if his own body were determined to accept defeat. He realized that the doctor was right. It was possible, even probable, that by the morning of Sábado de Gloria, only a few hours off, he might find himself deprived of the energy to set a foot out of the house. Rest he knew would not assist him; only prayer could help. In his mind he was perfectly aware that it was his already poor health, the acute strain of the last

299

few weeks on his nerves, and the worry and shock of Father Lasques' disappearance which were making their final assault. But he could not get it out of his head that he had fallen a victim to the power of suggestion. The Jefe's warning, the doctor's pessimism, Sam's fear, and the note itself must surely be responsible. There had been no other time in his life when Father Keogh remembered a more lonely and bitter fight. He felt incapable of carrying out his promise. He could believe himself a victim of thought-murder. He felt corruption of faith in his failure to pray. Not even Chela believed in his prayers. No one conceived that God would grant him the strength. Not even his friends had faith. He felt that he had lost it himself at times. He was assailed by crippling doubts once more; perhaps Chela was right and he should not attempt it. Perhaps it would be better if he did leave Quantana early in the morning so that at least if he failed to inspire faith he would have done nothing to destroy it further. If he had weakened to such an extent on the morrow that he could not ring the bell, if he failed to make the walk round the town, he would prove to Quantana once and for all that the power of God was less reliable than the spirit of Anacleto. He might even convince those who had been doubtful that the spirit existed. However legitimate his excuse for not carrying out his intentions might be, no matter from what natural causes his health might have failed, supernatural causes would be sure to be blamed. Then he as well as Vito would have added to the evil perpetuated in Malo's name. If he proved that, it would matter little whether his earthly body might survive or might not survive. He would feel himself dead as a priest if he could not summon up enough physical energy for his needs. His failure would have been due to lack of strength in faith.

The chances of salvation for the whole of Quantana might depend upon so material a matter as the endurance of his flesh. But again and again the feeling returned to him that the fight must be fought—by himself. At eight o'clock in the morning his breathing was difficult; he felt a dull cramp in his heart. He was near to collapse when he rose from his knees.

It was in the moment that Father Keogh rose that Father Lasques gave up hope. He could no longer mouth his prayers. His lips were too swollen and cracked. But he had seen in the distance the bright splash of the liquid-amber trees, that meant the edge of the forest. He could feel the flesh dying outside his mind but he must drag himself forward somehow. He moved no more than a foot at a time. The nearer he could leave his body the greater chance there would be of the diary's being found. He gave himself a target. He took off his Roman collar and threw it ahead of him to keep his course straight. Then with his eyes on its bloodstained whiteness he crawled towards it and threw it again. He despaired of reaching it the second time until, lifting his head, he saw a cross. Its black lines were cut boldly into the sunlight. He thought it a vision at first. It was the cross that marked Malo's grave. If he could reach it his body might be found. The black lines seemed to pull at him, urging him on. But the strain was too great for his powers. Vito Castillo was right. There was a clearing towards his left where the ground slightly rose. A straight course was no longer of use to him. He turned himself sideways and made for the rise. The added height gave more power to his throw. He sent the collar spinning towards the far-off sunlight that played on the forest edge. The collar fell sadly short of it. From the height he had a clearer view of the cross. It seemed a bitter thing to Father Lasques that the man whose body lay beneath it, in whom Father Keogh had managed to induce a spirit of penitence at the last, should be forced to act his enemy beyond the grave. It was a bitter thing too that his own body would not now be able to bear witness against those who profited by keeping the enmity alive. In spite of his struggles it would lie too deeply far back in the woods. It would lie with its valuable evidence of poison and murder hidden away to rot. He had no means but the collar of marking its place. It would need a more arresting signal than that. He prayed that a sign might be given to draw human eyes to the spot, that the searcher might then probe deeper and come on the body itself. He dared not separate the diary from it for fear that so small an object might be irrevocably lost.

He knew that time would not allow him to complete the Act of Contrition if he prayed for Father Keogh as well. He offered up the omission as a Holy Offering. Instead he used the fading seconds to ask that Father Keogh, deprived of the evidence a dead body could bring, might be granted other forms of assistance: that he might be fortified in his endurance, that he might not be left to feel alone in his fight. He sent the prayer for Father Keogh towards the cross on Malo's grave. He died with the impression of it in his eyes.

The streets of Quantana were lined. It was a silent, hostile crowd. Not a soul sent a friendly encouraging glance. No one waved a hand except Sam. Father Keogh felt a cold, depressive wall about him which seemed to exclude his God. The necessity to concentrate upon physical effort had numbed him. He felt no divine inspiration.

302

He felt only a weary determination to force himself to ring the bell. He was aware that it should not be so, that it cast a grave reflection upon his own personal sanctification, that in the hour for which he should have prepared himself he could not summon spiritual strength to his aid. He was the loneliest man in Quantana when he set out towards the church.

For Quantana he did not walk alone. It was almost as if the town could see two men. Malo was walking beside him as surely as if he were there in the flesh. Quantana was waiting to see who won—the dead or the living man.

Father Keogh was suddenly aware of the presence himself. The realization came simply and easily into his head. In the same instant he knew with certainty that Anacleto had confessed. There was no need to struggle for the memory. He recalled it with all doubts dispelled. Anacleto's voice had not followed the words of the Act of Contrition but to show that he acknowledged them he had pressed Father Keogh's hand. It gave Father Keogh unaccountable strength. He could feel the invisible friendship in step with him at last. Anacleto had died deserted by every other friend. He would never have forgiven a Judas. He was marching against his betrayers. He was giving support to Father Keogh to stop them profaning his name. Father Keogh felt no longer alone in the fight. He could sense in the revival of strength in himself, without which he could never reach the church, that his warning to Vito might yet be fulfilled. It could still be the spirit of Anacleto which kept Vito Castillo in jail.

When Father Keogh reached the church his breathing was free and his shoulders were straight but he had difficulty in ringing the heavy bronze bell. Its voice sent an echoing challenge into the heart of the town. Father Keogh waited twenty minutes before he commenced saying Mass. Nobody answered the call of the bell. He felt his failure double-edged. He had failed not only his God and himself and Quantana; he had failed the spirit of Anacleto which had supported him at last.

Sam fell into the church, out of breath. "Mac, you have to stay here until the Jefe brings an escort up. They've caught some sweetheart with a homemade bomb and it seems there could still be some others around."

Father Keogh refused to wait. He could not persuade Sam to stay in the church. "If there were medals for sticking your neck out you'd sure have a chestful, Mac." He jogged beside Father Keogh as they set out on the winding road back to the town. The jacaranda trees, shedding frail blossoms, made it seem as if the very skies had shattered and left fragments of blue on the ground. Once Father Keogh had wanted to die but now he was dreading death. He had no longer any hope that the younger priest might have survived. He must at all costs prevent the sacrifice from having been made in vain. There was work to be done in Quantana in Father Lasques' name. Father Keogh prayed to live. He suffered a paralyzing fear at every sheltered turning, at every twist in the dust-laden road. As they rounded the high white wall the vultures rose. Sam twisted his head to follow their clumsy black flight. "Those darn birds can smell blood already."

Father Keogh answered, "They're flying towards the hills. I hope it's not one of Alejo's goats—he's lost quite a few of the younger ones lately."

An explosion shivered the air above the town. Smoke rose and there followed a series of quick-firing reports. The Jefe must have opened fire on the bomb throwers, Father Keogh thought. There would be wounded and probably dying to attend. He summoned his last reserve of strength and ran towards the town.

Sam followed him, bargaining with God in his head. "Okay, so I came off the bloody wagon. I never said I could rate as a saint—but here's what I'll do—now here's the deal —maybe I'll try out that darned old church. . . ."

When Father Keogh came in sight of the plaza he could believe neither his wits nor his eyes. Four giant paper figures were strung across it. Fireworks were shooting off round them. They were burning the Judas figures. Someone had answered the call of the bell. There was no doubt whom the figures represented—Vito, fat Porfirio, Pablo, and the Jeep. The figures took weeks to make. Old Don Timoteo must have been secretly at work on them, believing the priests would win. Father Keogh had not been alone in his faith.

Several cheers went up to greet him. Domingo came excitedly forward to tell him, "The Presidente has been to the Jefe, and I myself went along to support him. Vito Castillo was not at the banquet that night and Pablo was not with him either. Quite a few are going up to the Jefe to tell what they know and have heard."

Many hands clutched at Father Keogh and patted his back, but there were still many who hung back undecided. The whole of Quantana was out and about. The band struggling into its uniform could not force its way through the crowd.

When Father Keogh spoke to them a respectful silence fell. At first only five people went down on their knees. There was still fear and lack of faith to fight, then twenty and finally forty knelt. It was not a magnificent triumph but he knew it to be a beginning again.

He directed his prayers towards the line of the sky.

Black circling dots could be seen. On the edge of the Great
Green Walk of Death the vultures were dropping upon
their prey. Alejo made off for the mountainside. He
thought the victim was one of his little goats.

(1)